Also by Vivian Conroy

Stationery Shop Mysteries
Last Pen Standing

Cornish Castle Mysteries
Rubies in the Roses
Death Plays a Part

Country Gift Shop Mysteries
Written into the Grave
Grand Prize: Murder!
Dead to Begin With

Lady Alkmene Callender Mysteries
Fatal Masquerade
Deadly Treasures
Diamonds of Death
A Proposal to Die For

Merriweather and Royston Mysteries
Death Comes to Dartmoor
The Butterfly Conspiracy

Murder Will Follow Mysteries
Ar
Ur
H
A

D0954267

For Letter or Worse

A Stationery Shop Mystery

VIVIAN CONROY

Poisoned Pen
PRESS

Published by Poisoned Pen Press, an imprint of Sourcebooks
P.O. Box 4410, Naperville, Illinois 60567-4410
(630) 961-3900
sourcebooks.com

Library of Congress Cataloging-in-Publication Data

Names: Conroy, Vivian, author.
Title: For letter or worse : a stationery shop mystery / Vivian Conroy.
Description: Naperville, IL : Poisoned Pen Press, 2020. | Series: The
  stationery shop mysteries
Identifiers: LCCN 2019059977 | (paperback)
Subjects: GSAFD: Mystery fiction.
Classification: LCC PS3601.V64 F67 2020 | DDC 813/.6--dc23
LC record available at https://lccn.loc.gov/2019059977

Printed and bound in Canada.
MBP 10 9 8 7 6 5 4 3 2 1

Chapter One

"Ahwawawawawa." Hazel's voice sounded muffled from beneath the counter she had crawled under, looking for her favorite scissors.

"What?" Delta called back, perching on a chair to dust the weapons rack that held their wrapping-paper display. With their stationery shop, Wanted, housed in a former sheriff's office on Mattock Street in historic Tundish, Montana, many of the elements were authentic. Hazel had decided to keep them when she originally rented the building for the shop.

One of the most eye-catching historic details was the heavy oak desk where Tundish sheriffs had sat, waiting for news about bank robberies or attacks on stagecoaches. A pair of old boots with spurs stood by the hearth as if the sheriff were ready to jump into them and ride out to catch some famous gang of outlaws. The former cells were still there, with their narrow, barred windows and wooden cots, now holding part of the stationery collection and decorative elements of Tundish's history as a gold-mining town. During the rush, it had boomed with prospectors flocking in to try their luck. No wonder criminals had followed suit, to get their greedy hands on the precious metal that was excavated. Old photographs on the cells' walls showed the various gangs that had roamed the Tundish area, and on a table, scales, clumps of fake gold, and a crinkled map harked back to those exciting days. A bigger map, with gold-find sites, sat under a glass slab forming the top of the counter.

"I think," Hazel said, pushing herself to her feet, "we should have tried harder to make the 3-D card–making workshop this afternoon into something special." She leaned back on her heels and whipped a lock of blond hair from her flustered face. She usually wore it cut at chin length but was currently growing it so she could pull it back into a ponytail.

"How do you mean 'special'?" Delta asked with a frown. "We're offering a good workshop, and that's really all there is to it."

"But we've never before had such high-profile guests: former models, wives of rich businessmen. I wonder what we got ourselves into."

At the mention, Delta's stomach wriggled with nerves. But she wasn't going to show that to Hazel. Her friend and co-owner of Wanted was nervous enough as it was. They had never before been asked to do a workshop at somebody's house, and this wasn't just any house, but one of the most expensive villas along Tundish's lake. The waterfront locations had been popular with rich families since the 1920s, when tourism to the area had started to boom. Doing a workshop at such a venue was good advertisement for the shop as well. *Provided it all goes well, of course.*

With a new flood of nerves inside, Delta wiped the last of the dust off the rack and sneezed. Blinking against the burn behind her eyes, she clambered down from the chair and went to the open door to shake out her dust cloth in the fresh air.

On the other side of the street, a truck stopped to deliver food supplies to Mine Forever, the restaurant that was famous around the area for its prizewinning coffee and friendly service. The owner stood in the street, gesturing to the truck driver to back up closer to the entrance so it would be easier to carry everything inside. His voice could be heard over the growling engine and the pulsing beats of music. Delta figured it came from the truck's open window, but once the truck had stopped and the driver had cut the engine, the music kept playing.

Her gaze wandered up to the top of the building, where an oversized mattock and sieve sat, immediately drawing attention to the restaurant's gold rush theme. Over time, this equipment had become quite rusty, and apparently, the restaurant's owner had decided some restoration work was in order during these fine October days. A guy in overalls was working energetically on the mattock's blade. Sunshine glinted off the cleaned area, and Delta narrowed her eyes against the piercing light. Although the leaf-peeping seasonal rush was over, tourists were still pouring out of buses to explore the historic sites around town. Soon the holiday season would start, with people coming in for the special Thanksgiving festivities centering on Tundish's first settlers and the run up to Christmas where the entire town bathed in colorful lights and musicians played Christmas songs live on the street corners. Delta and Hazel had made plans to tap into these activities with special offers at the store and holiday-themed workshops. Hopefully, they could wrap up the year with a bang, income-wise also. Although Delta was still rooming with Hazel at her cottage, she hoped to move into her own place somewhere down the line. Good seasonal sales could bring that step a bit closer.

With a loving look at the front of the building that housed her dreams, Delta turned back inside, where Hazel stood at the counter, staring into space. Her right hand toyed absentmindedly with the necklace dangling down her thick-knit sweater. "What?" Delta asked as she went to the sheriff's desk to dust between the stacks of notebooks. There were many with Christmas designs, with silver-foil trees, jumping deer silhouettes in gold, or nostalgic scenes of quintessentially British villages snuggled under a layer of snow that shimmered with added glitter.

"Maybe I should have had my brows done at the beauty parlor," Hazel replied and reached up to run a finger along her left brow. "I mean, with all of Lena Laroy's friends around this afternoon…"

"You're more than presentable, and you know it." Delta waved her dust cloth at her. "Besides, Lena might be a former top model and TV personality, but I heard she's been living a low-key life since she married."

"Low-key?" Hazel scoffed. She enumerated on her fingers. "The villa by the lake is one of her husband's many homes scattered across the country and abroad. His Drake Design company is rumored to net millions of dollars each year, restyling penthouses and country estates for the stars. He even rubs shoulders with royalty. They have a housekeeper at the villa, but still, the party snacks are coming from a reputed caterer. Lena has two prize poodles, which a professional dog walker walks for her." Hazel rolled her eyes. "I can't imagine why she wants a card-making workshop as part of her birthday celebrations."

"But she does, and she asked us to do the workshop for her. Great advertising. Besides"—Delta gestured at the cardboard box that stood beside the counter—"you've been packing and unpacking that box for days now, so you should be one hundred percent certain everything we need is in there."

Hazel sighed. "I'm worried it won't be enough. That her posh friends will let us know we're not high-class material."

"We or our cards?" Delta went over and gave her friend a hug. "Listen up. We know our craft. She hired us because she believes in us. We'll give her guests a great time."

"They've probably never made a card in their lives," Hazel squeaked.

"Exactly, which is why they're going to have fun."

"Hellooo!" Through the open shop door, a tall figure appeared in an orange woolen coat with a patterned scarf around her shoulders. A bouncy Yorkie ran ahead of her, nails scratching on the floorboards. Delta squatted to pat the dog. "Hey, Nugget, how are you?"

The Yorkie threw herself on her back to be patted on the stomach. When Delta rubbed her, she rolled from one side to the other, making satisfied sounds.

"Yes, you like that, don't you?" Delta cooed. "You like that."

"You're not bringing Nugget to the party, are you?" Hazel asked the dog's owner in a worried tone.

Orpa Cassidy made a scoffing sound. "Of course not. I know she has two poodles who would chase poor Nugget around the garden. They're not properly trained at all. I saw that dog walker the other day on the path by the lake, struggling to stay in control of the leashes. It's quite a young girl, just eighteen, I think. Maybe a student earning some extra cash by walking dogs for all those villa owners who don't have the time. They do have time to go out boating and drinking champagne with friends, of course." Mrs. Cassidy grimaced. "I can't imagine leaving Nugget in strange hands for hours on end, being away doing what I think is fun." Her expression brightened. "Then again, Nugget is extra special, aren't you, darling?"

Nugget sat up and barked, her head tilted to the side. Mrs. Cassidy smiled and scooped her off the floor. "I'll take her to Bessie at the boutique and pick up my lunch at the bakery. I wanted to ask if I can get you anything."

"I can't eat." Hazel sighed, but Delta tutted at her.

"Some of those pecan caramel buns would be great," she said to Mrs. Cassidy. "Isn't the deal of the week buy four, get one for free?"

"Consider it done." Mrs. Cassidy lowered her voice and added in a confidential tone, "Jane has been so excited about your workshop. She can't wait to hear everything about how that villa is decorated. They say Drake is a fan of modern art and has the most amazing pieces standing around."

"We're not there to peek into rooms," Hazel said, casting an anxious look at Delta.

Ever since they had told their crafting club, the Paper Posse, about the workshop with Lena Laroy, the ladies had been in a flutter of excitement, speculating about the villa's decor, the clothes Lena would be wearing to the party, and what important people might show up. Everyone, from Hollywood stars to royalty, had been suggested, and photos from gossip columns had been provided to enable Delta and Hazel to recognize these celebrities. The Posse expected a full report, one of them even suggesting they could sneak some pics with their phones to send through to the Paper Posse message group.

"And we certainly can't take photos," Delta stated in a firm tone. "We're there to represent Wanted."

"Of course," Mrs. Cassidy said with a determined nod. "I really don't understand all the excitement. If she had accomplished something extraordinary, like Amelia Earhart, who flew a plane across the Atlantic all by herself…" Her features got a dreamy expression as usual when she contemplated adventurous women from the past.

Delta grinned and gave her a little shove against the arm. "Get going."

"Right. I won't be long." Mrs. Cassidy broke her reverie and left the shop in a rush, almost bumping into Ray Taylor. The tall, ex-football player normally cut a fine figure with his broad shoulders, tan, and the twinkle in his eyes, betraying he didn't take life all that seriously, but today he looked extra smart in a crisp shirt with neat pants and leather shoes, carrying a bunch of pale pink roses in his hand.

Hazel spotted him and flushed, ducking behind the counter.

Delta had often heard Hazel claim she wasn't interested in Ray Taylor at all. Why would she be? He was a notorious ladies' man, who had dated a lot during his professional career. Now that he was retired—involuntarily, as an injury had ended his career—and back in Tundish, where his family ran the prestigious Lodge Hotel, he still couldn't complain about female attention, and Hazel, understandably, didn't feel like joining the queue.

But still, whenever Ray appeared anywhere within sight or earshot, she acted nervous, suggesting she did like him a little bit better than she claimed.

"Hey, Ray," Delta said, stepping into his path to cut off his route to the counter. "What gorgeous flowers."

"Yes, they're for a birthday girl. You're going to her party as well, right?"

Delta blinked a moment to process who he was referring to. "You mean Lena Laroy?"

"I should have known you know her," Hazel muttered, reappearing behind the counter and putting an unnecessary extra pen into the cardboard box with workshop supplies.

The corners of Ray's mouth twitched a moment, as if

he found her response amusing, and Delta made a mental note to tell Hazel she shouldn't let Ray rile her.

"I met her years ago at a party thrown by the club where I played at the time." Ray shrugged. "She was engaged to that singer then. What was his name?" He snapped the fingers of his free hand as if to help him recall. "He wasn't with her, though. Had some concert to do in Nashville, I think. All the boys wanted to dance with her. She was back from a shoot in Dubai or some other exotic destination. Had a fabulous tan."

"For something that happened years ago, you remember a remarkable amount of details about it," Hazel said.

Again, Ray seemed to be fighting a smile. Delta said, "So you're going to her birthday party now."

"Just because her husband invited me. Calvin Drake was at the hotel last week to talk to Rosalyn about changing our interior design. He has this plan to modernize it. You know, new couches in the lobby, different paintings on the wall."

"I heard he's rather pricey," Delta observed.

"Right, and I feel like he's trying to make money across our backs. Part of the Lodge's charm is that timeless feel. We don't need to go all twenty-first century. But Rosalyn felt very flattered that such a well-known man wants to get involved with the hotel, and she's seriously considering his offer."

Ray leaned over to Delta and added, "To be honest, he was so charming to her, I had the impression he was flirting."

"Then why didn't he invite Rosalyn to the birthday party?" Hazel asked.

Ray laughed softly. "Because during the party, while his wife is busy cutting out paper flowers with her friends, he's with Rosalyn. They're going boating this afternoon, to discuss the plans for changing the Lodge's interior look further."

Delta hitched a brow in disbelief. "Rosalyn makes that kind of appointment with a married man?"

"She must feel flattered. Or it's just business, and she thinks she can get his services for a sharp price. You never know with Rosalyn. Anyway…I'm ready to have a good time." Ray held up the bunch of roses.

"Are you going to papercraft as well, Mr. Taylor?" Mrs. Cassidy breezed back in, carrying two brown paper bags, which she handed to Delta and Hazel. "Your lunch before you leave."

Ray smiled at the prim elderly lady. "I would love to learn a crafting trick or two from you, Mrs. Cassidy, but I'm afraid I've agreed to lend a hand with *other* activities. See you later." And with a mock bow, he walked out of the door.

Mrs. Cassidy shook her head, and Hazel asked, "What other activities?" She gave the door, which was left half open after Ray's departure, a suspicious look.

Determined not to let their afternoon be spoiled by Ray's behavior, Delta opened the brown paper bag and breathed the inviting sweet scent of salted caramel–pecan buns. "Hmm, my favorite. Lunch first, and then to the workshop."

Chapter Two

THE VILLA LAY ON ONE OF THE MOST BEAUTIFUL SPOTS along the lakeside, overlooking the azure water with dense forest and snowcapped mountain peaks reaching up behind it. Two stone pillars, holding flowerpots with white roses, flanked a heavy gate that cut off access to the driveway. In one of the pillars, an intercom panel glinted in the sunshine.

Delta leaned out the window of Hazel's Mini Cooper to press the button for the intercom and report their arrival. The heavy, double wrought iron gates swung open slowly, and Hazel steered the car onto the gravel. It crunched beneath the car's tires as they drove down a long lane, sandwiched between waist-high box hedges and, every now and then, a trimmed shrub peacock or swan. In the distance, the drive turned away to the right, where a red sports car was disappearing around the bend. Hazel glanced at Delta. "There are no crumbs on my face, right?" She licked her lower lip as if to feel for sticky leftovers from lunch.

"No, and your hair looks perfect. Now stop fussing."

Hazel seemed to relax a moment until they came around the turn and saw the luxury cars parked before the villa's double garage. "That's a Porsche!" Hazel gasped. "And a Jaguar. I don't want to park closely to them. What if I scratch one?"

She passed the assembled car lovers' dreams and parked the Mini Cooper beside a van marked *Carver's Catering*. A guy in a white jacket pulled some plastic container boxes from the back and closed the door. He glanced in their direction and then carried his load around the garage.

Hazel took a deep breath. "We shouldn't have agreed to this. These people play roulette in Monaco, and we're going to tell them how to glue a cutout cottage to a greeting card? I bet they never ever sent cards. Not even at Christmas. They probably have bottles of champagne delivered to their friends with a message scribbled on the label with a diamond-encrusted pen."

"Relax." Delta put a reassuring hand on her arm. "Lena invited us. It was her choice. She probably enjoys doing something crafty. It reduces stress."

"Right now, it doesn't," Hazel said gloomily.

Delta pointed. "There's Mrs. Cassidy waiting for us." She got out and joined the elderly lady, who stood ready to go to the house. Hazel came over with the cardboard box in her arms and whispered, "Have you seen all those cars?"

Mrs. Cassidy nodded. "I think that gold-colored Porsche is rather tacky. I mean there must be more tasteful ways to show you have money."

Delta suppressed a grin, but Hazel pinched her arm. "We can't go through the front door as if we're guests. We'd better go around back like that catering man did." She scurried away along the garage's brick wall, clutching the cardboard box.

Mrs. Cassidy shook her head, but she and Delta followed. At the back of the garage, a smooth lawn stretched away to an edge of coniferous trees in the distance. Braziers gave some welcome warmth as the October air was chilly despite the sun overhead, and white party tents had been set up at regular intervals throughout the broad expanse of grass. One was marked with a gold sign: *Photo Shoot*, the next: *Nail Studio*. "Aha." Mrs. Cassidy pointed ahead. "I see *3-D Workshop* right there." She took the lead, striding across the immaculately cut grass.

Passing the tent marked *Nail Studio*, Delta heard the clatter of glass bottles inside and subdued female voices chatting. A cupcake-decorating tent stood brightly beside it. Lena had obviously wanted to provide a variety of activities for her guests.

Their tent was positioned close to a long table decked out with a gold damask cloth on which a few neatly wrapped boxes sat waiting. Delta assumed this was the gift table for their hostess, where the guests could put all their presents. She didn't see Ray's bunch of flowers, but maybe he wasn't there yet or he had handed off the roses to the housekeeper for her to put into water right away. It would be a shame to let them wilt.

Inside the tent, a small portable heater spread a comfortable warmth, and a white table was surrounded by six chairs. "Considering there are three of us, she doesn't expect many participants," Mrs. Cassidy observed. She leaned her hand on a chair's straight back and demonstrated that it wobbled a bit on the grass.

"Maybe she expects us to stand as we assist people," Hazel said in a forced cheerful tone. She opened the cardboard box and began to arrange the materials on the table. Plain backgrounds, patterns to cut elements out of, glue and foam pads that were sticky on both sides and could be cut into the right size to paste elements together with a 3-D effect. Glitter pens, beads, and ribbons could provide a finishing touch.

Mrs. Cassidy shrugged out of her long coat. "It's warm enough in here to do without this. I'm going to find the wardrobe. Can I also take your coats?"

Delta suspected she wanted to get inside the villa to see a bit of the house. To be honest, she was also curious how a famous interior designer would decorate his own home. But then this was one of many places where he spent time, and maybe Lena had done more on the furnishings than the big man himself.

Sharp barking resounded outside, and Delta left the tent to see what it was. A girl of about eighteen tried to pull a big, black poodle away from a screeching woman who held a purple box overhead. Delta closed in quickly and grabbed the poodle's collar to help tug at the strong animal. The woman with the box inched back and managed to get away, ducking into the tent marked *Cupcake Decoration*.

"They are completely addicted to sweet treats," the girl said in an apologetic tone. "It's so bad for them. I tell Mrs. Drake, but I don't think she really listens." She took a deep breath and added, "Thanks for helping me."

"No problem." Delta surveyed the girl's short, electric-blue dress, which didn't seem suitable for running around after willful dogs. The color was lovely, though, with her strawberry-blond hair, which was brushed back in a wet look, giving her a bit of a starlet air. "I'm Delta Douglas, of Wanted, the stationery shop in town."

"Zara Kingsley. I love notebooks. I've wanted to drop by your shop since I came into town. But there's a lot to do here, especially with the party preparations. The dogs get all wild." While speaking, Zara tugged on the collar of the poodle, who kept trying to wriggle away from her grasp.

"Where's the second one?" Delta asked, spying around.

"Under the…" Zara glanced to where a bright-pink blanket rested in the grass. Empty. "No, not again. Pearl! Where are you? Pearl!" She looked at Delta. "Could you hold Emerald for me while I go find Pearl? Thanks so much."

Before Delta knew it, the girl had taken off, leaving her with the struggling poodle. The animal wanted to go after the dog walker and dug her paws into the grass to provide extra traction. Delta had to use all her body weight to restrain the dog.

"Need a hand?" a deep voice asked.

Delta turned her head to find Jonas Nord right behind her. The wildlife guide, who was usually in the company of his retired K9 Spud, was now on his own, wearing a dark-blue suit with a deep-red tie.

"Very neat." Delta looked him over. "Were you invited by the husband as well?"

"As well?" Jonas hitched a brow.

"Yes, Ray Taylor is here too. Seems Mr. Drake asked him to attend his wife's birthday party while he's out on business."

Jonas's expression darkened at the mention of Ray. The two men didn't like each other, although they had to maintain somewhat friendly relations, since Jonas worked as a guide for the Lodge Hotel, taking guests to spot wildlife or improve their photography skills. He was an avid photographer himself, usually carrying his camera with its long lens whenever he went into the woods.

Jonas said, "Mr. Drake went on a bird-watching trip with me, and we got along well. He invited me to this party." It sounded quite sparse and not altogether convincing, especially with his stiff stance and gaze flicking away from her and across the white party tents, as if he was scanning for something. But Delta knew Jonas better than to press him for more information now. She could always ask about it later, when the party was over, and the pressure gone. Before coming to Tundish, Jonas had been a policeman and K9 handler, and he still had links with his old profession. He rehomed K9s who came out of active service and went into normal families. Spud helped him to give the dogs a taste of life without duties, and once they were good to go, they left for all parts of the country.

"Where's Spud? He might have helped us track Pearl," she said. Jonas patted Emerald, who gave him adoring looks and was no longer in any rush to get away.

"Spud isn't here. I wanted to bring him, but…" Jonas seemed to bite back something.

Delta tilted her head with a questioning look, but Jonas nodded past her toward their tent. "So, you'll be card-making with the ladies? Will Mrs. Drake be in with you?"

"I have no idea. To be honest, I thought she was having card-making and snacks for some close friends, but it seems to be a bigger event."

"Yes, well, she used to be a star." Jonas scratched the poodle behind her ears. He seemed to want to say more, but his expression suddenly became tense as he zoomed in on something.

Delta turned her head to find out what it was but only caught a flash of white near a bush. Probably a caterer carrying drinks and boxes with food.

Jonas said, "I'll take along the poodle and help look for the other one. I'll drop by later to see how you're doing."

Before Delta could respond, he had pulled the dog away from her grasp and led it to the back of the garden where the dog walker had disappeared in search of Pearl.

Delta exhaled. She had loved working with Jonas to ferret out the truth when, about a month ago, a murder had been committed at the Lodge Hotel, and Hazel's brother, Finn, had been incriminated. It had been a tense time for Hazel, but the sleuthing had provided an intellectual challenge Delta had enjoyed more than she could have imagined. Discussing the case with Jonas had been especially fun, but after they had successfully solved it and brought the killer to justice, Jonas had sort of disappeared from her life, busy with his wildlife-spotting tours. She had only seen him once or twice at Mine Forever on the other side of the street, and although she had wanted to go over and ask him how he was doing, her pride had prevented her from it. He could come over to her, right? Or give her a call?

That same brush of annoyance rushed through her now that he had left her standing there and had walked off to look for a dog. As if he couldn't have asked how she was settling into town and all. It had been a big change from having a desk job in the city to running her own business in a small town. A generous gift from her grandmother had enabled her to buy into Wanted and make her life-long dream of working with paper goods a reality. But the creative side of it—designing wrapping paper, thinking up workshops—was but one part. The business end came with a steep learning curve. There was stock to choose, decorations to decide on, paperwork to do, money to keep track of, both earned and spent. The cash register did part of the work for her, but still she needed to practice her skills to stay on top of things and not let Hazel, her co-owner, take the brunt of responsibility. It was awkward, feeling so out of her depth regularly, and sometimes she caught herself thinking she had felt much more in control of her old life, back in Cheyenne.

Delta shook her head as if to physically shed her unhappy feelings provoked by the brief encounter with

Jonas. He was just a very practical guy who probably thought his help was needed to resolve the issue with the unruly poodles. They were a handful for a college-aged girl on her own. Still, Delta wondered why a professional dog walker couldn't handle her charges.

"I handed off the coats to the wardrobe attendant," Mrs. Cassidy said, appearing by Delta's side and showing her a token she had received. "It all looks very professionally organized. Too bad I couldn't pretend to be lost and wander around a bit. I bet they have an amazing art collection. Paintings, drawings, silverware. Or china maybe. Drake has the money to buy some exquisite vases from a very old dynasty."

Delta frowned at her, and Mrs. Cassidy grinned. "I guess if I had gotten a chance to wander, I would have felt bad about invading the privacy of someone's home and not done it anyway. It would have felt odd to barge into rooms for a look around, as if you're at an art museum. But there are all these rumors going around about his collection. That it must contain very special, priceless pieces."

Delta knew that where rumors were concerned, Mrs. Cassidy was always in the know. Working at the town's gold-mining museum, she was part of a close-knit group of volunteers who shared what they saw and heard, and the line-dancing team with which she had won regional competitions also seemed to be a fertile ground for information. Not to mention the Paper Posse, who messaged each other about everything they found worth sharing. They all worked at shops or public places where they heard people talk all day, and what they didn't learn themselves, they could find out via friends who worked at the post office or a gas station.

"It's mainly because of Mr. Drake's sister," Mrs. Cassidy said with a pensive look. "She's an art expert, so you would expect him to have inside information on what works of art to buy and what to avoid. She used to live and work in Los Angeles, but a few days ago, she showed up here in Tundish. I'll point her out to you when I see her. Like Lena, she kept her maiden name when she married. She's Sally Drake still."

Delta nodded, although she wasn't really all that interested in the Drake family dynamics. "So, Lena Laroy kept her maiden name when she married?" she asked to keep the conversation going. "I heard some people call her Mrs. Drake."

"Yes, she answers to either, I assume. But Lena Laroy is almost a brand. Worth a lot of money even after her modeling career ended. Two years ago, she started this perfume line, and something with clothes too, I think. Wild Bunch Bessie mentioned having been to a fashion show with some of her items. Terribly expensive of course. High-end fashion it's called, I think."

A statuesque woman with platinum-blond hair glided toward them across the lawn. Delta really couldn't think of another word to describe the way in which she moved almost regally while she greeted people left and right. A turquoise dress with silver embroidery on the bodice fitted her like a glove. Silver high heels completed her ensemble. Her jewelry was kept simple: a single diamond dangled in her deeply cut neckline. It was encased in what looked like silver but was probably white gold. A plaited bracelet of the same material sat on her left arm. She wore no watch. With a wide smile, she descended upon them, her hand outstretched to Delta. "Hello, welcome to my home. How nice to meet you. Lena Laroy."

"Delta Douglas, of Wanted stationery store in town."

"Oh, yes, you have these gorgeous notebooks. I put two dozen in the tote bags for my friends." She gestured over her shoulder to the house. "They do enjoy a bit of sparkle."

Before Delta could say that their stock was mainly bought from Japan and Australia, ensuring novelties and rare items, Lena Laroy stared past her. She pointed a turquoise fingernail at the empty blanket and exclaimed, "Where are my little darlings?"

"I think the dog walker took them for a spin," Mrs. Cassidy said quickly, glancing at Delta.

"They are so cute," Delta enthused to divert attention. "Have you had them from the time they were puppies?"

"No, I got them later, through a friend who does shows with her poodles. But they have to be terribly well behaved to go to shows. Mine are spoiled rotten. My own fault, I suppose." She flashed a charming smile. "Oh, there they are."

From the back of the garden, Zara came holding one poodle by the leash, while Jonas walked the other. Delta suppressed a grin at the sight of his tall, suit-clad figure with the bouncy, trimmed poodle beside him. He looked like the butler of a rich lady.

"Jonas!" Lena Laroy rushed up to him, put her hand against his chest, leaned over, and pecked him on the cheek. "How nice to see you."

Delta didn't want to analyze the little stab she felt inside at the intimate scene. Jonas seemed a bit uncomfortable under the sudden attention, handing off the poodle to the girl and excusing himself. Lena gazed after him as he strode away. Then she snapped at Zara, "I do expect you to watch them by yourself and not need others to help you. If it's too much, I can always hire someone else."

"No, no, it's fine. I didn't ask for his help. He came over and said he knew a lot about dogs," the girl stammered and flushed.

Delta closed in and said, "Jonas is a former K9 handler, so he does know a lot about dogs. He really likes them and probably meant to get acquainted with your dogs."

Lena Laroy looked her over as if she wanted to comment on her intrusion but stopped herself in the last instant. "I have guests to attend to. Excuse me." She walked away.

The girl exhaled slowly.

Delta whispered, "Is she very demanding?"

Zara straightened up as if someone had prodded her in the back. "I'd better get going." She passed Delta and put the dogs back on the pink blanket.

"Sorry, I guess," Delta muttered with a sour expression and retreated to Mrs. Cassidy. "I thought I should help her a bit to escape her employer's wrath, but she doesn't seem to need any help. She looks rather classy in that dress. And the way she carries herself… Did she come here with the Drakes?"

Mrs. Cassidy shook her head. "She breezed into town just ahead of them. Spent a few days at the Lodge, then got the job with them and moved into the villa."

"Not bad." While the girl stayed at the Lodge, had she met Jonas, through a wildlife trip or something? He had seemed eager to help her.

"Delta!" Hazel waved at her from the party tent's entrance. "I'm set up." She pointed at her watch. "We should be ready for guests."

"Coming!" Good thing she would be busy all afternoon.

"Pffff." Hazel blew a lock of hair from her face. The small heater drove up the temperature in the tent's limited space, and the chairs around the table were glaringly empty. It seemed Mrs. Drake's high-profile friends weren't interested in making any 3-D cards.

Mrs. Cassidy had left a few minutes ago to see how the other tents were faring, and Delta stretched her shoulders and suppressed a yawn. "I had run through a couple of scenarios in my head, but nobody showing wasn't one of them."

"The only good thing," Hazel said, "is that we got paid already, simply for being here, so whether anybody turns up or not doesn't matter. Still, this is awkward. I feel like that kid in school who's last being chosen for gym teams."

"Hmmm. I know what you mean." Delta yawned again. "I'm getting a serious lack of oxygen, standing around here. I'll be back in a minute." She walked outside and ran into Mrs. Cassidy, who gave her a rueful grin. "The nail studio is doing great, with women waiting outside. But the cupcake ladies are not having much luck either. The only participants who showed up there are two little girls who are throwing fondant at each other and covering everything in unicorn sprinkles."

Delta had to laugh despite her mood. "Maybe Lena Laroy misjudged her friends. They are probably here to sample the champagne and cake and catch up with each other, not wanting to do anything but chat. But like Hazel said, we do get paid simply for being here, so…we'd better enjoy it."

"Oh, look, she's going to unwrap some gifts." Mrs. Cassidy pointed at the gift table where a crowd was gathering. The few presents that had been on it before were now surrounded by many more gifts, all wrapped up in beautiful paper and with ribbons on top and tags attached. Delta followed Mrs. Cassidy to stand in the back of the group to watch the unwrapping for a bit. A woman in turquoise came up to the table, and Delta briefly believed it was their hostess until she got a better look and decided the woman's hair wasn't blond enough. She didn't wear a single diamond pendant like Lena had, but a gem-studded double necklace with matching ring that caught the light as she lifted a hand to brush back her hair. Her dress was almost similar to Lena's, though—long, smooth, and flowing—with silver shoes. *Painful to appear at a party in a lookalike outfit…* Lena Laroy appeared from the other side on the arm of a man in a neat gray suit and let herself be led to the table. She threw the woman in the similar dress a vicious look and then stood with a smile to address her guests. "I'm so happy you're all here to celebrate my birthday. A milestone, well, we all know how that is. I'd rather not think of my actual age right now…"

Laughter rang out, and the man by her side said, "You don't look a day over thirty," and pressed a kiss on her hand. "Let's sing 'Happy Birthday,'" he encouraged the crowd.

The woman in the similar dress had taken her place among the guests. Looking her full in the face, Delta shivered under the intense expression in her eyes as she watched the hostess beam at the resounding "Happy Birthday" from all of her friends.

Mrs. Cassidy poked Delta's arm and said, loud enough to be heard through the singing, "That is Sally Drake, Calvin Drake's sister."

"She doesn't look very happy to be here." Delta tried to identify the emotion flickering in the woman's eyes. *Resentment?*

Or jealousy?

Was the similar dress not an unfortunate gaffe, but a conscious choice, to vie with the hostess?

After the hooray, hooray had died down, Lena looked across the table and picked up a parcel wrapped in baby-blue. She clawed at the tape with her too-long nails and then handed it off to her companion, who opened it for her.

"Who is the man beside Lena?" Delta asked Mrs. Cassidy.

"I don't know. Not Mr. Drake, in any case. I've seen him before, and he's older."

Delta recalled that Calvin was out boating with Rosalyn and glanced in the direction of where the lake was hidden from sight by the forest. The birthday girl's husband out for business… How odd when you came to think of it.

Lena looked into the opened box and laughed. She lifted out a bookend in the shape of an elephant. "I do hope I will have more time to read now that I'm not that busy anymore."

More presents were opened, revealing chocolates, a set of crystal glasses, and a hairdryer in the shape of a flamingo with the hot air coming from its open beak. Delta decided it was about time for her to get back to the hot tent and poor Hazel when Lena gave a cry. She stared at something in her hands.

Chapter Three

DELTA CRANED HER NECK TO SEE WHAT IT WAS. IT SEEMED to be a perfume bottle. Lena dropped it in the grass and walked away quickly. The man by her side gestured to the gathered people to back up, and they did, muttering and casting glances at the discarded bottle.

Jonas closed in quickly—Delta had not even seen him near—and leaned down to study the perfume bottle in the grass. He pulled a handkerchief from his pocket and used it to pick it up carefully. Holding it a little away from him, he carried it off.

People whispered among themselves, asking what he was doing and what for.

Lena had halted at the steps to the villa. She held her hands to her face while the man who accompanied her talked to her. Then he gestured to waiters to bring champagne to the guests, and as they handed out bubbling glasses, the party mood returned, and laughter reverberated on the air.

"What was that all about?" Delta asked Mrs. Cassidy.

"I have no idea. Maybe she's allergic to certain ingredients in perfumes?"

"But the smell can't get out through the bottle. She dropped it before she had even held it close to her face. Like it was a venomous snake or something. I'm going to look for Jonas and ask him what's up." *He has to have expected something to happen. He was so tense and watchful before.*

Delta crossed the lawn in the direction Jonas had vanished. The two-story, whitewashed house looked even more impressive than it had from the front, with the second-floor balconies resting on stone arches built into the first-floor structure. Classic and modern at the same time. There was an open door leading into the house. Delta went through, hesitating a moment as she stepped onto the thick, dark-blue carpet covering the floor. The mysterious perfume bottle was really none of her business. With Jonas, a former policeman, it would be in good hands. But that was just it: Jonas, who hated parties, being on the scene when something sinister happened. He had to have known more beforehand, and she wanted to know what it might have been. *Right. If anyone asks me what I'm doing here, I'll just claim to be looking for the bathroom.*

She spied into the first room on her right and saw Jonas standing at an oak table. The bottle he had picked up from the grass rested on it, half in his handkerchief, and he was placing a phone call. She heard him say, "Yes, it's better if you pick it up right away for analysis. I have no idea what it might be. Thanks."

He lowered the phone, looked at the door, and saw her standing there. His expression changed a moment from concerned to surprised. Then he said, "Nothing to see here, Delta."

"Come on." Delta stepped into the room. "From the moment I saw you here I knew something was up. You don't like parties. Especially not if you have to dress up for them. Are you here for a special reason? Is Mrs. Drake, I mean Lena Laroy, afraid of something?"

Jonas seemed to want to say something, then he exhaled and nodded at the table. At the bottle standing there.

Delta came over and looked at it. It was a perfume bottle from the Lena Laroy brand, but the name *DIVA* had been changed into *DEATH*, and the woman's face underneath was now a skull with hollow eye sockets.

"Nice birthday present, huh," Jonas said.

Delta frowned, her thoughts racing to make sense of events up to now. "You expected something like this, or you wouldn't have been here."

"When Mr. Drake went on a trip with me, he had hired me as his personal guide, so there were no others with us. I thought he didn't want people talking and disturbing the animals, as often happens in groups, but he told me that he didn't want to see deer at all, he was there to discuss his wife's safety. He had heard I had worked for the police before I came here. I told him I wasn't doing any such thing anymore, but he explained he didn't want professional security, just someone with knowledge and a keen eye to attend the birthday party and tell him a thing or two. You see…"

Jonas frowned, then continued. "I can't tell you the details, as they are private of course, and I don't want to betray his trust. But let's say there is…tension, and he doesn't know who he can trust."

"Has she received threats like this before?"

"I can't really discuss that with you, Delta. I've already said too much." Jonas rubbed his face. "I should have told Drake 'no' the minute he asked me to do it. I should have known it would lead to trouble. But I was intrigued by his story and…why not? Just an afternoon at a birthday party, doing a bit of surveillance. I didn't expect anything to happen really. I had concluded from Drake's story he was…a touch paranoid. Something you see more often when people have a reputation and wealth to protect."

"I see." Delta nodded. "But now there is a real threat."

She gestured at the perfume bottle's skull with its eerily empty sockets.

"I called the sheriff's office so they can come handle this. Not that they seem to take it very seriously. That deputy asked me what he can do about a perfume bottle with a skull on it. Take fingerprints maybe? See if he can figure out who sent it?" Jonas gestured impatiently.

"Come on." Delta shook her head. "He knows just as well as you that if someone sent something like this as a serious threat, they'd take care not to leave prints on it. They would've handled it with gloves. Everyone has gloves lying around."

"Sure, but not every criminal is necessarily that smart. If it's even a criminal, and not a disturbed fan or…someone who wants to give her a scare."

"You mentioned that Mr. Drake didn't know whom he could trust. So, it could be someone close to Lena Laroy, trying to scare her. Is someone trying to gaslight the former model? But why would someone near her try to manipulate her? Does Drake have concrete suspicions about someone in their circle?"

"I'm not saying one more word." Jonas gave her a stern look. "I'm staying here with this bottle until the police come to pick it up, and then I'm done with the whole thing. I should never have agreed to Drake's request."

But he had been unable to turn away from a chance to do his old job. He had loved it, and he still did. What on earth could have driven him away from the force? He had told her he had quit, but not why, and it had felt intrusive to ask. After all, there might be a very personal, painful reason for it, a traumatic event, like the violent death of a colleague. It couldn't have been a lack of passion for his job.

Jonas loved sleuthing. She had felt it in his every move when they were solving the murder case together. It had felt good to work as a team.

"Who's that guy who was with her? Not her husband, Mrs. Cassidy said."

"No, Calvin's older. It's her husband's nephew, Randall Drake."

"Does he also work in Drake's company? Hazel mentioned to me that Drake Design is doing very well."

"I don't think so. I heard in passing he's a software engineer. On vacation here."

"Oh." Delta pursed her lips. "I don't know, but he was acting like the master of the house, sort of directing everything. The crowd's happy birthday song for Lena, then when they had to back away from the table, and later telling the waiters to hand out more champagne. He had this take-charge attitude, like it was natural he was telling everyone what to do. Odd if he's here on vacation at his uncle's house." Had Drake left the house on purpose for the afternoon, so Jonas could see how his nephew acted around his wife? Did he suspect them of...an affair?

"Delta!" Ray waved at her from the door. "Would you like a drink and a spin around the garden? It's stuffy in here." He ignored Jonas as if he wasn't even there.

"Sure." Delta crossed to the door and accepted Ray's arm. She wasn't going to get any more from Jonas about the threats against Lena Laroy at this moment, and maybe Ray knew something about it.

As he walked her back out onto the lawn, she said, "I heard that the dog walker the Drakes employ lived at the Lodge for a bit. Do you know her?"

"Zara Kingsley, you mean? Nice girl."

Ray said it in a certain tone, and Delta glanced at him. "Did she like you?"

"She did mention she knew I had played professional football and all. I guess she wanted to flirt. But she's a bit young for me." Ray leaned over and added, "I'm saying it before you do."

Delta flushed in annoyance. "It's none of my business really who you hang out with, but it does seem remarkable that Zara came to town for sightseeing and then immediately landed this job with the Drakes."

"Who says she came to town for sightseeing? She stayed at the Lodge, yes, but maybe with the intention of scoring a job here, at one of the villas. She obviously wants to move up in the world." Ray shrugged. "I got the impression it doesn't matter much to her how she does it. Had I encouraged her, she would have thrown herself right at me. Then she did the same thing with Calvin Drake."

"Drake? He's more than friendly with his wife's dog walker?"

"Well, let's say I saw them at the Lodge together, and he put an arm around her shoulders. I couldn't see much more, as they walked away."

"So, he hired a girl he's been seeing at the Lodge to move into the villa?" Delta whistled softly. "I wonder if Lena knows about that." She thought of the woman's tone toward the dog walker earlier. "Maybe she does. But then why doesn't she fire Zara and send her away? With her money, she must be able to hire a new dog walker in a heartbeat."

"She can send her away from the villa but not pack her out of town. Maybe she thinks it's better to keep her close where she can see exactly what is happening." Ray shrugged.

"I'm surprised, though. Calvin Drake was rumored to be absolutely mad about Lena when he married her. Why would he suddenly go after a college girl? Oh, wait a sec. I see Lee Turner there. I have to ask him something. I'll be back in a minute, okay? Hang tight."

Ray walked away from her to greet an elderly man. Delta accepted a glass of apple juice from a passing waiter and retreated a few paces to stand in the warmth of a red lamp attached to a tall oak tree. With those lamps everywhere, and the heaters in the party tents, it was perfectly possible to have a garden party in October. Clever. Expensive too, probably, but then the Drakes could afford such a thing.

Delta glanced around her as she sipped her drink. She caught a glimpse of a woman in a turquoise dress disappearing into some brush. Lena Laroy? Had she overcome her shock over the sinister perfume bottle so quickly? Or was it the sister-in-law, Sally, who was dressed similarly?

Too bad Jonas wasn't here to see this. He was hired to keep his eyes open for mysterious stuff, but he was now inside, guarding the incriminating perfume bottle.

Delta's hand clutched the glass. What if the perfume bottle had been a distraction, to get Jonas away from the party scene, so whoever targeted Lena could strike?

She followed the woman and stood at the brush, peering in. On the other side, she heard voices. A man said, "I told you before I won't let it go. You know what I want, and you give it to me. Tonight."

"I can't." The female voice was brittle and desperate. "Give me more time."

"I'm tired of your lousy excuses. It's tonight or else."

Delta chewed her lip. She could barge into the brush and disturb the conversation, but then the aggressive-sounding man might do something to hurt the woman. And was it even Lena Laroy speaking?

"You wandered off." A hand landed on her shoulder, and she almost yelped. Spinning around, she was face-to-face with Ray. "You gave me a scare."

"Sorry. I thought you'd wait for me while I chatted with Turner. He might be able to get us a new piano for the Lodge at a good price. The old one is out of tune permanently. Rosalyn's attached to it, but I'm not so sentimental. What are you looking at anyway?" He peered past her.

Delta was certain the man and woman would have heard them and removed themselves. She exhaled. "Nothing. Just some air. Nice about that new piano."

"It's not a done deal yet. He'll call me later. Didn't want to do business at a party." Ray rolled his eyes.

"Speaking of business," Delta said, "I should really get back to Hazel and Mrs. Cassidy. I feel like I'm letting them down, wandering around like I'm here as a guest rather than a hired entertainer."

"I'll walk with you." Ray swung his arms as he walked by her side. Delta was tempted to ask him what he thought of Lena Laroy's response to the perfume bottle, but as he had seen her briefly with Jonas and might have noticed the bottle on the table, it was better not to say anything. Else Ray might suspect Jonas of knowing more about the situation.

"Hello, Hazel," Ray said, stepping into the tent. He glanced around. "I see it's not exactly packed with crafters."

"Do you want to make a 3-D card?" Mrs. Cassidy asked sweetly. "Lena never said it was just for women."

"I could never cut anything straight," Ray said, raising both hands in a dismissive gesture. "Ask my kindergarten teacher." And he fled.

Mrs. Cassidy chuckled. When she saw Hazel's expression, she sobered and said, "Don't take it so hard. It's not your workshop. People have other matters on their minds. Especially after the strange gift." She perked up. "Is that a siren I hear?"

Delta listened. "I think so."

Moments later, the blare became overwhelming, and brakes squealed. Delta peeked out of the tent and saw two deputies rushing across the lawn to the gift table. One of them was holding a roll of crime-scene tape and started to string it from one tree to another, fencing off a wide area around the table. The other told people to step away.

Delta frowned. Jonas had told her the deputy he had talked to didn't see the need to come out for a mere perfume bottle with a skull on it. Now they were suddenly acting like there was a serious threat?

"What's happening?" Mrs. Cassidy asked over her shoulder. "Look, the sheriff himself."

Delta saw Sheriff West striding across the lawn, pausing at a group to ask a question. The congregated partygoers pointed to the villa with serious expressions and started to talk among themselves as soon as he walked away. "Maybe Jonas suspects the contents of the bottle are poisonous or combustible and called them in to remove it with special care," Mrs. Cassidy mused. "He can hardly throw it in the trash without them having had a look at it. Nobody knows what it might be."

The potential threat had to be serious if the sheriff was coming out like this. Sheriff West didn't like Jonas and would sooner ignore him than act on something he said.

Nerves tingled in Delta's stomach. Was something violent about to happen at this party? With so many people around, it could turn into a disaster.

The two deputies had cordoned off the gift table, and one of them pulled out his phone and was taking pics of the items on the table. There was a strange and unsettling contrast between his stern uniform and the cheerful parcels with ribbons and bows he was snapping.

The other deputy joined a group of people at a safe distance from the table and was taking down information in a notebook.

"What on earth is happening here?" A tall woman with black hair worked into an ingenious bun and an ankle-length purple dress marched up to the gift table and gestured at the deputy taking pictures. "What are you doing disturbing the party like this?"

The deputy quietly explained something to her. "Outrageous," she called out. "There's nothing wrong here. Who placed that call?"

"Who's she?" Delta asked Mrs. Cassidy.

"Una Edel. Drake's right-hand woman. She's one of his top designers and built the Drake Design company with him. I heard that before Lena Laroy came on the scene, she had hoped to become the third Mrs. Drake. But that could have been an idle rumor. She strikes me as far too independent to tie herself to a man."

As Mrs. Cassidy said it, Una Edel was ushering the deputy away from the gift table and toward the house. She gestured with her left hand, which held a bunch of keys on a sparkling key chain with a pendant in the shape of a flying bird. The blue gemstones in its wings caught the light of the afternoon sun.

"A force to be reckoned with," Mrs. Cassidy said.

Sheriff West exited the house and met Una Edel and his deputy halfway. He sent the deputy back to the gift table with a mere nod of his head. The poor man seemed totally confused by the contradictory orders as he jogged back and resumed taking photos.

Una Edel argued with the sheriff, but he brushed past her and gave instructions to the other deputy, who was interviewing guests. Una clutched her key ring and disappeared into the house with short, angry steps.

Mrs. Cassidy wormed past Delta and said, "I'll go and listen in on what West is saying." She took care to stay out of his line of vision and approached the group via a wide circle. Delta shook her head at her surreptitious tactics but had to admit she also wanted to know what was up.

Two little girls with red fondant on their faces and sprinkles all over their hands ran up and asked, "Can we make cards here?" Without waiting for Delta's reply, they ducked under her arm into the tent. Chairs rattled against the table, and Hazel said, "Hey, look out. You're tipping over the whole thing."

Delta quickly turned inside to help ensure some great cards were made.

———————————

"Now I know," Hazel said, when the two girls had run off with their cards clutched in their hands, "why I won't be doing kids' parties. They are fun but so exhausting."

Delta crawled across the floor to gather discarded stickers, tubes of glitter, and candy wrappers. Popping up with two hands full, she said, "I wonder how far the sheriff is with his investigation, or what exactly he's investigating among those party gifts. When put like that, it sounds a bit laughable, but I assume he doesn't come out with sirens blazing for nothing."

She put the items in the cardboard box Hazel had used to transport the materials. "I'm going to have a look. Can I bring you some juice?"

"Yes, please. I feel drained." Hazel sank on a chair and rubbed her face, leaving glitter on her cheek. Delta motioned at her to scratch it off, and Hazel dived into her purse to look for her mini mirror.

Delta stepped out and looked around. Most people had gone inside, and at the gift table, the police tape moved in the growing wind. It looked like an abandoned crime scene, and Delta shivered involuntarily.

In the distance, a man in—what she assumed to be—the white catering uniform walked about with an empty tray. Delta went over to ask for two glasses of juice. But as she neared, certain he had seen her waving at him, he suddenly made a U-turn and disappeared around the house. It seemed everyone was flustered by the sudden party disruption. *Let's see if there's a drink to be had indoors.*

Delta entered the house through the same door she had used before and peeked into the room where Jonas had been with the sinister perfume bottle. He was gone, and the table was clean. *Where is everyone?*

She followed the corridor, peeking into another empty room with beautiful paintings on the wall lit by special, overhead lights. A spotlight shone on a bronze statue of a woman picking flowers, which dominated the far end of the room. The metal had been worked by an expert hand, creating an illusion of movement as the woman leaned down. It seemed her dress moved in the breeze, and her head was just about to come up again as she rose to continue walking. *This must be Drake's rumored art collection...* Delta heard voices and turned away from the art, to follow the sound to a large living room where all the missing party guests stood and sat in groups, talking. She figured they must have been rounded up by the police for questioning, but their conversation seemed casual, and she scanned the room for the police officers she had seen earlier. No uniforms in sight.

She did spot Jonas, standing beside a huge potted plant, and went over. "Have the police already left?"

"I never meant for them to come out like that, with blaring sirens and all. Lena is upset her party is ruined. I bet her husband will be mad at me too. I had better leave before he turns up."

"But he asked you to help out. You only reported the bottle to have them take it in for analysis. With your knowledge of Calvin Drake's worries about his wife's safety, you could hardly have ignored it."

"Yes, but you know how bad my relationship with West is. I bet he figured that I was hired to do security here, and he didn't like it. To ruin my relationship with the Drakes, he came rushing in and disturbed the party."

"I can't imagine—" Delta said, but Jonas cut her off.

"He's interviewing people now upstairs in the study. I was first on his list. I don't know what has gotten into him. Except for a need to fight it out with me."

"I'm sure he has a good reason to do this," Delta said, although she clearly remembered that in the murder case at the Lodge Hotel, West had arrested and charged Hazel's brother, Finn, without having much hard evidence to do so.

As she searched for something encouraging to say to Jonas, her gaze wandered and fell on Una Edel, who came in through another door and scanned the room. She walked about, muttering to herself, her eyes searching, and then disappeared again. On the clock beside the door it was ten past six. Delta's stomach growled, and she wondered how long they'd have to stay here. She could do with a hot meal.

Jonas straightened up. "Well, all I can do is tell Drake what happened, and he has to draw his own conclusions. I should never have let myself be talked into this in the first place."

"But you must admit it is fascinating." Delta touched his arm. "Who sent her that bottle? Can it be someone present right now? People arrived and put their gifts on the table." *Imagine someone sitting here, acting innocent, while they knew...* Suddenly, she thought of Sally Drake and the look in her eyes as people sang Happy Birthday for Lena.

"The garden is open in the back, leading into the forest." Jonas glanced at her. "Someone could have come in, added a present, and vanished again. It need not have been a party guest."

"You said something about a disturbed fan. Are you thinking of anyone in particular?"

"There were several people sending her frequent messages and presents while she was still modeling. That was even in the papers." Jonas leaned back on his heels, studying the people in the room. "But why would they continue after she quit?"

"The skull was taped to a perfume bottle. Do you think that's because perfume is an acceptable birthday gift, or because Lena is now in the perfume business? To show her that although she's no longer a model, she's still..."

"A target?" Jonas nodded. "I have considered that. I took it seriously, which is why I phoned the station. I wish now I never had."

One of the deputies entered and beckoned forward a new guest to be questioned.

Jonas hid his face in his hands and rubbed it. "What a mess," he muttered.

A handsome man in his sixties, clean-shaven, with an energetic air, came into the room and asked someone close to the door a question. He was pointed up.

Jonas peeked through his fingers, whispering, "That's Drake himself. He must be back from his business meeting."

"Yes, Ray mentioned something about Drake coming to the Lodge this afternoon to discuss furnishings with Rosalyn." Delta thought it might be better not to mention Ray's suggestion that Drake and Rosalyn had gotten along very well. Ray had a bit of a difficult relationship with his eldest sister after they had been estranged for a while, and maybe he had been pulling Delta's leg by suggesting something. In any case, she wasn't about to spread a rumor like that.

Drake went around, shaking hands with a few people, and then disappeared upstairs. Halfway up, he ran into Una Edel, who stopped him. Her emphatic voice carried across the buzz of people talking. "It has gone too far."

Did she mean the threat to Lena? Or Lena's response to it and the arrival of the police, ruining the party?

Drake shook his head emphatically and although Una looked ready for an argument, she let him pass and came all the way down, continuing to look about her as if still searching for something or someone.

"Well," Delta said, "I guess I should really go and help Hazel clean up." She did want to know more about this, but she could hardly let her friend wonder where she had disappeared to.

Just as she wanted to step away, Zara Kingsley, the dog walker, came running into the room. Her face was pale, her eyes wide, and she screamed, "Help, help! Police!"

Una Edel went over and grabbed her by the shoulders, shaking her. "Calm down."

Zara screamed even louder. "Police! She's dead."

Everyone had gone silent and stared at the two women.

"Who's dead?" Una asked.

Zara gasped for breath. "Pearl had run off. I went after her. She was at the dead rose bushes in the back of the garden. She tried to dig there. When I went up to her to catch her collar, I saw the"—she swallowed hard—"dead body."

"Don't be silly, girl. From a distance, you may have seen a branch or something. A mossed-over tree trunk. Get yourself together."

"It was a dead body."

West came banging down the stairs. "Did someone call for the police?"

Una turned to him. "The silly girl thinks she saw a dead body. Merely stress, Sheriff, I assure you."

"I'll be the judge of that. What did you see?"

"At the rose bushes, in the back," Zara said shakily. "A dead body. It's Sally."

"Sally?" Una repeated.

"Sally," Delta mouthed to Jonas, who widened his eyes. The woman who had dressed similarly to their hostess, Lena Laroy. A mistaken killing?

"You take me to the dead body," West decided. "Everybody else stays here. You too." He growled the latter at Una Edel, who seemed eager to fall in step with him.

"This is outrageous, Sheriff," she snarled.

"I said you stay here." West marched off.

There was a mutter among the guests. Una raised her hands and spoke loudly. "Nothing has happened. We'll soon hear it was a simple mistake. Please stay calm."

Jonas leaned over to Delta and whispered, "I don't think you can mistake a branch or even a mossed-over tree trunk for a dead body. Sally Drake wore a conspicuous turquoise dress."

"Yes, looking a lot like Lena's." Delta held his gaze. "Do you think…"

"I'm not thinking anything until I have some facts." Jonas shifted his weight.

"Admit it, you'd just love to go out there now and see it all for yourself."

"I quit that kind of thing."

"Yeah, which is why you agreed right away when Drake hired you for some security."

Jonas nodded past her, and Delta turned to see Drake rush down the stairs. "Where's my wife? I heard something about a dead body. Where is she?"

Una said, "I was with her a few minutes ago. She's fine."

Drake didn't seem to hear her. "Where is she?" he cried.

Lena Laroy entered the room through the other door off the corridor. She looked about her as if she was suddenly conscious of people in her home. "Is everything all right?" she asked.

Drake ran for her and locked her in his arms. "Darling…"

She leaned her head on his shoulder and closed her eyes.

Delta looked from the embracing couple to Una Edel, who studied them with a strange expression. What exactly flashed in her eyes? Jealousy? Or suspicion? Or was it exasperation, as if Una didn't buy into their little act of affection? Because she herself was in love with Drake and had wanted to be with him? Because she saw the other woman as a rival?

Stop it, Delta admonished herself, *you know nothing about them. Just rumors and assumptions.*

One of the deputies prowled by the door, and his phone beeped. Everybody looked at him. It was like the entire room held its breath. He read the message on screen and then turned to the assembled people. "There has been a dead body discovered on the grounds," he said. "I have to ask all of you to remain where you are."

Drake looked at him over the head of his wife, who pressed herself closely against him. "A dead body, who?"

"They think it's Sally," Una said.

Drake's face drained of color. "Sally? No." He let go of his wife and attempted to rush to the door. But the deputy blocked his path.

"No one is leaving. This is a murder investigation now."

"Murder?" Drake gasped. "You mean, it isn't a heart attack or…"

Delta thought it was odd he would assume death by natural causes, especially since he had been worried enough about his wife's safety to have hired Jonas, but maybe in a moment of crisis, people didn't think straight.

"Everybody stays here," the deputy said. He gestured at Jonas. "You help us contain them."

Jonas hitched a brow. "Am I suddenly one of you?"

"I'd like to think you are."

Jonas held the deputy's gaze and then said, "Okay. I'll help where I can." He glanced at Delta. "Looks like we have another murder on our hands."

Chapter Four

DELTA SAT OPPOSITE SHERIFF WEST IN THE STUDY upstairs. The shelves along the walls were filled with books, and the atmosphere was stuffy. A door onto a balcony let in a welcome breeze, moving the wine-red velvet curtains that were half-drawn.

Sheriff West stared with a frown at his notebook. "So, you saw the deceased at the party, moving into the brush?"

"It could have been her. It could also have been Lena Laroy. They both wore similar turquoise dresses and have blond hair. I overheard a bit of conversation between this woman and a man. The man threatened her to give him something or else. I couldn't make out who the man was... maybe he's the one who killed Sally."

Sheriff West sighed. "This is all very vague. You're not even sure it was the victim you overheard."

"I know, but at least now you know she may have been under threat."

West frowned and muttered, "I wonder if the perfume bottle was also meant for her."

"But it was a birthday gift for Mrs. Drake, I mean, Lena Laroy, right? It was on the gift table among the other presents." Delta didn't know what Jonas might already have told the sheriff, so she added, "I heard a rumor at the party that Lena Laroy was threatened before. By a disturbed fan. When she was still modeling."

"I'm well aware of her past." West put out his chest. "Which is why I responded to a reported threat during the party. I think her husband also appreciates us being vigilant."

Delta didn't comment that Drake's sister, Sally, might have been killed while West and his men were on the premises. Or had the murder happened earlier? Maybe the spot where the body had been discovered was so remote the death could have gone unnoticed for a while?

The door opened, and a deputy walked in with a plastic evidence bag in his hand. He put it on the desk in front of West and said, "We found this in the dead woman's hand. We don't know if it was hers, but maybe you can ask Mr. Drake about it?"

Delta stared at the glimmer through the plastic. Keys on a chain with a bird-shaped hanger full of blue gemstones. "I saw Una Edel walking about with it. That bird shape with the gems is very distinctive. Maybe she was looking for Sally Drake to return it to her? If it does belong to her."

"You saw Una Edel with this set of keys?"

"Yes, she carried them in her hand, quite ostentatiously. So maybe she found them lying somewhere and wanted to return them to their owner."

"Or they are hers, and the victim tore them from her in their struggle when she killed her," the deputy enthused.

West shot him a murderous look. "Thank you. Carry on."

The deputy grimaced and retreated to the door.

West prodded the evidence bag with his pen. "Well, well," he said, "Una Edel." He glanced up at Delta. "Do you know her?"

"Miss Edel? Not at all. I saw her walking about. She had a very take-charge attitude." Delta could still see Una shake Zara when she had come in all upset about having found the dead body. And her remark to Calvin Drake that it had gone too far... Not a woman who minced her words.

"Yeah, yeah." West made a dismissive gesture. "I think that was all. Send in that friend of yours."

Delta rose to her feet. "Is it okay if I go fetch our things from the tent outside?"

"As long as you don't come anywhere near the gift table or the murder scene…" West surveyed her through narrowed eyes. "Last time I let your interference pass because you were concerned for your friend and that brother of hers, but this time I might not be so lenient."

"I don't want to get involved in any way." Delta left the room and ran down the stairs. Hazel came for her at once.

"What did he say?"

"Only some questions about this afternoon. You better go up now."

"I don't like this. It reminds me too much of last time, with Finn and all." Hazel rubbed her hands together.

Delta's heart clenched for her friend. In the previous murder case, Hazel's brother, Finn, had been accused of involvement, and Hazel had been held at the police station because she hadn't been entirely truthful about what had happened right before the dead body had been found. She had done it to protect Finn, of course, but it had muddled the waters and put Hazel behind bars.

"This time it's totally different." She gave her friend a reassuring pat on the shoulder. "We have nothing to do with the victim or the people here. Tell him that you were in the tent most of the time and haven't seen anything worthwhile. Then we can go home and have some dinner. My stomach is growling."

Hazel dragged herself up the stairs, and Delta looked around. Most people had been interviewed already and left, it seemed. She caught sight of Drake sitting in a leather armchair, staring ahead with a vacant look in his eyes. She walked over and said, "My condolences on the death of your sister, Mr. Drake."

With a jerk, he looked up at her and blinked. "Excuse me, you are?"

"Delta Douglas. Your wife hired me and my friend Hazel to do a cardmaking workshop here this afternoon. I saw your sister only in passing but…" *She seemed like a nice person?* What to say that wouldn't sound silly? "I'm sure this will be a heavy loss for you, and I just wanted to say I'm so sorry."

"Thank you." Drake sat up a bit. "It's sad, you know. She had just quit her job to make a fresh start. Now…" His eyes filled with tears.

"Yes, I heard she worked in Los Angeles as an art expert," Delta said. "I also heard she advised you about the art you have here in the house. She had exceptionally good taste." She gestured around her at the paintings on the wall.

Drake shook his head. "Sally wasn't into paintings. Sculptures were her thing. Bronzes and all such. She got me the lady picking flowers, in the other room. She had contacts all over the world." His jaw tightened. "Too bad that no-good husband had to ruin it for her."

Delta didn't quite know what to say.

Drake continued as if he was speaking to himself. "She worked so hard to get to where she was, art advisor at a museum, buying pieces for galleries, while he spent the money she earned on trips with his friends. Betrayed her too, of course. Finally, she couldn't take any more and broke up with him. But then he spread false accusations about her, and she lost her job…" He swallowed hard. "Poor Sally. The injustice of it all ate at her. She had come out here to try and start over, but there really isn't much to do artwise here in Tundish." He gave Delta a sad look. "Sorry to be rambling on about this."

"I understand. Her death came as a complete shock."

"It must be that bastard." Drake shot upright. "I told the police. He must have followed her here to ask her for money again, and when she refused to give him any, he must have killed her." He formed his hands into fists and banged on the armrests of his chair. "Bastard. If I get my hands on him…"

"Do you know if your brother-in-law is here in Tundish?" Delta asked, fascinated by the possibility.

"Yes, Sally mentioned to me that Abe would be coming over and that I shouldn't agree to give him any money. Like I ever would." Drake inhaled hard. "He's a louse. He used her, and he couldn't stand her leaving him and starting a new life without him. He killed her."

"I'm sure the police will look into that possibility." Delta stepped back. "I must be going now. Good night." She went out the side door she had come in and headed for their tent. The white structures spread across the lawn seemed eerie in the dim light of the lamps. At the cordoned-off gift table, the wind played with the ribbons on the still-wrapped presents. A party quickly ended by a looming threat and then a murder.

Delta stood staring at the gift table with a deep frown. One woman threatened and another killed. Unrelated events? Or connected? It seemed illogical that at the same party two unconnected incidents would happen. *There must be some link.*

But then again, Drake had told her how Sally had been facing her own problems, having lost her job and wanting to divorce her husband. Maybe the threat to Lena and the murder were indeed acts from different persons, each for their own reasons. Pure coincidence.

Delta went to their tent and collected the cardboard box with leftover materials. She looked down ruefully at the unicorn sprinkles left on the table's surface by the two crafting girls. It could have been so much fun. And it had ended in disaster.

Leaving the tent, she almost collided with Ray. He slipped something into his pocket and retracted his hand with a quick, caught-red-handed movement. "Delta! I had no idea you were still here. Did West grill you?"

"Yes, but I hardly know anything. I've never even met Sally Drake. Did you know her well?"

Ray shrugged. "I knew she had been here for a few days. And she does something artsy for a living. That's about it."

It sounded evasive, and Delta gave him a closer look. "You never met her personally?"

"No, why would I?" Ray shrugged and walked past her. "I'm off to the Lodge. Rosalyn will be shocked to hear her good friend Calvin lost his sister." Half turning to her, he added with a cynical smile, "Maybe she'll want to come out here and comfort him, huh?"

"He has his wife to do that," Delta said automatically and then realized she hadn't seen Lena anywhere near Drake, who was left sitting distraught in his armchair. *How odd, when such a tragedy has hit, you'd assume she'd be at her husband's side... Where is she?*

Maybe she has a headache and is in bed, Delta admonished herself. There could be any number of reasons.

Ray waved a hand at her and marched off. Watching his tall, athletic figure, she wondered what he had put in his pocket. Why be so secretive about it?

Maybe he was feeling for his wallet or something. Stop attaching meaning to every little thing.

Turning around to carry the cardboard box to the house where Hazel should be about done with the sheriff's questions, she saw a figure near the gift table, ducking beneath the crime-scene tape. "Hey, you there!" She ran over.

The man turned to her. Delta clenched her jaw, recognizing Marc LeDuc, a pit bull–style reporter who'd do anything—including break the law—to get a story for his online news site. He had given her and Hazel a hard time with the previous murder when Finn had been under investigation, and the mere sight of him still raised her hackles. "Out for a scoop?" she asked sweetly. "West will arrest you if he sees you violating the crime scene."

"I don't see West anywhere around." Marc gave her a challenging stare. "Are you going to report me to him?"

"I might." Delta reached into her pocket for her phone. She wasn't too keen on West, but she liked Marc even less, and he might ruin valuable evidence.

"No need." Marc raised a hand in a placating gesture. "You can give me more than an underlit pic of this table, hey? Was the body found underneath?" He pointed at the damask cloth hanging down from the table. "Was it a big scene? Like when the hostess wanted to unwrap a gift, suddenly a dead hand appeared, and she started screaming? Give me something to entice my readers. A headline that will draw in thousands of clicks."

Delta shook her head. "No comment." She almost had to laugh at the thought of him writing such nonsense, but given the fact that there had been a very real death, her amusement faded instantly. "The sheriff has a lot to look into, and I don't think you snooping around will help any."

Marc tilted his head. "Come on, the public has a right to know what happened here. Do you know who it is? Did you get a glimpse of the corpse? I need not mention your name. I can quote you as a source who wishes to remain anonymous. A source close to the fire, that would give my report some credit."

"Sorry, I really don't know anything."

Marc ducked under the tape again and came to stand beside her. "Look, I know we didn't exactly meet under the best of circumstances. Your friend was wrongly accused, and that is a terrible thing. But that's all solved now. No need to carry grudges anymore."

"I'm not carrying a grudge; I'm telling you I don't know anything."

Marc wanted to say something, but he glanced past her, and his expression changed. He straightened up and snapped, "Too late, Dad. All the action is over. The body is removed from underneath the table, and the suspects have been taken to the police station already. If you want anything from the sheriff, you better go there."

Marc's father, Sven LeDuc, dressed as usual in a jacket with elbow patches, closed in quickly. He carried his ever-present notebook in his hand. His newspaper, the *Tundish Trader*, claimed to be a reliable news source since 1887. When Marc had come back to town to join the paper, his ideas about new media had clashed with his father's old-school approach. The two had split up in anger and were fighting for scoops ever since. Marc usually won because he put things online the moment he heard them, regardless of whether they were facts or not, but that didn't stop his father from trying to outwit him. LeDuc Senior glanced at Delta. "Is she an eyewitness? Can I talk to her?"

"No way." Marc shook his head. "Her story belongs to me."

"My story belongs to nobody, because there is no story to give," Delta said to LeDuc Senior. "The sheriff is still at the villa, interviewing people. You can talk to him there if you want to."

"So, you lied to me," LeDuc Senior shot to Junior. "My own flesh and blood lies to me, for a scoop."

"You trained me like that," Marc retorted with a grimace.

LeDuc Senior rushed off to the villa with its brightly lit windows.

"Why did you have to tell him that?" Marc asked. "I would have loved to see him race to the station only to find no one there."

"Your competition is very childish." Delta shook her head at him. "If you were a real journalist, you'd handle this completely differently."

"Oh, yeah?" Marc leaned back on his heels. "How?"

"You'd wait until there was factual, confirmed information instead of spreading a ton of nonsense."

Marc laughed softly. His eyes twinkled as he studied her. "People don't want facts. They want to know what others believe, think, feel. They want to be there on the scene, as it were. I can't just sit at home, waiting for some statement to come through. You know what West is going to say? That in the interest of the ongoing investigation, he can't comment on anything. Come on. There's enough to find if you look in the right places. I mean, a dead body popping up on the lawn of this villa…during a party. How poignant."

Delta decided he was a lost cause and feigned

understanding. "You're right. It's just like *The Body in the Library*. In that book, someone dumped a dead body in a respectable family's library to hurt their reputation. Terrible." She thought Marc would see right through her forced weighty tone.

But he nodded in earnest and said, "Drake did make enemies here."

"In Tundish?" Delta asked, surprised.

"Yes. Seems locals are considering him for their interior design all of a sudden, and others who might have been eligible for the job are suddenly dropped like a hot potato. They are not happy, I can tell you."

"What others? Does Tundish even have a decent interior-design agency?"

"Don't you know them?" Marc tutted. "LyCla Design worked on the community center. All that eye-catching red with the white and black geometric patterns, it really divided the council. Some think it's the latest in good taste; others claim it hurts the eye and should be redone."

He leaned over and added in a conspiratorial whisper, "LyCla Design is run by two women, who fight with any means available to them. They tried to team up with Drake, and when he wouldn't budge, they vowed to destroy him. Or in any case, chase him out of town. And this body on his lawn sounds like a perfectly good reason to leave. Right?"

Delta made a mental note to look closer at these designing ladies, but first she wanted to kid Marc, just a little. She nodded, feigning awe. "Which one of them do you think sacrificed herself for the good cause?"

He stared at her. "Excuse me?"

"Well, to have a dead body to put on the lawn, someone

has to die. Do you think they drew straws to see which one of them…"

His expression changed as he realized she was riling him up. "Very funny. But I'll get to the bottom of this. You bet on it." He walked to the house with long, angry strides.

Delta suppressed a grin. Hazel appeared in the doorway and ran for her. "That was easy," she said with a relieved smile. "Let's go home and pop some pizza in the oven." She rolled back her shoulders. "I can't believe it, another murder as we're doing an event. But this time Finn didn't find the body, and nobody can claim we had anything to do with it. West can look into it all he wants."

During the drive home, Delta heard her phone beep several times, but she didn't look at it. She simply wanted to enjoy the quiet of the evening around them and dream about what dessert to have after the promised pizza. There was triple chocolate ice cream in the freezer, but she might also dig into that salted caramel pudding in the fridge. Just thinking of it, her mouth watered, and she couldn't wait for their cottage to come into view. The small but cozy cabin-style home had a well-equipped kitchen where Hazel preheated the oven while Delta cleared the table in the living room for their dinner plates and drinks. She glanced at her phone's screen before putting it away and noticed several new messages from the Paper Posse group. Rattlesnake Rita said, "I heard the police were out in full force at the Drake villa by the lake. What happened?"

Mrs. Cassidy responded, "Someone died."

"Foul play?" Wild Bunch Bessie asked.

"I think so, or they wouldn't be questioning everybody."

"Was it a local or one of Mrs. Drake's high-profile friends? I saw their cars breeze through town. Must be a million-worth standing in her driveway."

"The golden Porsche was too tacky for me."

"I'd love to have seen it up close. Why didn't you snap a pic for us?"

Calamity Jane intervened, "I heard there was something wrong about the gifts. Were they not what she had ordered? Or was it the catering? Was that deceased person poisoned?"

"I have no idea," Mrs. Cassidy replied. "It will be in the papers tomorrow, I suppose."

Delta replied, "Yes, it will, because both Sven LeDuc and his son, Marc, were there. Marc seemed to think the dead body was under the gift table, and he believes it was planted there to drive the Drakes away from town. Something about a vendetta between interior designers? Do you know anything about that?"

Calamity Jane responded at once. "He must mean Lydia and Clara from LyCla Design. They are regulars at the bakery. They love sweet treats. A few weeks ago, Clara rushed in with a grin on her face, claiming something wonderful was about to happen. She didn't want to say too much about it, but she did suggest it had to do with their business getting a huge boost. Maybe that had something to do with Calvin Drake?"

"I heard," Wild Bunch Bessie said, "that one of them got awfully close with Drake, and his wife didn't like it. Maybe their planned cooperation tanked because of her?"

"And then they wanted revenge," Rattlesnake Rita wrote with lots of exclamation points and open-mouthed emojis. "But I don't think they would actually kill someone for it. They seem the type to simply send a box with a big spider in it to give Mrs. Drake a scare."

Delta thought about the perfume bottle with the skull and the word *DEATH* and wondered if Lydia and Clara had anything to do with that. They could have decided to use it to put their own kind of pressure on Mrs. Drake.

"Put aside that phone and have some appetizers," Hazel said, shoving a bowl of walnuts in Delta's direction. "The pizza will be ready soon."

Delta sighed. "I know you said this one has nothing to do with us, and it's a relief that it doesn't, but I must admit I'm fascinated by the dynamics. Lena Laroy, a former model now married to a hugely successful interior designer who has women smiling up at him everywhere he goes. That must create bad blood."

"Not enough to kill for, I suppose. And it wasn't Lena dying, but Drake's sister." Hazel popped a slice of cheese into her mouth. "Do you want some ice tea?" Without waiting for a reply, she opened the fridge and pulled out a pitcher.

Delta got two glasses from the cupboard. "It's odd that Sally is the one who died. I mean, the party was for Lena's birthday, so all those people present were her friends. Did they even know Sally? Why would someone who hardly knew her want to kill her?"

"I'd assume the killer did know her. So, it has to be someone from the Drakes' inner circle." Hazel nodded as she filled the glasses. "I think the dog walker is very suspicious. I heard she found the body and acted like she was in a panic."

"*Acted?*" Delta echoed. "Did you think she wasn't then?"

"I don't know. I was in the tent cleaning up when it happened, but I heard Una Edel say that Zara's panic was overdone."

Delta recalled the woman shaking the girl. She seemed to have little patience with emotions.

Hazel said, "I thought about it and it could be true. I mean, when we saw her earlier in the afternoon, with the poodles, something about her struck me as a bit…too much. The whole air of the young twenty-something who doesn't really know what she's doing. Like she can't handle the dogs and all. She got the job, so she must know something about taking care of them."

"Not necessarily," Delta said with a grimace. "Ray told me he saw her and Drake at the Lodge, and Drake put his arm around her. He may have hired her not for her experience with dogs but because he liked her."

"See." Hazel passed Delta a glass of ice tea and returned the pitcher to the fridge. "There's more to Zara Kingsley than meets the eye."

"But why would she kill Sally? If she's after Drake, you'd think she'd kill his wife. If she would want to kill anyone at all. It's so drastic."

"Maybe Sally had seen them together and threatened to tell Mrs. Drake. Zara would have been fired then and not been able to see her lover anymore."

Delta sipped her drink, considering this theory. As Sally had been staying at the villa, she could of course have seen or heard something. "If Drake really likes her, they could stay in touch, even if she no longer worked for them. No, I think if she killed Sally for anything, to keep her job, she must want the job for another reason than being near Drake."

"That's it." Hazel pointed a finger at her. "She wormed

her way in by flirting with Drake while she has some ulterior motive. Vengeance against the Drake company for some injustice done in the past…"

Delta waved a hand. "That is all pure speculation because you think she's more than an ordinary dog walker. And the Paper Posse"—she pointed at her phone, which was still beeping every thirty seconds—"is discussing what Lydia and Clara from a Tundish design agency might have to do with it. Wild Bunch Bessie said she heard that one of them was close with Drake. I admit he's a handsome man, if you like the type, but he can't have been having affairs left and right. I mean, Ray also told me Drake was close with Rosalyn. Seems he wants to modernize the Lodge's interior look. Not all of these can be true, right?"

"I don't see anything wrong with the Lodge's furnishings as they are right now," Hazel said with a sour expression. "Maybe Rosalyn does like him and is using changes to the Lodge as a reason for seeing him."

"Nah, I don't believe it." Delta shook her head. "He's a charming man, and people read far too much into that. Right now, he's very upset about his sister's death. He mentioned to me she had such a hard time, losing her job, and with her marriage ending as well… Seems her husband harassed her to get money off her."

"I see. Is he here in Tundish? He might have asked her for money again, and when she refused, killed her. Not that he meant to, just in anger, you know. Those things happen." Hazel looked into the oven. "I think it's done. Let's eat."

Delta picked up her phone. "I'll turn this off. I want to eat in peace and then dive in for a nice long night. We can better leave the speculating to Marc LeDuc and his news hunters."

Chapter Five

THE NEXT MORNING, WHEN DELTA AWOKE, SHE REMEMBERED snippets of dreams that had plagued her all night. In them, she had been chasing a black poodle, who ran off with a 3-D card in her mouth before jumping into the lake and swimming away while glitter rained down from the trees on the bank. On the other side of the water, someone was calling for Delta, but she couldn't make out who it was or what it was about.

So much for a quiet night. She rubbed her sandpaper eyes and stretched, then sat on the edge of the bed, wriggling her toes. The dream images still whirled through her mind, and she took a couple of deep breaths to restore some calm. Her gaze fell to the small rug she had brought with her from Cheyenne. The text on it read: *follow your dreams.* A smile spread across her face. Yes, even when she had still been in an office job, she had believed in following her dreams. And in moving to Tundish and joining Wanted, she had made her biggest dream come true. All thanks to Gran, who had given her the money to buy into the shop. *I'll send her a message to say how happy I am every day for that chance!*

With a grin, she turned on her phone. *Over one hundred twenty messages?*

The Paper Posse had been busy.

Delta wanted to swipe away without even looking at what they were talking about, but curiosity got the better of her, and she went to the website of Marc LeDuc's online newspaper. The headline read: *Who sabotaged former model's birthday party?* with a smaller caption underneath: *Gift table turns into crime scene.*

There was a badly lit picture of the table in question, no doubt illegally snapped with Marc's cell phone when she had seen him skulking about the night before, but Delta doubted people would really mind the photo's quality, as the accompanying piece was full of clickbait—exaggerated statements about tension brewing during the party as the guests had gathered for what was a birthday "resting under a cloud of bad feelings."

Delta read the next bit half aloud, "Tundish residents feel like Mr. Drake swept in last July and claimed too much space, both with his villa, which dominates the lake view, and his professional enterprises, encroaching on some locals' very livelihoods."

She frowned. When they had been invited to do the workshop, Mrs. Cassidy had told them in passing that the villa had been built in the forties, right after the second world war. So why blame Drake for the way in which it dominated the lake view? The original builder had chosen that site.

Shaking her head at LeDuc's total lack of accuracy, she read on. "But also, personally, the Drakes never felt at ease. Lena's previous engagement ended abruptly for reasons undisclosed, and one can't help but wonder if her new husband discovered the same thing her ex-fiancé already knew *after* their recent marriage vows. The big secret that led her ex-fiancé to ask the model to return his diamond engagement ring."

She frowned, recalling Ray's mention, when he had popped into the shop with his bouquet for the birthday girl, of Lena being with some musician when they had first met at a team party, years ago. So, this bit could contain some truth. However, Marc would have to give more substance to the "big secret" before she could judge whether there was anything there that would have upset Drake.

She continued reading. "One of the reasons for retreating to the quiet of Montana was the constant pressure from the media, who often wrote unkindly about the former model's tendency to team up with men with the reputations and wealth to boost her career. While her previous interest was music and her ex-fiancé an award-winning musician who had already arranged a record deal for her, her current husband allowed her to dabble in interior design, and there are rumors she was to come into his company, Drake Design, as a partner. Perhaps even taking the place of current right-hand woman, Una Edel."

Delta whistled. "First thing I've heard about that," she said to herself and scrolled through the rest of the article. Lena Laroy was painted as an opportunistic woman who made friends one day and dropped them the next when someone more advantageous came along. Someone with enemies who might have wanted to plant a dead body at her party to ruin it all for her and drive her away from her mountain hideout.

Apart from the overdone tone of the article, Delta had to admit that Marc LeDuc had managed to unearth quite a lot about Lena's past and current relationships and turn it into a piece people would be talking about. Still, knowing the deceased had been Calvin Drake's sister and not some randomly planted dead body, she had a hard time believing the murder had happened only to ruin Lena's birthday party. It seemed more likely that someone had wanted to remove Sally from the scene.

But why?

Why Sally?

Having showered and dressed, Delta came downstairs to find a big breakfast laid out on the table. Yogurt with fresh fruit flanked nuts, cheese, cold cuts, and a platter of hot toast, while Hazel stood at the stove, making scrambled eggs. "Good morning," her friend called out to her. "I figured you'd like something substantial before we hit the store. We need to do a lot of unpacking today."

"Right. New washi tape and erasers. Can't wait to see them. Especially the animal line with the llamas and pandas. They looked spectacular in the catalog." Delta sat down. "Did you have a look at the news?"

"About yesterday? No, of course not. I want to stay far away from it." Hazel shivered. "I was locked up last time. I dreamed about it again. I don't want to think of anything remotely involving murder."

With a pang of sympathy for her friend, and guilt that she had looked already and was sort of intrigued by the revelations, Delta nodded. "I understand." She picked up some warm toast and scooped jelly onto it. "Did you know Lena Laroy had been engaged before?"

"Done, I think." Hazel took the pan with scrambled eggs off the stove and came to the table. "With that musician guy, you mean?"

"Yes. A musician or a singer." Ray had mentioned meeting Lena at a football party and all his teammates wanting to dance with her. Her boyfriend had not been with her because he was doing a concert in Nashville. "Who was that exactly?"

Hazel frowned as she shoved the eggs onto her plate. "You don't want some, huh?"

Delta shook her head. "Sweet things for me, thanks."

"I think he was a country star. Probably still is. I'm not really into all that celebrity news. But she was engaged to him. It ended quite suddenly, and nobody knew why. Usually, there is someone talking after the breakup, one of the two exes, or a friend of them, a management person who wants to set the record straight. But they never said a word. Odd thing." Hazel gestured at Delta with the spatula. "I know, because Mrs. Cassidy told me all about it yesterday. We had enough time to chat as we sat waiting for those workshop participants that never showed." Frustration lined her voice.

Delta smiled encouragingly. "The little girls liked it."

"Liked sprinkling everything with glitter, you mean. I think when the company comes to remove the party tents, ours will leave a circle of glitter on the grass." Hazel half-grinned and sat down to eat. "I hope we won't get asked for birthday parties for eight-year-olds now. I do love kids, but they can get everything so messy in a heartbeat. Rosalyn won't allow us to do it at the Lodge, and we don't have the space in the shop." She dug into her eggs and chewed with an expression of bliss. "Just right." Tilting her head, she asked, "Is that your phone beeping?"

"Yes, the Paper Posse are sending a gazillion messages. Probably about the murder. But as you said you don't want to hear about it, I won't be looking at what they say."

"Good." Hazel nodded and ate on. The beeping continued.

"I wonder what they can be messaging about," Hazel said. She glanced nervously at the phone on the sideboard. "The sheriff was quite friendly to me yesterday when he asked for a brief statement, but I still feel like he's angry he was wrong last time and wants to get even with us."

"I suppose he's trying to do a good job and save some face. He came out to the villa to look at that perfume bottle with the threat on it, and then someone died..." Delta pulled a face. "If you think about it, it doesn't put him in a very favorable light. If Sally died right before her dead body was discovered, his men were at the villa when it happened."

"In that case the perfume bottle and the murder can't be related. You don't have the police come and then kill someone." Hazel gestured with her fork. "It makes no sense."

The phone rang. Delta shot to her feet. "I'll answer it now."

"Sure."

She picked it up. "Hello?"

"Jonas here. I suppose you will want to be going to the shop soon, but could we meet up briefly? I have something to discuss that I can't say over the phone."

"Um, sure. One moment." Delta looked at Hazel. "Jonas wants to meet me about something important. Can you drop me off at the Lodge with my mountain bike and then go to Wanted to open up? I'll bike into town later. I can do with the exercise."

"Sure."

Delta told Jonas she'd meet him at the Lodge in half an hour, and they finished their breakfast. Hazel winked at her. "I wonder what that is all about."

Delta shrugged. "Don't get anything into your head."

"Oh, come on, Delta, Jonas is perfect for you." Hazel leaned back. "You can at least try."

"How do you mean try?"

"To show him you like him. That you think he's attractive. To maybe get him to go on a date with you sometime. I don't know. Don't you like him?"

"Sure, but…" Delta felt her cheeks flush. "He has been so distant lately. I think he has his work and his dogs and that is enough for him. We're just friends, and that's fine with me. I'm not risking it by playing for anything more that might not work out."

Hazel rolled her eyes. "Maybe Jonas is thinking the same thing."

Delta got up. "I'm going to change. You eat up, and then we leave."

"Put on that red sweater. That looks so good on you."

Delta ran up the stairs. Her friend's attempts to pair her off were no doubt well meant, but also a bit embarrassing. Jonas and she were…

She opened her closet and reached for the gray sweater she had intended to wear today. Then she hesitated, looking at the red one. Did it look better?

Did it matter?

With a sigh, she picked the red one and pulled it over her head.

"Have fun." Hazel squeezed Delta's shoulder before diving back into the Mini Cooper and driving off. Delta steered her mountain bike to a nearby tree and leaned it against it.

"Morning."

She jumped at hearing Jonas's voice. She hoped he hadn't caught Hazel's parting words. In combination with her suggestive look, it might convey the wrong impression. But Jonas had wanted to meet her, so…

"Good morning. Here I am. What's up? Hey, Spud." She leaned down to pat the German shepherd. He wagged his tail and barked once. "You had to stay at home yesterday, right? I bet you could have caught the killer if you had been there. Good boy."

Jonas gestured for her to walk by his side across the parking lot. He folded his hands on his back and said, "I told you yesterday that Drake asked me to have a look around at the party. I didn't tell you exactly what he said when he hired me..."

"Because it was too personal. I know."

"But you should know now."

"Why?" Delta studied his tense profile.

"Because I need your help. You did such a good job with the previous murder case and...I wouldn't ask you if it wasn't really important."

Jonas halted. Spud sat down by his side and looked up at Delta with earnest brown eyes, as if he wanted to support his human's request.

"You see..." Jonas sighed. "I shouldn't have taken Drake's case. I'm not a PI, and... But he flattered me, saying he knew I was really good, and he only wanted me to keep an eye out for anything suspicious during the party. He told me that his wife was under serious strain from someone harassing her with cryptic messages. He had only found out the other day during a grocery delivery. Apparently, it contained a package of cookies and a smoothie. Lena had become agitated and said that she had not ordered them. She didn't know what they were doing there, that it had to be some mistake, but later she was in tears, and Drake concluded that someone had sent them to her on purpose. I asked him why he thought it was on purpose, whether there had been anything special about them, something threatening added to them, like with the perfume bottle. But he said that the groceries were innocent looking. However, he had noticed Lena was different after they had arrived, very nervous and looking out of the window all of the time."

"As if she suspected someone was watching her," Delta supplied.

"Exactly. Drake thought that the delivery was meant to demonstrate that someone she had been avoiding had finally found her, even here in this remote place, and was watching her. He wanted me to find out who that was."

Jonas shook his head. "I fell for it, Delta, while I knew I shouldn't. Like I said, he flattered me and… It was dumb. Look what happened now."

"This isn't your fault, and who says the murder is even connected?"

"The perfume bottle seemed to be exactly what Drake was afraid of, and I called in the police because they can analyze evidence, take prints and follow up. I hoped they would find out who had sent the bottle and could do something about it, as I obviously can't. But by involving West, I got him into trouble. The time of death has been established as between five thirty and six, so Sally Drake was actually killed while the local police were around, looking into the bottle. Drake is outraged, and…he wants to file some sort of charge for incompetence and get West removed from his post as sheriff. You can understand how West now thinks I set this up with Drake. We've never seen eye to eye, but I won't have West lose his job because of some judgment mistake I made."

Some mess. Delta looked him over. "So, what do you propose?"

"That I find out how it all fits together. The bottle with the skull, the murder. The groceries earlier. I need all the information I can get about the party, and I thought you might know a thing or two." He gave her a hopeful look. "Hazel was there too, and Mrs. Cassidy."

"Hazel wants nothing to do with this investigation. She dreamed again about being locked up when Finn was accused of Vera White's murder." Delta bit her lip. "I'd hoped we could put all of that behind us. I feel so sorry for her."

"Okay, leave Hazel out of it then. Ask Mrs. Cassidy and that outlaw group of hers."

"They're already on the case." Delta sighed. "I have about two hundred messages on my phone."

"Great, can I see?" Jonas sounded eager to unearth a major clue.

"Sure." Delta pulled out the phone and handed it over. Jonas started to read. After a while, he glanced up. "It's not really facts they deal in, huh?"

Delta had to laugh. "Last time they did unearth a lot of useful stuff. They have eyes and ears in all public places. I hate the saying: 'Where there is smoke, there's fire.' But it turns out to be true at times. And you can see there are already some claims in here that might be useful. Take Calvin Drake and Zara Kingsley—he got that girl into his home as a dog walker for his wife's poodles. They seem to have met at the Lodge where Calvin Drake put an arm around her in a pretty friendly way, suggesting she's not just some student he offered a job to."

Technically, Delta had gotten this information from Ray, but knowing how Jonas felt about Ray and the Taylors in general, she wasn't going to specify that. Instead she added, "Oh, and you could go talk to Lydia and Clara of that design agency to see what their gripe was with Drake."

"Could you do that?" Jonas handed back the phone. "Maybe as an excuse for contacting them, you can fake interest in interior design for Wanted?"

"I don't think we can afford anything like that." Delta looked him over. She really wanted to help out, but she had a suspicious feeling Jonas was going to load a ton of jobs onto her. "What are you going to do?"

"Take a group birding." He gave her an apologetic smile. "My schedule was filled up weeks in advance, so I can only sleuth in my free moments. I was hoping to rely on you and the crafting ladies."

Delta sighed. Irritation fought with excitement that they could go sleuthing again, like they had before. She had missed it. Had missed him. "I must admit I'm super intrigued, and I want to help you. But I can't promise any results. I mean, last time I could easily ask a question here and there, since my link to Hazel and Finn explained why I was so interested in the murder and I wanted to clear their names. But I hardly know the people involved now, and…it might look very nosy."

"The murder will be the talk of the town. You can listen well. Your friends are at the important places: bakery, boutique, mining museum. They will hear things."

"I know, I know." Delta gestured. "Shall I add you to the message group so you can hear our discussions firsthand?"

"No, please." Jonas put up both hands, palms outward. "I have an idea how those discussions go. You condense it and share it with me. You made a very nice concise overview last time. We can uh…meet up for regular strategic discussions?"

She looked into his probing eyes. Was this really about the case or…? Hazel had said Jonas liked her, and she should take the opportunity to get to know him better. Date. Discussing a murder case wasn't dating, of course, but still… It was a chance to spend time together and see how they got along.

"Sure, strategic discussions sound good."

Jonas's expression relaxed into a relieved smile. "I knew I could count on you. Thanks so much. We'll be in touch." He backed up and waved at her. "See you later. Come along, Spud." And with the dog trotting by his side, he walked off.

Delta exhaled. *Did he even notice what sweater I'm wearing?*

Still, he had called her earlier contributions valuable. And that smile when he had said he had known he could count on her…

They were officially on a case again.

Together.

A wave of excitement ran through her chest, and with a grin, she jumped on her mountain bike to race into town.

On the last bit downhill, carried by the forward momentum and the wind at her back, Delta was contemplating the good in her life when a big, black shape shot out into the road ahead of her. In a reflex, she hit the brakes of her bicycle and steered away, sending the bike skidding across the concrete and veering into the bank. She managed to stay in her seat but didn't have enough control to avoid the bushes. Twigs broke all around her, and the bike hit an exposed root and came to a full stop. With adrenaline pumping through her system, Delta reached up to wipe the sweat off her face. A burning sensation in her left cheek suggested twigs had grazed the skin off. She took a deep breath and turned her head to check how her neck was functioning.

"I'm so sorry! Are you all right?"

Delta twisted her upper body toward the voice and saw Zara Kingsley staring at her with a worried frown. Her strawberry-blond hair looked fiery in the morning sun. She wore a short leather jacket with skinny jeans and sneakers. By her side, one of Lena Laroy's poodles tore at the leash. The other one was nowhere in sight.

Delta sighed. "That black thing running right in front of my bike was your other dog?"

"Pearl. She's off again. I can't control her." Zara burst into tears.

Delta untangled herself from the bike and bushes. Plucking twigs from her sweater, she went over to the girl. As she put a hand on her shoulder, it struck her how ironic it was that *she* was the one almost in an accident because of the runway dog, and she was now comforting the dog walker. But it had all ended reasonably well, so no need to upset the girl any further.

"They do seem to be a handful," she said, leaning down to calm Emerald.

"They are monsters," Zara burst out. "They don't obey; they are practically untrained. They are spoiled rotten and think everyone exists purely for them."

"Doesn't sound like you like dogs at all." Delta tilted her head.

"Oh, I do. Just not these two. They are so badly behaved." Zara sniffed. "They should have hired a dog trainer instead of a dog walker."

"If you can't control them, you have to stay away from the road. Suppose Pearl had run right in front of a car. If the driver had panicked and steered away..." Delta grimaced. "You can take them for walks in the forest behind the villa, right?"

"Where the murder happened? No way." Zara hugged herself. "I could be next."

"You think the killer is some maniac targeting random women?"

"Why not? It's full of tourists here." Zara swallowed hard. "I can't see why someone would want to kill Sally Drake. She was a quiet person. Not likely to get into an argument."

"I heard she had trouble with her ex-husband."

"I don't know anything about that. She left the place where she lived and came here. Maybe for vacation?" Zara shrugged. She stood with her head down, staring at her feet.

"Don't we have to look for Pearl?" Delta asked. Her heart clenched at the idea of the poodle running into trouble. Maybe the dog had never been trained properly, but that was not the animal's fault. Out on her own, she could get hit by a car or hurt, and Zara didn't even seem to care.

"I don't know where she might be. Maybe she ran home?" Zara sounded less than enthusiastic about a search for the missing poodle.

"You could give the villa a call to ask if the dog has come home," Delta suggested.

Zara's head shot upright. "Are you crazy? I can't tell them I lost her. Then I will get fired."

"If you can't handle the dogs and believe they are monsters, why don't you look for another job anyway? It can't be much fun to have to work this way."

"It's not about fun. I…need the money." Zara gave her a pleading look. "You won't tell them either, will you?"

"No, I won't call them right away, but…it can't go on like this."

"I'll look for Pearl." Zara turned away and pulled the other poodle along. "Pearl! Where are you?"

Delta shook her head. She went back to the bush and extracted the bike, straightening the handlebars. Then she climbed back on it and tested it to see if she could move the pedals without trouble. Everything seemed to function all right. She put the bike into motion and called out, "Pearl! Pearl, good girl, come here."

When Delta arrived at Wanted, Hazel's voice rang out, "There you are. I was just thinking I'd have to do it by myself. There is this fun package with… What happened to you?" She closed in on Delta and put a hand on her arm, scanning her face with a worried expression. "Your forehead looks all red, and there is this odd graze on your left cheek."

"One of Lena Laroy's poodles ran into the road ahead of my bike, and I sort of crashed. It was nothing serious, but Zara was rather upset, and I helped her catch the dog."

"*Zara* was upset? How about you?" Hazel gestured for her to come along into the kitchen area in the back. "That graze needs to be washed with hot water."

While Hazel poured water onto a cotton pad, Delta sat on a chair, telling the full story. "Pearl hadn't gone far. She was simply walking about in circles, barking. She doesn't seem to be a truly badly behaved dog; she's just naughty and testing how far she can get with Zara."

"Zara doesn't seem very experienced as a dog walker," Hazel stated. "Now hold your breath, this may sting." She applied the cotton pad to the graze.

Delta hissed a moment, then relaxed. "Zara asked me

not to tell a thing to Lena or her husband. Apparently, she needs the job because of the money involved. I guess she does really need it for something, since she seems so unhappy with her work but is still determined to stick it out." The graze burned, and she sucked in air. "Of course, I could hardly ask her *why* money was such an issue. I mean that would have been rude, and she wouldn't have told me the truth anyway. Especially not if she's having an affair with Drake. Him being married and a lot older than she is."

"Right." Hazel threw the pad in the wastebasket. "That should be a bit better. I don't have any disinfectant here."

"No need for it. It's just a little graze. It could have been much worse, so I'm happy. Too bad the chat with Zara didn't deliver the jackpot for Jonas." She told Hazel what Jonas had shared with her about wanting to look into Sally Drake's death because of his assignment for Drake.

Hazel whistled. "So, Lena Laroy was seriously under threat, even before the party? Maybe the wrong woman was killed."

Delta made a so-so gesture. "They wore dresses of a similar style and color, but that doesn't make them identical twins. If you want to kill Lena and you've been targeting her for some time, you don't suddenly come and kill the wrong woman."

"Maybe the killer was waiting for Lena, and then Sally showed up and recognized him, and he had to kill her to silence her."

"Recognized him?" Delta tilted her head.

"Yes, maybe she had seen him before, hanging around, or she knew who he was from a prior occasion. She was Drake's sister; she might have stayed with them before."

"Good thinking. As Drake's sister, she must have known about a lot of things. And rumor has it she wanted into the company as well. She might not have known a lot about interior design, but her brother might have taken her on board purely to support her after her old job ended." Delta frowned hard. "Drake mentioned to me that Sally had left her job. It sounded as if that had been her own decision. But then he also said her husband had maligned her, and she had been fired. So, did she leave of her own accord or not?"

"Does that matter?" Hazel perked up as a tinny ring sang through the shop. "The store bell. I'll go serve the customers; you sit quietly for a bit to get over the shock of the near accident. Oh, there's a pie in the fridge. Jane brought it right before you came. It's a new idea from the bakery we have to test."

Delta's mouth watered. It was the best thing to have a baker's wife for a friend.

Hazel disappeared into the front, and Delta peeked into the fridge. The pie looked amazing, with a chocolate cake layer, cream with raspberries, meringue, and chocolate chunks on top. She took it out of the fridge, cut off two large slices, and put them onto plates. She then poured coffee into two mugs and put everything on a tray. She peeked into the shop. Two women were just leaving, Hazel guiding them to the door and saying goodbye. As she turned into the shop again, Delta carried out the tray with their coffee and pie. Hazel grinned at her. "Perfect timing. Oh, that does look good. Jane said to evaluate how we like it."

Delta dug her fork into the meringue and took a bite. "I already like it," she mumbled.

For a few minutes they ate their pie, sipped their coffee,

and enjoyed the sun slanting into the shop, shining light on the notebooks for sale. Delta took in the newest display, an array of planner fillings. It was a recent addition to the shop, so people could vary the color and pattern of the sheets in their planner. Delta had fallen in love with the botanical designs and purchased two, even though she didn't own a planner. But the paper was too pretty to resist.

She closed her eyes a moment and enjoyed the happiness of being in her own shop among the scent of paper and ink, eating pie with her best friend in the whole world. This was the perfect life.

The graze on her cheek stung, and opening her eyes again, she realized with a sigh of regret that even in the perfect life not everything went as planned, and with a dead body found at a party, things were getting complicated again—fast. The only good thing was that this time Finn wasn't involved, and via him, Hazel, so their shop wasn't caught in the line of fire. She had barely completed the thought when the door opened, and Marc LeDuc rushed in. He held out his phone and moved it up and down as if scanning for something. He came to the counter and eyed the pie. "Celebrating, are you? A bit callous after a death."

"We're testing a new pie for the bakery," Hazel snapped. "And what do you want?"

"Information about the party yesterday." He held the phone close to her. "You gave a workshop there. You must have noticed something. Did you see Sally Drake's ex-husband there?"

"Her ex-husband? I thought he was in LA." Delta knew very well that Drake had told her the day before how his brother-in-law had popped up in Tundish, but she wanted to find out exactly how much Marc knew. And what was more, how he knew it. Who was tipping him off? Delta studied Marc. "Do you know for certain he is around town?"

"I'm asking you questions."

"Well, you can share a little. It would be pretty sensational. After all, their marriage ended, so why would he want to come after her?"

"For money maybe?" Marc leaned back on his heels. "It seems that he's a big spender, and her job at the museum and various art galleries provided for his needs. But after she left, well…" He tutted. "It's not nice to be cut off, I guess."

"So, you think he would have been…persuasive to get her to start paying again?"

"But why would he kill her?" Hazel intervened. "That makes no sense at all. If she has to pay him money, he would only be hurting his own interests."

"Unless he knew he'd inherit from her. They had only recently split up, and the divorce hadn't come through yet. Maybe she hadn't changed her will either. You know how spouses often make each other their beneficiary…" Marc beamed. "I think it's a very interesting angle. He could actually have killed her to get the money before the divorce ensured he lost it all."

"Yes, but I don't see why you're here then. Naturally, Sally Drake didn't discuss her upcoming divorce or a possible change of her will with us." Delta took a sip of coffee. "We barely saw her at the party."

"That's odd, because someone told me she had been looking forward to the 3-D card–making. Wasn't that what *you* offered?" Marc leaned in. "I bet she came into your party tent and made a card, and while working on it, talked a lot. Like women do when they're at the hairdresser's and all."

"There was a nail studio there," Hazel said in a musing

tone. "Maybe she had her nails done and spilled about her unhappy situation? The tension with her husband, how he hounded her."

Marc shot upright. "Really? That would be… Bye then. Talk to you later." And he raced out of the door.

Hazel laughed softly. "The pie does taste better when he is not around."

"He seems to be full on top of this." Delta stared at the closed door.

"Nothing much of interest happens in Tundish. This is his chance. Also to aggravate his father, who will be chasing the same leads."

Delta hemmed. "Marc could be onto something with that will. I understood from what Drake said about his sister that she had left her husband only a short while ago, because he was spending her money and was unfaithful to her. The husband then spread false stories that made her lose her job and come here to Tundish to start over. Maybe she never thought to change her will. It's not a pleasant subject to think about."

"Plus, it costs money to change it," Hazel said. "And if she made a joint will with her ex, like Marc suggested, she might have figured she couldn't even change it without him finding out. Maybe she thought she'd have time off here to think things over and make decisions without him coming after her."

"Only she never got around to that, and now he inherits the lot." Delta nodded slowly. "That's some motive for murder. We have to find out if there was anything to inherit. If it made it worthwhile to…"

"Kill her?" Hazel shivered. "I think her brother would know or could guess, but we're not going to ask him. It would be rude."

"Agreed. I'll let Jonas know about this possibility, and he'll have to follow up on it. He has PI friends, so who knows what they can turn up?"

Delta finished her pie. "This is delicious. I'll pop over to the bakery to tell Jane. I won't be long. We really need to unwrap all that new stock and give it a nice place."

She left the shop and crossed the street. At Mine Forever, a radio was blasting from the roof, and the same man from the other day was working on cleaning the mining utensils. Delta grimaced at the tearing electric guitars from his music and hurried into the bakery. Several customers were waiting for their turn, but Jane's daughter was helping, and Jane gestured to Delta to step into the back a moment. Under her apron, she wore one of her trademark, long dresses with an intricate, French-lily pattern. Her dark hair was braided, and the braids were rolled around her head. She leaned over and asked, "Are you all right? I heard from someone you fell off your bike. He had seen it in passing as he went up to the Lodge to deliver something. He wanted to stop to see if you were okay, but there was a girl with a dog going over to you, so he figured you had help if you needed any. His delivery was rather an urgent thing, food that had to go into the Lodge's breakfast offering so…"

"That's totally fine. I wasn't injured or anything. Just this." Delta gestured across the left side of her face. "And yes, Zara Kingsley came over to help me, mainly because it was one of the dogs she was walking who caused it all." She sighed. "Those poodles are really naughty."

Jane nodded. "I heard Lena is spoiling them, treating them almost like her children. They sleep on her bed, and they pinch food from the kitchens, and nobody is allowed to say anything about it or she gets upset and cries."

She hesitated a moment and then continued, "It's a nasty thing to repeat, but some people claim she loves her dogs more than she does her husband."

"I really don't know. I barely saw her yesterday. And Calvin Drake wasn't at the party, so I couldn't see the dynamics between them." Delta recalled the dashing young man by Lena's side, smiling at her, unwrapping gifts for her and playing the crowd, both before and after the sinister perfume bottle had been discovered. "When she went to unwrap the gifts, she was with her husband's nephew, though. I think his name's Randall Drake?"

"Oh, him. He came over in a gorgeous old car. A black Buick Electra with those fins on the back. Took it to the local garage to have them check it over. They were salivating. An icon from the fifties, their head mechanic called it. Told me that Randall Drake is quite a normal guy, even though he has money."

"What does he do?" Jonas had mentioned that Randall was a software engineer, but it couldn't hurt to check that information.

"I don't think he has to do anything, job-wise, I mean. He has money from his family."

"Oh, but Calvin is a self-made man, right? He earned his wealth from his design company?"

"That's right. He had to fend for himself, because his father disinherited him when he was younger. Everything went to his brother, Randall Drake's father. Imagine what he must have felt." Jane shook her head. "It had been all over Marc LeDuc's website when Calvin bought the villa here. Something about an eerie resemblance between his fate in life and that of the industrialist who originally built the villa."

"Oh." Delta filed this tidbit away to look into later. Who had built that villa, and why would there be a resemblance between that person and Calvin? "Judging by that inheritance matter, you'd expect Calvin wouldn't be on very good terms with Randall then. Doesn't he blame him that he got everything handed to him on a silver platter while Calvin had to work for it?"

"I have no idea. Maybe Lena convinced Calvin to reconcile with Randall? After all, Calvin doesn't have any contact with his own children from his first marriage."

"So, Randall is like a sort of surrogate son to him?" Deep in thought, Delta touched her cheek. *Ouch!* She retracted her hand quickly. "Maybe he can help Zara with those dogs, since he's so close to the couple. I advised Zara to walk them in the forest behind the villa where there isn't a road, but she said she was worried she would also be murdered. She seems to think the killer was a maniac lurking in the trees, waiting for victims."

"Could be." Jane pursed her lips. "This wouldn't be the first tourist town to draw in criminals. Usually it's con men with sob stories meant to empty an unsuspecting lady's pockets, or credit card fraud. But it could be more serious this time."

Delta tilted her head. "You don't believe the murder was meant to dispose of Sally Drake specifically? I mean, that it was done by someone she knew?"

"I don't know. I heard from all around she was this nice, quiet person who wouldn't hurt a fly, so why would anyone hate her and hurt her? It seems to make no sense."

"I've heard that before, about her being so nice and all, but when Lena was unwrapping her presents, Sally gave her a decidedly evil look. Whether it was resentment or jealousy, I can't tell, but it felt like they didn't get along. Well, anyway, your meringue pie was delicious, and you should start selling it pronto so we can buy it. And keep your eyes and ears open to let us know anything you might pick up. Jonas asked me to help as...uh...it seems West might be in some trouble. Calvin is angry that the murder happened after the police arrived at the villa, and he wants to complain and make life hard for West."

"Jonas told you that? And he wants us to help West? I thought they didn't get along."

"They don't, but Jonas never meant for West to get into trouble because of the call he placed to the station about that perfume bottle. He feels responsible for all this."

Jane nodded pensively. "If only we knew who had put that on the table. All the guests put their presents there, right? Wasn't there a camera somewhere that could have picked it up? Most villas have security, right?"

"I suppose if there is footage, the Drakes will turn it over to the police. I have to run. Hazel is waiting for me with a ton of new stock. See you later." Delta left the bakery, mulling over the new information she had learned. Calvin had been disinherited by his father and all the money had gone to his brother. How about their sister, Sally? Had she played a part in the situation that led to the disinheritance? How had she felt about meeting Randall at the villa? Could there have been tension between them?

And did the close relationship between Lena and Randall factor into the murder? If Lena had urged Calvin to reconcile with his nephew, like Jane had suggested, only to discover that Randall was now awfully close with his wife, this could have caused major friction. Had Calvin stayed away from the party for that reason, not wanting to see Randall play master of the house? Or to give Jonas a chance to see something incriminating? He had suggested the danger might come from close to home.

She had to write all of this down into what Jonas had called "a nice concise overview."

Chapter Six

"So that was the last package." Hazel sighed as she stretched her back and waved her arms in the air.

"Good." Delta let her gaze roam across the glass jars with washi tape atop what had once been the cot in a prisoner's cell. She grinned as she pointed at the new washi tape with a panda design. "I bet that will be a hit. We should already order more."

"Did it this morning." Rolling back her shoulders, Hazel walked to the window and peered out into the street. "Didn't you say something last night about the Paper Posse speculating about the ladies from an interior design agency here in town? Possible cooperation with Calvin Drake gone wrong and such, them being vengeful?"

"Yes. Lydia and Clara from LyCla Design." Delta nodded. "How come?"

Hazel pointed out of the window. "That's their car on the other side of the road. It has their logo emblazoned on the side. I thought you might run over and ask them to have a look inside here. Just a free consultation about changes to our interior design?" She underlined "free" with a cheeky wink.

"I doubt anything they do will be for free," Delta said, studying the BMW with a tasteful golden logo. "And can we really pretend to be listening to pro tips for bigger lamps or different carpet, while we throw in supposedly innocent questions about their relationship with Calvin Drake and the murder of his sister? I have a feeling they will smell a rat in a heartbeat."

"There's one of them now," Hazel exclaimed. "You have to do it."

A tall, dark-haired woman in a purple pantsuit exited the bakery and headed to the car. Delta recalled Jane sharing in the Paper Posse message group that the women loved sweet treats and were regulars at the bakery. Delta dashed from Wanted's entrance and managed to reach the BMW as the woman was about to close the door. "Excuse me. Jane"—she gestured at the bakery—"mentioned you to us. That you have this design agency and all. I'm new to town. I help Hazel run Wanted. I'd love for you to give a professional opinion about the store. Just have a look to see what we might change, to make it more on trend?"

The woman's immaculate eyebrows rose a moment as if she wasn't quite sure about the request, but then her face relaxed in an accommodating smile. "Of course." She got out of the BMW and extended her hand. "Clara Ritter, of LyCla Design."

"Delta Douglas." Delta got a whiff of an expensive perfume. She shook Clara's hand with a vague sense of guilt, because Hazel and she had no intentions of changing anything about the shop and certainly wouldn't spend serious money on it. "You do have to understand," she rushed to add, "that we are a small business and we can't afford to uh…"

"Splurge on expensive changes." Clara flashed her pearly smile again. "Of course not. We're aware of that. As a small-town agency, we try to offer what a big-city agency would for prices that are affordable to the local business owner. Often, the end costs depend heavily on how you have the work done. What workers you engage and what materials you choose. I'll come over and have a look right away if that's okay with you." She swung her purse over her shoulder with energy.

"Perfect," Delta said, resisting the urge to show too much enthusiasm and give herself away.

Clara locked the car and followed her to Wanted in a clatter of her high heels. "Such a nice, authentic old building," she gushed. "And you've kept it all in that old-West style, I see."

"Yes, that's what makes Tundish so charming, don't you think? I came here from Cheyenne, where I worked in advertising. I hear Lydia and you aren't locals, either?"

Clara shook her head. "We moved here three years ago. It seemed like a risky move to some, but it turned out very well for us. We recently did a renovation on the community center's boardroom."

"Yes, so I heard. And with all the villas by the lake getting bought by rich holidayers, you must be swimming in assignments. Aren't you working with Calvin Drake as well? I was at his home just the other day."

Clara seemed to tighten a moment, her friendly expression setting. But her voice was steady as she replied, "We haven't worked on his home. He has his own company, after all. His sister wants to join in, as does his wife. Enough voices clamoring about how it should all turn out. I don't think we should try and mingle in that."

"Well, his sister won't be joining anything anymore," Delta said in a light tone, but keeping her eye on the other's features. "She died yesterday."

"I read about it." Clara nodded. "It was probably a heart attack. She was under a lot of stress because she lost her job at some art museum, and her marriage was over too."

"Oh, you knew her personally?"

"No, Calvin, I mean Mr. Drake, told me, in passing."

Clara flushed. "He was very worried about her. I'm so sorry for him." Her voice was unsteady a moment, and Delta wondered if Clara had been the LyCla partner seen with Drake and sparking gossip about a relationship.

"The newspapers are writing it was murder. Didn't you have time to read them this morning? I can imagine you lead a very busy life."

"Probably Marc LeDuc, trying to make more of it than it was. He desperately needs exposure for his online newspaper." Clara snorted. "I wonder if he ever completed any kind of journalism degree. He seems to be very free with his facts."

"Yes, well, he claims that people love to hear opinions, not necessarily facts."

"It can be very hurtful," Clara said.

Her tone made Delta perk up. Was Clara worried about Sally Drake's murder harming Calvin Drake, with whom she might be close, or was she referring to something else? Had Marc also written about the LyCla Design agency? Maybe about the controversy over their renovation of the community center's boardroom? She'd have to look online to check and see.

They entered Wanted, and Hazel came over to shake Clara's hand. "So nice to meet you. I've heard so much about you. Of course, I did most of the changes here myself and…I hope it's not too bad by your standards."

"Not at all." Clara looked around. "You kept it all in one theme, which is good. Too many different things can make it look disjointed. I would have opted for more airiness, probably. One white wall can do so much for a room. And light…" She glanced up. "A few nice industrial lamps would change the whole atmosphere of the place."

"Industrial?" Hazel mouthed to Delta, who grimaced. Clara was walking around, measuring spaces with her widespread hands and muttering to herself.

"Did you also come to Lena Laroy's party yesterday?" Hazel asked.

"I was invited, but I had to cancel, as I had this important business meeting out of town." Clara flashed a quick and not very sincere-looking smile. "Lydia went, though. You might have seen her?"

"I don't know her by sight," Hazel said. She threw Delta an excited look. So, one of the two ladies of the design agency had been at the party. Delta bet Hazel was wondering the same thing as she was. Had Lydia put the sinister perfume bottle on the gift table? Marc LeDuc had claimed that both Lydia and Clara hated Drake and had vowed to chase him out of town. But if Clara had been close with Drake, maybe she didn't hate him quite so much, and Lydia had decided to take action on her own.

Hazel said, "I think Lena Laroy is ever so elegant and charming. I had so little chance to talk to her really. You must have asked her sometime about her modeling career."

"Actually, no. I guess it gets very tiresome for her to talk about it over and over. She's done with that really."

"Her perfume line then?" Delta noticed that the woman's shoulders stiffened a bit at the word "perfume," but that could also be her imagination.

"Sorry, no." Clara shook her head. She eyed Delta. "Shall I make a design idea for your shop? It's merely a concept, you need not let us do the actual work if you don't like it. It only costs a hundred dollars."

Delta glanced at Hazel. Hazel glanced back.

"That's a deal then," Clara enthused. She snapped a few

pics with her state-of-the-art phone and then clattered to the door on her high heels. "I'll mail it to you in a few days. Bye."

Hazel exhaled slowly. "A hundred dollars for the little she told us."

"We do know Lydia was at the party."

"We could have found out about that in a cheaper way, I'm sure."

"At least we'll hear what she thinks it needs. We won't give them the assignment, but if we do like elements of it, we can buy a lamp or two, I suppose." Delta looked around. "I couldn't quite determine whether her praise was genuine, or she hated everything about this place but didn't want to tell us."

"I don't know if personal taste even factors in these people's evaluations. Maybe they can see a concept and how it should turn out. Based on the building, the space, existing elements. I think it's fascinating." Hazel's expression turned dreamy. "I would have wanted to do something creative like that."

"Yeah, but you're always at the heart of a discussion. What one person loves, the other thinks the ugliest imaginable. Anyway, we have to wait and see what she comes up with. I'm going to sit down now and open a new case file. I wanted to do it when I came in from the bakery, but then you sent me out after Clara."

"Case file?" Hazel echoed.

Delta nodded and extracted her sketchbook from her purse. She always carried it with her to make little drawings of scenes she came across or ideas that popped into her head. Hazel and she were looking into the possibility of starting their own stationery line to carry in the shop, and the wrapping paper and notebooks would then display Delta's designs. She had so many she wasn't quite sure yet which to choose first.

In the murder case at the Lodge, she had used the back of the sketchbook to make a case file, using stationery items to create a makeshift police whiteboard, with the victim, suspects, and leads. It had worked well, so she might as well try again for Sally Drake's murder.

She sat down and drew the shape of a human body in the center of two white pages and wrote: *Sally Drake, formerly lived in Los Angeles, an art advisor for museums and galleries, left her husband, Abe, lost her job (quit or got dismissed?), came to Tundish, wanted to join her brother Calvin Drake's design company.*

She then sketched Calvin Drake in his suit and wrote beside him: *Calvin Drake of Drake Design wasn't at the party but at the Lodge, discussing changes with Rosalyn. Twice married before, seems to have lost touch with the children from his first marriage. Believed his wife to be threatened (mysterious grocery delivery, which had Lena in hysterics), and hired Jonas to keep an eye on her at the party.*

She drew Una Edel with her key chain in her hand and wrote: *right-hand woman in Drake Design.*

She connected Una and Sally with a bit of washi tape, writing on it: *Was Sally competition for Una? What was Una's key chain doing in Sally's hand?*

Then she drew Lena Laroy and wrote down a number of questions: *Threatened by whom? Can we establish who placed the perfume bottle on the gift table? Camera footage? Why did her previous relationship end suddenly and without a reason provided? Did she marry Drake solely for his money and to get a place in his company?*

She connected the figure of Lena to Drake with a bit of tape, reading *married* and to Sally with a note: *What was their relationship like? Sally resentful/jealous during the gift unwrapping?*

Hazel watched over her shoulder as Delta added Clara of LyCla Design in her purple pant suit and put up a note asking: *Was she friendly with Drake? She wasn't at the party, Lydia was.*

She sketched in Lydia as a vague figure, since she hadn't seen her yet.

More vague figures appeared: Sally's husband, Abe, with *in town?*, and the guy who had been with Lena at the party, Drake's nephew Randall. *His father inherited the family fortune, cutting out Calvin. What was Sally's role in this? What was her relationship with Randall?* Come to think of it, Delta wondered if Sally's hateful looks at Lena during the gift unwrapping had been prompted by Randall's presence by her side. Had she disliked her nephew's closeness with her sister-in-law?

"Don't forget Zara," Hazel reminded her. She went to fetch something and returned with a sheet of foam stickers representing various dog breeds. "Look, Pearl and Emerald."

Delta grinned as Hazel peeled two poodles away from the sheet and handed them to her. "I will use the rest of the sheet to create a mock scrapbooking page for the shop."

Nodding, Delta pasted the poodles beside the figure of Zara: *Did she know Drake even before she came to work at the villa? The two of them met at the Lodge, and he wrapped his arm around her. Why is she a dog walker if she can't control the dogs? She claims to need money, for what?*

"Seems there are enough questions and rather odd things," Hazel said, looking across the sheets. "I mean, it

seems everyone wanted to get into Drake's company—
Sally, Lena, LyCla, maybe even Zara. But can they even? I
mean, I can want to work at a bank or as a rock-climbing
instructor, but I'd need an education for that, right?"

"Lena could bring her celebrity status, and Sally may
have appealed to Calvin's sense of family loyalty. He did
appreciate her art advice for the villa. Maybe she really could
have made a contribution to his interior designs doing the
art side of things. Which would make her the real rival for
Una. Not Lena." Delta pursed her lips. "We have to zoom in
on why those keys were in Sally's hand. And what about her
husband, Abe? Do we know for sure he's in town? Calvin
said so to me, but Jonas should check on that. And even if
he's in town, he could have an ironclad alibi, having been at
his hotel all afternoon or something. Maybe we can exclude
him right away?" Delta picked up her phone and sent Jonas
a text message. She also mentioned having spoken to Clara
Ritter and recalled the thought flashing through her head
while Clara had been in the shop with them: Had Marc
LeDuc written something unpleasant about the designing
ladies?

She went online to his news site and searched for the
name of the design agency. She didn't have to look far to
find a picture of Drake and Clara toasting each other with
wine. They were seated on a terrace somewhere along the
lake, maybe the Lodge. They smiled broadly.

The headline asked whether good times were ahead for
a local design agency as a major deal was struck with nation-
ally acclaimed Drake Design. Delta studied the photo for a
while, wondering if this really was business or something
more personal. If so, Clara couldn't have been happy with it
going public. And how about Drake? He was married, after

all. Had Lena Laroy seen this photo and put pressure on her husband not to do business with the ladies anymore? Was Lydia angry at Lena for the deal falling through? Or maybe at Clara for risking their business by being so friendly with Drake?

The doorbell jangled, and customers filed in, a dozen women, who chatted busily about going to see the gold-mining museum after lunch. The one in the lead explained to Hazel they had ten minutes before lunch to shop, and she wanted to see the paper goodies, because those were simply too good to resist. Hazel said she'd try her best to serve them all in ten minutes.

Delta's eyes went wide as she watched the ladies rush through the shop, grabbing notebooks here, washi tape there, stickers, wrapping paper, and pens. One added two expensive calligraphy sets to her purchase, explaining she'd give those to her mother and mother-in-law over Christmas.

Hazel manned the cash register while Delta gift-wrapped the items at a speed she had never managed before. As she handed out the last paper bag to the final customer, the first ladies had already left to claim their places at Mine Forever for lunch. The door shut, and Hazel released breath in a long huff. "That was…fast."

Delta burst out laughing. "Normally, we'd sell this much in two or three days, and now we sold it in less than a quarter of an hour."

"I don't think we have to change anything about this store." Hazel grinned. "It's perfect the way it is."

Chapter Seven

THEY WERE ABOUT TO CLOSE UP SHOP WHEN JONAS appeared. "Listen, there have been some developments in the case, and I wondered…if you'd go to dinner with me to discuss them."

Delta focused on some notebooks on a display table. "I uh…Hazel and I…"

"I've got leftovers I can warm up." Hazel sounded brisk. "You go. Fine with me."

Delta knew there were no leftovers, but her friend was apparently eager to see her leave with Jonas. Recalling how little interest he had had that morning for her outfit, or anything else for that matter, she wondered if Hazel wasn't mistaking Jonas's professional zeal about the murder case for something more romantic.

Jonas said, "Are you ready to leave? I wanted to go to this little place I discovered along the lake. They have great fish dishes. If you like fish."

"I eat almost anything." Delta looked at Hazel. "Okay for you to lock up on your own?"

"Sure, no problem. Have a good time."

Delta got her purse and coat and followed Jonas out of the shop. His Jeep was parked right in front, which was actually forbidden, but at this hour there was no deputy in sight to put a ticket on it. He opened the passenger door for her. Delta clambered in and buckled up. She patted her coat, which lay across her knee. She was suddenly a bit nervous about this whole thing, which was silly, as she had spent time with Jonas before. But dinner together was just a bit more…

Jonas started the engine. "I can answer that question you texted to me."

Delta had to think a few moments to know what he was referring to. "Oh. About Sally Drake's husband. Whether he's in town."

"Yes. He is. And I know exactly where."

"Ah. I see." Suddenly Delta got it all. "You're taking me to dinner in the restaurant of the hotel where this guy is staying, so you can survey him. Clever." She didn't want to admit to herself she was a little disappointed at this idea.

"Nope, that's not it."

"Oh." Her sense of excitement returned with a flutter in her stomach. "So where is he staying then?"

"In a cell at the police station."

She glanced at him. "He's in jail? So, he can't have committed the murder if he was locked up already. What for anyway?"

"They arrested him this afternoon." Jonas glanced at her. "Someone declared they had seen a man skulking about in the forest near the villa. They assumed it was him. That he had waited for Sally Drake and then, when he had her alone, he fought with her over money and killed her."

"I see. But do they think it was an impromptu killing then, unplanned? He got angry and hurt her… Or is it about the inheritance? Does the sheriff know he will now inherit her property?"

"The sheriff did look into the matter of the wills. Or rather, Calvin Drake readily told him that his sister had been about to make a new will, as she didn't want her husband to get anything of hers, but she hadn't done so yet. So, currently he does inherit."

"I see. That could mean he knew that she was going to cut him off, and he acted before that. But it seems a bit stupid to kill someone when you're clearly the one profiting off the death; you're immediately in the police spotlight."

"Right. From what I heard, he's protesting his innocence with all his might. But West locked him up anyway." Jonas grimaced. "We know he isn't always right in those decisions."

"You doubt it was the husband?"

"I don't know. I haven't met the guy. I don't know if he carried a grudge or was angry at her for leaving LA. She kept her maiden name, never wanted to call herself Jarvis—that's his name, Abe Jarvis. Some men take rejection badly. He might have resented her independent attitude before, and he may have killed her because he didn't want her to be free. Those cases happen from time to time."

"But you're not convinced?"

Jonas hemmed. "There was so much going on. Lena being threatened, Drake telling me he didn't know whom he could trust. So, the threat might not have come from the outside, but from someone near. Who did he mean?"

"Have you asked him?"

"I tried to call him, but he's not answering his phone. I guess the media are hot on his trail, and he's lying low for a bit."

"I can understand that." Delta nodded. "The death seemed to have hit him hard. Do you know if he was close with Sally?"

"When we met to discuss the threats against his wife and my role at the party, he did mention her in passing. That it was great she was staying with them because she was so positive despite her sad circumstances. I guess he felt she provided a welcome distraction, maybe also for Lena."

"But did Lena and Sally get along? I thought it was odd they both wore a turquoise dress. Ladies who live under the same roof can prevent their clothing looking too similar. I mean, as soon as you see the other one, you can say 'Oh, we seem to have the same great taste, but we don't need to look like twins, do we? Could you maybe select another dress?'"

Jonas glanced at her. "Speaking from experience?"

"Not really." Delta laughed. "I can't recall Hazel and I ever wearing something similar, not even in college. We have different tastes, I guess. I wonder if Sally bought a dress similar to Lena's to spite her. You know what they say about not wearing white to a wedding because you'd take attention away from the bride? What if Sally wanted to take attention away from the birthday girl?"

"A sort of strife between the ladies? Maybe for Calvin Drake's affection? But he wasn't even at the party." Jonas shook his head. "There could be a simple explanation for it. Sally wasn't as well to do as her brother and his wife. Maybe she only had this dress to wear."

"But her family has money, right? Calvin Drake was cut off, but not his brother, so why wouldn't Sally have inherited money too? That fortune is exactly what her husband is supposed to be after. Then again"—Delta glanced out of the window. Light was fading fast—"we really don't know a whole lot about her."

"I can help you there. I talked to a former colleague of hers at the museum where she gave advice about their collection."

"Oh, you've been busy." Delta shifted her weight in the seat. "What did that colleague tell you?"

"That she was a very nice person to work with, knowledgeable and friendly. That her husband wasn't so pleasant, though. She had called Sally once or twice, before the split, and when her husband answered the phone, he growled at her that she shouldn't make calls outside working hours."

"Couldn't she call on Sally's cell?"

"She did. He apparently picked that up as well. Could indicate that he tried to control her life."

"And what did he discover when he looked in her phone? You often hear people check each other's messages to find proof of infidelity. If Abe found something on her phone before she left him, it might have made him mad enough to follow her here and hurt her."

Jonas nodded while he steered the Jeep around a bend in the road. "Especially if he figured that she was waiting for her new love, a little away from the party."

Delta's thoughts raced. "Did Calvin Drake tell you anything about a new love for Sally? Oh, no, he can't have. You said he only mentioned his sister in passing and you haven't been able to reach him since the murder."

"Right. I did ask the colleague if she knew more about Sally's reasons for divorcing her husband and leaving town. She said it had come as a shock to all of them that Sally was leaving, but that her boss had said it was for a good reason. She guessed that Sally might've wanted to make 'a fresh start as her husband was pushy.' Quote unquote."

"I see." Delta surveyed the specks of lights in the distance, probably lit windows of holiday homes on the other side of the lake. "So, everything you found out strengthens the case against Sally's husband, who is now locked up by the police. Well, maybe West can solve the case quickly, and Calvin Drake will be happy with him and decide not to file charges against the station."

"I don't know. Isn't it all too neat? The husband, who

was harassing her, who couldn't accept she had walked away, following her here, her turning up dead, him being arrested? And it still doesn't account for Lena and the perfume threat."

"I'm sure West will look at fingerprints on the weapon and see how the presumed killer might have gotten hold of that weapon. Do you know what the weapon was?"

Jonas nodded. "A knife that was lying on one of the tables to be used to cut up cake."

"So, anyone at the party could have picked it up…" Delta frowned. "But didn't you say the husband allegedly came from outside the party? That he lurked in waiting for her in the forest on the edge of the villa's grounds?"

"He could have walked to the table and picked up the knife. There were about seventy people milling about, including staff, caterers, and workshop presenters like you and Hazel. Nobody would have paid much attention to a single person going to a table."

"Okay. Did Drake have security images he could give to the police?"

"Yes, he has a system that records several key places around the house—the driveway, part of the lawn, and all the entrances." Jonas braked as they came up behind a slow-moving truck. "But he doesn't have a camera on the forest, so we have no images of the actual murder scene."

"That would have been too easy, right?" Delta pursed her lips. "If we could simply have looked at some footage and see someone do it." She shivered. "It must be gruesome."

"It probably happened very quickly. I doubt she noticed much."

"And the killer could have been male or female?"

"Yes, definitely."

"That means Una Edel isn't off the hook. Remember, her key chain was found in the dead woman's hands. How does she explain that?"

"She claims they are not her keys, but a bunch of spare keys used around the house. Front door, garage, that sort of thing. Lena used that set from time to time when she couldn't find her own. Zara the dog walker used them too, and apparently Sally as well while she stayed there."

"Sally had the house keys in her hand to use." Delta tilted her head. "Does that mean she wanted to get inside somewhere? But she was found outside at the edge of the forest. What was there to unlock?"

Jonas shrugged. The truck in front of them turned into a side road, and he accelerated again. "I haven't heard about anything she might have wanted to unlock. There's a path through that forest leading back to the lake. When the villa was built, it also had a boathouse, but it was demolished later. It's a plain dock now. No cover there, let alone anything with a lock on it. The sheriff assumes Sally never intended to go into the forest or down to the lake, but was just there, perhaps waiting for someone, away from the party."

"And then her husband found her first and killed her..." Delta stared into the darkness. She recalled the moment when Zara Kingsley had run into the living room, screaming about a dead body. She had given a few details about how she had found it, and something had struck Delta as important at the time. But her mind refused to recall the exact wording.

"We're almost there." Jonas turned into a gravel side road. "I hope I didn't spoil your appetite with all this murder talk."

"Not at all. I find it rather... Exciting is the wrong word, as someone died and that's terrible, but the riddle of it, searching for answers, is thrilling." She added, "But if the sheriff is right this time with his first arrest, there is no more case already."

Jonas braked. "I doubt it. Abe Jarvis is too easy a suspect. And was he really anywhere near the party? Maybe he can come up with an alibi and clear himself. The murder happened between five thirty and six o'clock. Pretty narrow window, so if Jarvis can prove he was, say, getting gas on the other side of town…" He pointed ahead. "What do you think?"

The lit windows of the restaurant seemed to wink at them with a friendly shine. It was a two-story building, mainly constructed out of wood, with stone elements at its base. Antlers sat over the entry doors, and a year was carved into the lintel—*1963.*

"They have a great terrace by the water," Jonas said, "but it's not summer now, so we'll have to sit indoors. Come on." He got out and Delta followed suit. A friendly waiter welcomed them and led them to a table against the far wall, at a window. In the sill were small cacti in pots, and on the table, colorful candles flickered in glass jars.

Jonas gave her chair that little polite push in place, and for a moment, Delta felt like this was truly a date. But it was a case discussion, really, and that was fine with her. After all, she had just told Jonas how exciting it was to hunt for clues. Together.

After they had ordered drinks from the waiter, Delta pulled her notebook from her purse and showed Jonas her case file. "Don't laugh. I know it doesn't look as professional as your whiteboard at the police station did, but it helps a lot to keep everything straight. I'm adding Sally's husband's full name—Abe Jarvis. If I could only find my pen." She dug through her purse.

"I'm not laughing. After all, I asked you to help me." Jonas gave the sheets a quick once-over and nodded with a satisfied expression. "Not bad at all. Here." He handed her a ballpoint from his pocket. "Also add the information I gave you about the will and the husband coming off as controlling before they split."

"According to that colleague from the museum," Delta added with a bit of rebuttal.

"You think she may have a reason to lie?" Jonas sounded incredulous.

"Not to *lie* maybe, but…after you heard something, you can see the things you experienced earlier in a different light. Maybe when the husband answered the phone, the colleague didn't think anything of it. But now it's proof he was controlling his wife. You get my point?"

"Yes, of course. You're right." With a suddenly very serious frown, Jonas straightened the cutlery beside his plate. Discomfort crackled in his tense movements. "I'm guilty of that myself. Right after the murder, I recalled seeing Sally Drake in town, talking to a man whom she seemed to want to shake off. She walked away, and he was following her, pleading with her it seemed. I mentioned this to one of the deputies at the party. When I heard they had Abe Jarvis locked up, I called to ask if my description of this man in the street matched Jarvis, but the deputy said it didn't. So, my idea that Jarvis had harassed her before and had then come to the party was totally wrong."

Delta frowned. "Sally wanted to shake off another man besides her husband?"

"Yes, it seemed so at the time. But maybe I'm influenced by the knowledge she was murdered. Maybe he asked her for the way to the museum and she said she didn't know since she was new to town, and he walked along, asking if she could then tell him where to find tourist information or something like that. It could have been innocent."

"Still, what did that guy look like?"

"Tall, blond, in his forties. Her husband is also in his forties, but he's short, thickset, and dark-haired."

"I see." Delta drew a new figure on the lower side of her case file sheets and wrote beside him: *tall, blond, forties, mystery man, accosted (?) Sally Drake in the street.* "And did you ever see this man again?"

"Can't say I have, but I will keep an eye out for him."

The tone of his voice made her glance up. "You're laughing at me."

"No, no, I think your enthusiasm for it all is rather cute."

Cute, huh? Delta looked down quickly and pretended to be sketching in some details.

The waiter brought the drinks, and Jonas lifted his glass. "To a good night."

"To a great night. You chose a beautiful place."

"Like I said, it's even better in summer when you can sit outside, but we'll have to make do. Let's have a look at the menu."

Delta sipped her mineral water while leafing through the extensive menu of delicious salads, great fish dishes, vegetarian burgers, and desserts. The desserts especially drew her attention, and she salivated at the idea of triple chocolate ice cream with pecan nuts drizzled with salted caramel. Or meringue with caramelized pear. Or warm apple crumble with vanilla ice cream and whipped cream. Or...

"Do you want to start with dessert?" Jonas asked with a twinkle in his eye.

"Never eat with a former policeman, because he sees

everything," Delta countered. "I will be good and start with a salad, okay?" The idea of a leisurely dinner with Jonas, hours of his time, made her feel all warm and comfy, like the world was right as it should be.

A low beep rang out, and Jonas reached for his pocket. Pulling up his phone, he said, "This won't take long" and before she knew it, he had left the table to take the call.

Hmm. Nothing was perfect, right? She watched Jonas's back, as if his stance could betray something about the conversation. *Why does he have to be so busy? Can't they leave him in peace for a night?*

He came back already and reseated himself. He held up the phone to Delta. "Just what I wanted to hear."

"What?" Delta had been about to sip her drink but held her glass midair, waiting for a spectacular revelation.

Jonas leaned back, stretching the suspense.

"What?" Delta pressed.

"Well, you can guess that West isn't eager to share anything with me. Regardless of whether his deputy asked me to help out with all the guests yesterday, or the fact that Drake hired me to look after his wife at the party. He's not giving me much, certainly not about the specific details in the case. Fortunately, I have a few contacts I can tap into when I really have to, and I thought I should know about this. Because it's so important when we're assuming motive."

Delta still clutched the glass on its way to her mouth. "Yes?"

"That will Sally Drake made, which left everything to her husband…"

"Isn't valid anymore," Delta guessed. "She made a new will anyway, and the husband doesn't get a thing. But if he didn't know that…"

Jonas shook his head. "It's still valid all right. But he doesn't get much. Sally Drake didn't have anything worthwhile to her name. The house in LA, which she left, is her husband's. Her bank account is about empty. She even has a few overdrawn credit cards. She apparently paid for their luxury lifestyle—think dinners, city trips, and even biannual cruises. Her salary at the museum was too modest for that, so she must have been spending her family's money until there was nothing left."

"Meaning Abe Jarvis is actually going to be paying for her debts?"

"Exactly. And he knew about that, because Sally had already hired a lawyer to start divorce proceedings, and the financial situation had been discussed and seemed simple to handle, mainly because the house was his, and they didn't have a business together. There were no children either, so the lawyer thought it could be arranged fairly quickly."

Delta stared at Jonas. "Her husband had no reason to kill her, because even though he would still inherit from her, there was nothing worthwhile to get."

"Exactly." Jonas pocketed his phone. "I'm not saying it excludes him as the killer, because he might have just been too angry to think straight once he saw her again, or she told him anew why she wanted to leave him. What do I know about the strain on their relationship after she left? But from all sides, I heard he wanted money from her. He had sponged off her during the marriage, letting her pay the bills, so why would he kill her and then be left with nothing?"

Delta finally took that sip and put the glass back on the table. "The main question is: If he wanted money, and he knew that Sally was practically broke, why come after her? There was nothing to get from her."

"Maybe he expected Calvin Drake to give her money?"

"Or gifts, because he felt sorry for her." Delta sat up. "I recall she wore an expensive-looking necklace and a ring with gemstones. If they are real, they could be valuable."

Jonas looked at her. "Hey, that is a very good suggestion. What if she came here with virtually nothing, and brother Calvin took pity on her and bought her some things? Nice jewelry. Might be worth something. Hubby sees it and wants to have it. He threatens her with a knife to hand it over, and it goes wrong."

"There you have it. West could be barking up the right tree and we're looking at all other angles because we like to be thorough." *And because I wouldn't want to miss this night for the world.* She toasted him again. "To all other angles."

Jonas halted the Jeep in the drive of Hazel's cottage and looked at her. Delta's cheeks were warm from her dessert— she had finally decided on the apple crumble—and she felt more relaxed and happier than she had in a long time.

"Thanks for a fun evening."

"I had a great time." Jonas's blue eyes searched her expression as if he was looking for something there. She was too rosy and comfy to move and sat in the seat, vaguely aware she should be getting out but not wanting to.

"So...good night." He smiled at her. "Dream something nice, huh. No chasing killers along the lake." He reached out and brushed the graze on her cheek. "Or cycling into poodles."

"I didn't come anywhere near that dog." Delta said it softly, holding Jonas's gaze. Her skin tingled where his fingertips had touched her. It seemed he was waiting for something, wavering maybe, making up his mind if... When...

Then he sat up and said, "I'll uh...call you later, huh? About the case." The tension broke, bringing her back to reality. *This is business, not personal.*

"Yeah, sure, the case." *What was I even thinking?* "Talk to you later. Good night." She opened the door and slipped out. The evening air felt chill, and she shivered. He backed up the Jeep and waved at her. Then the car vanished into the night.

She dug into her collar and unlocked the front door, trying to be as quiet as possible. Hazel had already gone to bed, probably, and she didn't want to wake her. No questions about how it had been. Delta didn't want to put into words how she had felt, what it had been like. She couldn't talk about it.

Suddenly, the light in the hallway went on, and Delta blinked furiously. At the top of the stairs, Hazel stood in a flaming-red dressing gown, looking down on her. "Did he kiss you?"

"Who?" Delta shaded her eyes against the stabbing bright light.

"Jonas. Did he kiss you? The Jeep stood there for a few minutes before he pulled out."

Delta recalled them having these kinds of discussions in college after dates, and it had never bothered her then. Indeed, being so in love back then, she could have talked about the chosen one for hours on end. Now, she was annoyed that Hazel was awake and wanted to get into bed as fast as possible.

"You're flushing," Hazel teased.

"We're just friends." Delta hung her coat on the rack and carried her purse up the stairs. She brushed past Hazel. "I don't like it when friendship is put under pressure by the immediate assumption that it has to be more. Not every man and woman who get together once in a while become a couple, you know."

"Sorry. I thought you liked him. And he likes you."

"Jonas isn't the type to really let on," Delta said, trying not to think of the moments in the Jeep when he had caressed her cheek and she had believed he was going to kiss her. Maybe she had mistaken a friendly gesture for more.

"I'm really tired. Let's chat in the morning, okay?" She went to her bedroom door.

"Okay." Hazel sounded disappointed. "Sleep tight then."

"You too." Delta closed her door behind her and stood a moment, not quite knowing how she felt. Or, rather, why she felt what she felt. Was she really angry at Hazel for asking questions she had often asked before when they had roomed together in college? Or was she conscious that her relationship with Jonas was something different, not a date, a fun time with a guy she liked? Life was more serious now, of course; she was no longer a student but a business owner in a small town where people looked at you and followed along with the developments in your life. Was she worried about what people might say when they believed she liked Jonas and he didn't like her back, or at least not in the way she wanted him to?

Afraid of losing face? Or more?

Delta sighed in frustration and started to undress. All those questions could be analyzed some other time. Right now, she needed at least eight hours of undisturbed sleep.

The little girl picked up the jar of tinsel and threw it in the air. "No!" Delta shouted, but it was too late: the jar burst into a thousand pieces, and a sparkly shower rained down over her. The glitter kept falling until she was knee deep in it. She tried to walk away, but the shimmering mass sucked her down. Lena Laroy stood a few paces away, and Delta called out to her, "Help me. Throw me a line or something."

Lena smiled enigmatically and kept watching as Delta sank into the glimmer up to her waist, then her neck.

With a gasp, Delta opened her eyes and stared into the darkness. A dream. A nightmare. She pushed the duvet away and tried to breathe evenly. The cold air in the room brushed her bare arms, and she shivered, pulling the duvet back in place. What time was it anyway? She looked at the alarm clock's illuminated numbers. Almost seven o'clock. She was sure she'd never get back to sleep now, and with the sweat on her back, a shower would be bliss. She slipped out of bed and tiptoed across the landing to the bathroom.

When she wanted to return to her room, to make the bed, she heard noises downstairs. Was Hazel up already? She rushed down the stairs and found her friend in the kitchen, mixing batter. "I thought I'd make pancakes." Hazel smiled at her. "To make up."

"For what?"

"Last night. I shouldn't have jumped at you like I did. I'm sorry."

Delta looked at her friend's apologetic expression and the mess in the kitchen at this hour, but she didn't laugh like she normally would have. She felt very tired and sat down at the table, supporting her head in her hands.

"Is something wrong?" Hazel asked. "I don't mean to pry, but you're not yourself."

Delta took a deep breath. "I don't know. A new murder, and Jonas asking me to help out... Maybe we shouldn't have gotten involved. It will create tension around town. Imagine, we about hired a design agency just so we could ask questions about the Drakes."

"We're paying Clara Ritter a hundred bucks for her initial design advice, so it's not like we did her any harm." Hazel grimaced. "In fact, I had a feeling she sensed what we were after. Or maybe that was my guilty conscience prodding me." She returned her attention to the batter. "I'm really sorry about last night."

"That's okay. I guess I'm not ready to talk about it. To even think about it. I like how Jonas and I can work together and...feelings are going to spoil all that." Delta rubbed her face and leaned back. *I don't want to care too much.*

Hazel nodded and poured batter into the buttered frying pan. A hissing sound spread, and soon the smell of fresh pancakes wafted through the kitchen. Hazel put butter, syrup, jelly, and sugar on the table. As she was about to give the first pancake to Delta, there was a knock at the back door. Hazel put the pan down on the counter and went to see who it was. She came back with Mrs. Cassidy and Nugget. The Yorkie sniffed the air and whined, clawing with a paw.

"She wants some, but she can't have any," Mrs. Cassidy said with a look at the dog which was half-indulging and half-reproaching.

"But *you* must have some," Hazel said, getting an extra plate from the cupboard.

"Thanks, that would be most welcome. I've been up and about for an hour already. An elderly friend of mine is moving to a new house, and I went over to help her pack the last few boxes and make sure everything is ready for the movers. She's only going to the other side of town, but still, to her, it's a big deal, and she wants it to go down smoothly."

"I see." Hazel gave the pancake she had intended for Delta to Mrs. Cassidy and gestured to the jelly and sugar. "Have what you like."

Mrs. Cassidy spread a liberal amount of strawberry jelly across the pancake and inhaled the scent. "Delicious. I do feel a bit guilty I'm eating your breakfast." She glanced at Delta.

"There's enough for everyone," Hazel assured her. "But why are you here? I assume you didn't knock in the hopes of a free breakfast."

"No, I actually have some news about the case." Mrs. Cassidy pointed her fork at Delta. "You talked to Jonas last night, I heard. Did he have anything new to reveal?"

Delta flushed at the idea that her dinner with Jonas had gotten around so quickly, but then the Paper Posse were well connected. And as long as they thought it was just friendly sleuthing talk…

"Yes, he told me a thing or two about the husband. Abe Jarvis."

Mrs. Cassidy raised a hand. "Let me see if we found out the same things as Jonas. The guy is arrested; West thinks he's guilty because he had followed her here to put pressure on her to rethink the decision to divorce him. Oh, and the life insurance of course."

"Life insurance?" Delta echoed.

"Yes. The murdered woman and her husband had taken out insurance on each other's lives. So now that she's dead, he's getting a lot of money."

"What?" Delta's eyes widened, and she shot upright in

her chair. "So, he profits off her death anyway. Jonas thought he didn't, because he is heir to her estate, but she owns virtually nothing. He didn't mention any life insurance to me."

"Victory," Mrs. Cassidy said with a grin. "I admit we had an unfair advantage. Bessie talked to Tammy at Mine Forever, and she told me that Sally Drake had met her husband there and they had argued over coffee. Something about that life insurance. She wanted to make someone else the beneficiary. Her brother Calvin, I think."

"Oh. That might make sense if she was going to stay here and was going to work in her brother's company. Maybe she even offered to put the death benefit in his name in exchange for a place in the company? Might have been an inducement. Would explain why Una Edel hadn't liked Sally at all. Moving in, with no knowledge of design, and buying her way into the Drake Design company. I'll have to tell Jonas about this right away."

"After breakfast." With a stern look, Hazel gave her a pancake and poured new batter into the pan. "Did Tammy have anything else to reveal?"

"Yes," Delta mumbled around a bite. "Did she also see Sally with another man? Not her dark-haired, stocky husband, but a tall, blond guy?"

"I don't think so." Mrs. Cassidy frowned. "Is that her new boyfriend?"

"No…" Delta paused before she could underline her answer. Why not? Jonas had said the blond guy had seemed to plead with her. Maybe she did have a new boyfriend around here, and they had fallen out with one another? About the husband appearing? Had the new boyfriend maybe worried the husband would be persuasive enough to get Sally to give him another chance?

"Could it be her boyfriend?" she mused aloud. "Has anyone heard anything about Sally Drake having a boyfriend here in Tundish?"

Mrs. Cassidy shrugged. "She had only been here for a short while. But I have no idea how fast people get attached these days. I read something in the newspaper about a couple meeting and marrying within fourteen days. A bit fast if you ask me. How much do you know about each other then?"

Hazel leaned against the sink with a pensive look. "Everybody thought Sally came here because her brother has his villa here, and she wanted to come and work for him now that she had lost her LA job. But what if she met another man, maybe months ago, and then decided to leave her husband and her work at the art museum behind and come here to be with this new lover?"

"I heard she got fired from her job and didn't leave of her own accord," Delta said.

But Hazel continued, waving the whisk, "The new lover had never meant for her to be quite so drastic right away, and didn't want her to come here. Or he did want her to come here and then commit to him, while she was still having second thoughts. Enough potential for conflict, especially with her husband in town."

Delta said, "We don't know much as long as we have no idea who the blond guy is. These pancakes are really delicious."

"Pancakes!" Hazel swirled around and dove for the pan. "Phew, saved it before it burned to the bottom of the pan. Who wants one more?"

They ate and chatted for a while, Delta also digging out her notebook and adding the life insurance information to the case file. Mrs. Cassidy took her leave, saying she would message them with anything new she heard. "See you tonight for rehearsal." Nugget ran after her, disgruntled that she hadn't gotten any sweet goodies.

"Rehearsal. I had almost forgotten all about that," Delta said. Hazel and she had agreed, almost on a whim, to be part of the Paper Posse's performance at Tundish's annual town festival the first weekend of November. They got together once a week to rehearse at the community center.

"Me too." Hazel sank on a chair and whisked a lock of hair from her face. She tried to pull it back into a ponytail, but it was still too short to fit an elastic band around it. With a sigh, she let it fall back in place. "This case has a lot of angles, it seems. The more we learn about Sally, the more people we find who might have been at odds with her."

"And then to think people told us she was so quiet, and everybody liked her." Delta tapped the figure of Zara Kingsley in her file. "We should find out if she already knew Drake before she came to work for the family. Why she came to work for the family. She told me she needs the money, but does this job really deliver so much more in pay than something else?"

"She won't tell us herself, and we can hardly phone Drake about it. He's devastated over his sister's death."

Delta nodded. She picked up her phone and checked the website of Marc LeDuc's online paper. Despite her annoyance at his tactics, she had to admit he managed to dig up information, and some silly thing he said might actually lead them to a real clue. "Wow, listen to this. 'Murder villa up for sale? Rumor has it that Calvin Drake of Drake Design will put his villa up for sale after the recent gruesome crime on his premises. Two days ago, his sister, Sally

Drake, was killed during a party where most of his friends and acquaintances were gathered. The woman, who was staying at the villa throughout messy divorce proceedings, was found stabbed in the back of the garden on the edge of the forest. It's poignant to note that shortly before the dead body was discovered, the police had arrived on the scene to investigate a threat against the hostess and birthday girl, Lena Laroy, Drake's third wife. The question now is: Was the threat really directed against the murder victim, and were the police looking in the wrong direction? Or is the entire Drake family a target? Calvin Drake's decision to sell off the villa right away seems to suggest he is feeling the evil influence of the place.'"

"Evil influence," Hazel scoffed. "It's merely a house by the water."

"Apparently not. Marc isn't done yet. Listen to this bit of in-depth research he did." Delta continued to read in a weighty tone as if narrating a documentary, "'The villa dates back to the forties, built by a rich industrialist who aimed to use it as a holiday home. On the evening of May 19, 1959, at the boathouse that once resided on the grounds, the dead body of Athena Barrows, the industrialist's new bride, who had only wed him seven weeks before, was discovered. She was stabbed to death, and her killer has never been found. Barrows demolished the boathouse shortly after, haunted by his wife's untimely death there. He sold the villa in 1961. Is there a sinister connection between this earlier unsolved crime and the current murder of Sally Drake?'"

"Does Marc mean that it might be the same killer still lurking about?" Hazel asked with wide eyes. "It's over sixty years ago. That guy must be eighty!"

Delta pursed her lips. "He seems to mean that the house

is a bad place to live. I have heard of people who investigate before they buy a house as to whether a violent death happened there, because they don't want to live in such a place. I can imagine it's kind of creepy, especially if the crime was never solved."

"I see." Hazel nodded. "But Drake wasn't afraid."

"Or he didn't know. I wonder if he ever heard that story about the boathouse murder in the fifties. Especially with the boathouse being demolished, there might not have been a reason to say anything about it. And as it's so long ago, the real estate agent might not even have known it. I wonder how Marc found out about it."

"Ask him," Hazel wriggled her brows.

"Please." Delta shook her head. "I don't want to talk to him about anything. Maybe there are mentions of it online? I'll have a look." She entered the words *boathouse murder Tundish 1959* into the search engine. "Ah. Here it is. Marc got it from his own father's newspaper. The *Tundish Trader* reported on it in May 1959. The old editions are digitalized and accessible via the local library, if you have a library card. I can only see the headlines now. I have to log in to read the actual article."

"Excellent reason to get a library card," Hazel said. "I've been meaning to get one ever since I moved here, but you know how those things go. I never got around to it. But now you can go and get one, and then you can read that article and borrow some nice books to read."

"Great idea." Delta put down her phone. "Off to the library then."

Chapter Eight

TUNDISH'S LIBRARY SAT IN THE SHADOW OF THE COMMU-
nity center. The modest entry led into an inviting reception
area with a bulletin board where Mine Forever and the gold-
mining museum had put up flyers about their activities.
Delta made a mental note to add a leaflet with information
about their next workshop. She went to the desk and asked
the librarian for a library card. The woman, in her fifties,
with a long vest, corduroy pants, and a badge that read *Ethel*,
quickly prepared the card for her, asking for her personal
information and entering it into the computer. Delta said,
"I can look into the archives with this, right?"

"Yes, we have a lot of digitalized information about
Tundish. Students helped us out last year as part of their grad-
uation project. Are you looking for anything in particular?"

"Yes, the boathouse murder in 1959. A woman named
Athena Barrows was stabbed in a boathouse by the lake. It
was never solved. I mean, the killer wasn't caught."

"I see." The librarian handed her the card. "You can use
it right away if you like. There are computers over there.
Feel free to ask me if you don't get the right results."

"Thanks." Delta crossed to the computers and sat
down. She entered her library card number and could
search the digitalized archives. She discovered that the
boathouse murder had been a hot item for days on end, and
the *Tundish Trader* had written about it with a sort of sen-
sationalist glee she hadn't expected in the fifties. But then
Barrows, the house owner, had been a well-known person,

and his wife—judging by the information about her—a sort of star. A young socialite who had done some modeling work and then met Barrows during a summer vacation on Rhode Island. Glamour at its finest.

The resemblance to Lena Laroy couldn't be overlooked. Again, Delta wondered if she had been the one meant to die, and Sally had been killed by mistake. But while the dresses had been similar in color and style, they hadn't been exactly the same, and the two women had been quite different in build as well. Still, she and Jonas had to keep the possibility in mind. If Lena had been the intended victim and Sally had been killed only by mistake, it made no sense to look for the killer by investigating motives of people who might have wanted Sally dead. What were the motives for wanting Lena dead?

Delta stared in deep thought at the computer screen. Had the old murder at the boathouse given the killer an idea? Had he or she meant to set it up the same way? Lure the victim away from the party and then attack at an isolated spot?

But what had Athena Barrows been doing at that boathouse? And what had Sally been doing alone at the back of the garden? A secret meeting? With her husband? A new lover? Someone else altogether?

"Have you found what you're looking for?" The librarian popped up by her side and looked at the screen.

"Yes, thank you." Delta smiled up at her. "You don't happen to know if there is any more information on this boathouse murder? I mean, in a book or something? These newspaper reports are rather haphazard. Not much was known at the time, and as the killer was never caught, there wasn't a trial or anything where they could establish the facts."

"No, of course not; that does sound rather complicated." The librarian chewed on her lower lip. "I don't know if it made it into a book. If there were so few facts... But we have a bit of a historian here in Tundish. Mr. Coldard. He might be able to help you. He wrote several books about the area. If anybody knows a bit more about this boathouse murder, it's likely to be him."

"Great. Can you give me his contact information?"

"I wouldn't call him if I were you. He's quite deaf, and you have to yell to get through to him. I'd drop by his place. He loves visitors. And he doesn't go out much anymore, so there is a good chance you'll find him at home. I'll write down the address for you." She crossed to her desk and wrote something on a notepad, then tore off the sheet. "There you go."

Delta logged off and came to her to fetch the sheet. "Thanks so much."

"Any time."

Outside, in the crisp air of a late autumn morning, Delta wondered if she should go and see Coldard right away. The librarian had kindly added directions to his address, and it didn't seem to be far if she went by car. She did feel a bit guilty about not doing her bit at the shop, but she would try and catch up later. Right now, this link with the fifties unresolved crime intrigued her, and she wanted to get right on it. With a grin, she crossed the street to the parking lot beside the church.

Delta parked her car beside the dirt path leading to the cabin in the distance. It was a wooden structure on a brick base, with a porch full of empty hanging baskets, swinging in the breeze. Delta got out of the car with her phone in her hand and walked down the path. There was an eerie silence in the forest around her, and she again thought of the lurking killer in Tundish, making her glance over her shoulder. Perhaps it had been a better idea to take along Jonas?

She stopped and texted him: "I'm at a rather isolated cabin in the woods, belonging to a guy named Coldard, a local historian who should be able to give me some information that might be useful in the case. I'll text you again in ten minutes." She wanted to add: *If I don't, come look for me*, but she thought that might look overdramatic.

A twig snapped, and she almost jumped.

"Just a bird." The high-pitched voice came from the porch. A frail, elderly man came to the top of the steps. He waved at her. "Come over, girl."

Delta walked over, clutching the phone. She spoke loudly and clearly. "Mr. Coldard? I'm Delta Douglas. I live in Tundish and run a stationery store. I want to ask you something about local history. At the library, they said to find you here."

Coldard reached out his hand. "Coldard. You live in Tundish? I never saw you before."

"I moved to town recently."

"You don't have to shout." Coldard smiled at her. "Nothing wrong with my hearing."

Like some elderly people she had met before, he probably ignored his hearing trouble. She continued to speak loudly and clearly. "I want to ask you something about the villa that was owned by Barrows, the industrialist."

"I said that you don't have to shout." Coldard winked at her. "Mrs. Sheffield, the head librarian, wants to turn me into a project. Have hot meals delivered and my house cleaned up. I pretend I can't understand what she's asking. There is nothing wrong here."

Delta looked at his hanging baskets. "Those had better come off before winter hits. You should store them indoors, and then you can use them again in the spring. Shall I take them down? In exchange for the information."

"As long as it's an even deal, young lady. No favors toward an old man. I'm not a sad case. Yes, my wife died, and things haven't been as tidy as they used to, but I can still take care of myself."

Delta had to admit he was dressed neatly and looked sharp and alert. On a table on the porch were stacks of books and an old typewriter. "You sit out here to work? Isn't that cold?"

"I dress up warm and put a blanket across the old legs. I like being out-of-doors. More oxygen, you know, good for the brain." He gestured at the paper in the typewriter. "I'm writing a new book."

"Oh, good for you." Delta reached up and took down the first hanging basket. She took out the inner plastic pot with some dry earth in it and put it on the porch while placing the basket to the side. "You can tell me a bit about the Barrows villa."

"Barrows left it a long time ago," Coldard said while he seated himself in the chair. It creaked in protest. "It belongs to another rich man now. What is his name? Dragon. No, Drake. He's an architect of some sort."

"Interior designer," Delta said. "This man Barrows was an industrialist?"

"Yes, he had factories, and he invested in railways and airports. He was into everything, really. A self-made millionaire. With a beautiful young wife who got murdered."

Coldard observed her with his pale eyes. "Are you here for details on that murder?"

Delta took her time to extract a plastic pot with some dead plant remains from a basket. The pot had a crack all round and was really ready for the trash.

"Did Marc LeDuc send you?"

She turned to him in a surprised jerk. "No, not at all. Has he contacted you too?"

Coldard grimaced. "He was so indoctrinated that I don't hear well, he had written his request down on paper. In capitals. He showed it to me like I'm some kind of idiot. I pretended I couldn't read it. He looked about him with a sort of disgusted air and left again."

"I'm sorry to hear that. I'm hardly friends with Marc LeDuc. My best friend was in some trouble a few weeks ago, and he wrote nasty things about her in his paper. It could have hurt her very badly had it not been cleared up quickly. I avoid him where I can."

Coldard nodded. "That makes sense. He's as cold as ice. I used to know his father quite well. He let me write columns for the *Tundish Trader* about local history. But a few years ago, he told me I was getting too old for it and people wanted something new. Practical tips and all that, a baking column or something about gardening." He snorted. "No wonder his sales are going down."

"Can you tell me more about the murder of Athena Barrows?"

"Huh?" Coldard peered at her. "Oh, yes, the beautiful young wife. It was very tragic. She died in the boathouse. Stabbed. They never found the killer. They thought he went away by boat. Across the water. Nobody saw anything, though. Or nobody was willing to come forward. There was this feeling Barrows was an outsider, and the locals all sided with one another."

"So, the killer might have been a local?"

"Well, there were rumors at the time that she had fallen in love with that Taylor boy."

"Taylor?" Delta said, shocked that the name of the most influential family in town had popped up. "You mean, the Taylors who run the Lodge Hotel?"

"Yes. Not the grandfather of the current young people who try to modernize the lot." Coldard looked sour. "I don't like changes. Why can't things stay the way they always were? We had nice card nights there. Good games. But they had to change it to having bands over with loud music and dancing."

"Not the grandfather," Delta coaxed him back to his tale, "but…a relative?"

"His brother Anthony. Everybody called him Tony. He was in college, and he came over that summer to help at the hotel, make some money. He wrote poetry. They whispered that Athena Barrows inspired him."

"But she had married Barrows. She can't have…"

"Fallen in love with another?" Coldard laughed softly. "Barrows was twenty years older than she was. He had chosen her to be an asset to his house here. Much like you choose furniture. She had to be pretty, be there for him when he wanted her to be, while he could ignore her if he didn't feel like spending time with her. They had absolutely nothing in common. She was a romantic girl who had dreamed of making it onto the big screen. Becoming a Hollywood star. Instead, she had to play housewife at the beck and call of a domineering older man. Then comes along this young poet with his golden hair and fiery words. Calling her his muse. She fell in love all right."

"You know this for sure?"

"For sure? What is for sure, after so many years?" Coldard leaned his green-veined hands on the table's edge. "I use my imagination. I speculate. And mind you, the police never got any further than speculating either. They looked at similar cases in the region to establish a pattern."

"Pattern?"

"Yes, two weeks before Athena Barrows was stabbed at the boathouse, a waitress died at a roadside cafe. She took a break from work, wandered away a bit under the trees, and was stabbed in the back with a narrow-bladed knife. Looked kind of the same."

"So, the police believed it was a serial killer?"

"They thought in that direction."

"They didn't look closer to home? At people who knew Athena Barrows and lived with her? Friends, relations, maybe in the household even?"

"I looked at those." Coldard focused on her. "There was a housekeeper she had threatened with dismissal. Athena didn't like her scrambled eggs." He clicked his tongue. "Silly young thing, pretentious and vain. But she didn't deserve to die for that, you know."

Delta's phone beeped. It was Jonas, asking her why she hadn't texted him again. "Is something wrong?"

Her earlier uneasy feeling about the isolated location had vanished under the intriguing chat with Coldard, and she felt rather silly now for having taken the precaution to let Jonas know where she was. *Good thing he didn't decide to come blazing to the rescue.*

She quickly replied: "All good, am chatting with Coldard. Will report my findings as soon as I'm done."

Looking up, she caught Coldard's questioning look and

said quickly, "Just a friend I'm meeting later today." She took down a few more baskets. "And what else did you discover?"

"The poet, of course. Anthony Taylor, thinking he was the new Ovid. Had the two young lovers quarreled? Had he asked her, on impulse, to go away with him and had she laughed at him, practical or greedy as she was? I don't think she would have exchanged her life of luxury with Barrows for a life of uncertainty with a man who didn't even have a college degree yet. Who believed his words could make him famous, but what were those words worth at the time?"

Delta nodded. "So, you can see the lover as the killer? An act of passion, when he felt spurned?"

"Misunderstood, his grand love rejected. Tony Taylor was a very sensitive and emotional boy."

"What became of him after the murder?"

"He wanted to come to the funeral and recite a poem he had written for her on her untimely death, but his brother, who was much more levelheaded, persuaded him not to. He left town; he was basically shipped back to college, and he found a wealthy lady who gave him a sponsorship to go to Italy and write poetry there. He went to Rome for inspiration and dived into a fountain. Got pneumonia and died."

"What?" Delta tilted her head. "You're pulling my leg."

"No, he did die. Whether it was of pneumonia is hard to tell. His family might have said that to hide a scandal. It seems he had found another muse there, and her family didn't like it. Might have beaten him up to teach him a lesson."

"Wouldn't there have been a police investigation in such a case?"

"I don't know. Anyway, I could be wrong. Maybe he did die of pneumonia. A rather lackluster ending to a promising young life, don't you think?"

"There. All done." Delta stacked the empty hanging baskets and came to sit opposite Coldard. "Do you think that Tony Taylor killed Mrs. Barrows?" She asked it with some trepidation, as it was a Taylor relative, and she didn't feel like crossing the wealthy family again. Once had been enough.

"I don't know." He shrugged his narrow shoulders, pulling his blanket better over his legs. "They may have quarreled, yes. But would he stab her? Where would he get a knife? He wasn't an outdoor man who carried a pocket-knife or comparable weapon. Was something at hand in the boathouse? Your guess is as good as mine. The weapon was never found, although they dredged the water for it. That supported the sheriff's serial killer theory. Such a killer would take the weapon along to use in the next crime. The sheriff even claimed at the time that the killer was attached to his weapon, and using the same blade contributed to his sense of accomplishment in committing the crimes."

Delta took in the story quietly, looking at the sunshine playing around the cabin, lighting on the bark of the trees. "You have a lovely place here."

"Which is why I don't want to leave. You won't tell Mrs. Sheffield my hearing isn't all that bad, will you?"

"Of course not. As long as you do take care of your-self." Delta cast a reluctant glance at the door into the house. What if it was really messy in there?

Coldard lifted a hand. "I have someone visiting me regularly to make sure the books don't pile up to the ceiling, and I have some meals in the freezer that I can heat up in the microwave. I'm not a sad case."

"That's good." Delta smiled at him. "Thanks so much for telling me about Mrs. Barrows."

"What's your interest in her story?"

Delta considered a quick lie, but said honestly, "I was at the party two days ago, at the Drake villa, where Sally Drake died. She was stabbed. Some people see a link with the Barrows murder."

"Some people as in Marc LeDuc?" Coldard asked skeptically.

"I did find the information about the Barrows murder on his website, but I'm not working with him or anything. I want to… A friend asked me to look into it because he made Calvin Drake a promise. I can't tell you much more. But I'm doing this for a good cause really."

"You don't have to win me over." Coldard gestured with both hands. "I already told you about it. I wouldn't have if I had believed LeDuc Junior was involved. He's a disgrace to any journalistic standards. His father should straighten him out." He surveyed her with a frown. "In the murder case, have you asked yourself who stood to lose the most?"

"What do you mean?"

He smiled. "Just the musings of an old man. Thank you for taking down my baskets. They will be better off indoors when the weather turns cold. Stretching and reaching up is not my strong suit." He peered at the typewriter. "High time I start a new chapter."

"Yes, well, thank you for your time." Delta rose and hesitated a moment. His fingers were already resting on the keys, and it felt rude to linger. But she wasn't sure what he had meant with that final question. Have you asked yourself who stood to lose the most?

In the Barrows case?

Or in the present-day murder?

Chapter Nine

WHEN DELTA CAME BACK TO WANTED, SHE FOUND BESSIE Rider there, owner of Bessie's Boutique, where both Delta and Hazel bought a lot of clothes and accessories. She was a member of the Paper Posse, nicknamed Wild Bunch, and always in for a little sleuthing on the side. Even when there wasn't a murder case, Bessie knew everything that was going on in her customers' lives, mainly because they liked to chat with her whenever they visited her store. She took the time to listen to their stories about broken nights with a teething baby or an argument with their mother-in-law, and gave advice on the side.

"Hello." Bessie waved at Delta with a long-beaded necklace. "The one you wanted came in at last. It's such a shame I can't order them individually. I mean, half the time I get twenty of the same ones, and of course the design the customers like the least. But I have the one with the bird pendant now. How do you like it? You only saw a picture of it. You don't have to buy it if it isn't what you imagined."

Delta took the necklace in her hands and studied it up close. "It looks great. I love the different glass beads; the colors are so pretty." She ran her thumb across the berry hues. "And the pendant is even better than I imagined. You can see it's a robin right away. That red on the chest is so vivid. I'll have it." She dug into her purse for the loose bill she had spotted in there earlier.

Bessie said, "Things are really heating up with the murder case, aren't they? Imagine killing your wife for the life insurance." She stared into the distance with a focused frown. "I do think it's stupid. I mean, the police are going to check on things like that right away, and Abe Jarvis could have figured he'd be picked up in a heartbeat."

"There you go." Delta handed her the bill. "Bring the change around some other time. You must be in a rush to get back to the store."

"Not really. My cousin is here for a few days, and she's helping me out. She used to work in a store, but she's retired now. Really misses it, so I'm actually doing her a favor letting her run it for a bit." Bessie picked up a set to make paper bunting. "This looks like fun."

"We're going to do a workshop about creating your own bunting, for a baby shower, birthday, or anniversary." Hazel gestured at her from behind the counter. "I'll let you know when. Won't be this year anymore, probably, as we're focusing on seasonal stuff for the rest of the time. But in January, who knows."

Bessie nodded. "Fine with me." She turned her head and looked out into the street. "Oh, there he is again." She rushed to the door and stood there, craning her neck. "I saw him when I was walking over here. Guy in a neat suit, with a briefcase, scanning the street like he was looking for something. I was about to help him out when he asked the hardware-store owner instead."

"Why does this guy interest you?" Hazel asked with a confused expression.

"He is an outsider, and he has 'insurance' written all over him. I bet they rushed into town now that the guy who did it is behind bars. They want to make sure that Jarvis doesn't get a dime."

"There are businessmen having coffee at Mine Forever

128   VIVIAN CONROY

all the time," Hazel protested. "That he wears a suit and carries a briefcase doesn't say much."

"All right, I cheated." Bessie grinned. "He got out of a car with a company logo. Investo Insurance."

Delta suppressed a laugh. "That way we can all be Sherlock Holmes."

Bessie pretended to be hurt and pouted, but her eyes betrayed her laughter as well. "I would love to have stopped him and asked a few questions. But of course, you can't. And he isn't the type to pop into my store to buy something. If only they had sent a woman... She might have fallen for one of those silk scarves I have on display outside. I would have advised her about the best colors to suit her complexion and slipped in a few innocent questions about why she was here. Oh, well, you can't have everything, I suppose." She walked to the door. "I'll pick up a few of those delicious salted caramel–pecan braids at Jane's for my cousin and me. If they have any left. Else banana-apricot bread will have to do. My cousin is watching her calories anyway."

She half turned to them. "She doesn't have any interest in western stuff, else I'd give her a perfect Old West name. See, her last name is Gunner, so we could call her Old Gun Gunner. But she doesn't even want to go see the mining museum. Oh well..." The door fell to a close behind Bessie's back.

"Can you believe that?" Hazel shook her head. "She actually wanted to ask that insurance man direct questions. That would really be taking it too far. I do understand we're trying to help with the murder case, but... We can't poke our noses into everything. And if that guy is really here about the life insurance policy Sally Drake took out, he should talk to West. They can compare notes and maybe close the case against the husband."

"Hmmm." Only half-listening, Delta pulled out her phone and looked for Investo Insurance. She found their website right away. As the header banner rolled into full focus, she whistled.

Hazel looked up from the cash register she was filling with some more loose change. "What?"

"That guy is not here about life insurance. Investo is a specialized company. And you can have three guesses what they specialize in."

"Um…" Hazel pursed her lips. "No idea."

"Come on, what do people have insured?"

"Valuable objects?"

"Yes, such as…"

Hazel drummed the counter as if to jog her brain into thinking up the answer. "Art?"

"Right. And Investo doesn't insure just any art." Delta waited a moment to reach full effect with her revelation. "Museum art."

Delta expected Hazel to rush over and want to have a look at the website as well, but she looked puzzled sooner than excited. "Oh. But we don't have an art museum here in Tundish. Only the gold-mining museum, and their gold nuggets may be real, but not worth a fortune. Can't call them art either. Could they be here for the estate of that copper magnate? There's art there, I'm sure."

"No, of course not." Delta gestured impatiently. "Remember what Drake told me about his sister Sally? What she had done before coming here? She advised a museum in LA about their art collection. He specifically mentioned to me that she was an expert on statues. That she had advised him to buy that bronze statue in his living room, of a woman picking flowers."

"You think the guy is here because of Sally? But she's dead."

"Exactly. Which makes it all the more poignant. He can't want to talk to her. Unless he doesn't know she's dead yet."

"That could be it." Hazel pointed a finger at Delta. "Sally gave her expert opinion on pieces of art, right? I imagine she confirmed their age or value. That's important for insurance as well. Now how could that have led to her death? Maybe someone wanted to remove her so she wouldn't find out certain art was fake and tell the insurance company?"

"But Sally had already left LA."

"Maybe she left because she had discovered something?"

"Calvin Drake told me she had left because her marriage had crumbled, and she had lost her job."

"She need not have told him what was really up." Hazel seemed determined to press her point. "I mean, if she didn't work for the museum anymore, why would the insurance company want to contact her now?"

Delta stared at the website's banner. Some of the pieces displayed immediately conveyed value with gold and gemstones, but others looked quite ordinary. A polished wooden statue of some figure. Maybe an ancient hero or god? Coming across it in a secondhand store, Delta wouldn't have given it a second glance. But apparently it was worth a lot of money. Could something like that have to do with Sally's death? Had she seen something maybe, recognized a valuable art object here in Tundish? Had she contacted Investo to come and talk to her about it, and before she could actually meet with the insurance company's representative, she had been killed.

"I have to tell Jonas about this," she said, screenshotting the site to pass on to Jonas. "He can ask Calvin Drake what this is all about. Or wouldn't Calvin know either?"

Hazel came over to her. "If Sally did discover something at the museum where she worked was actually a fake, maybe she felt afraid to address the issue while she worked there. Or maybe she was even fired because she raised doubts? She took refuge here to think about the next step. But someone followed her and made sure she never told the truth."

"Would someone really kill over an art object?"

"If it could harm the reputation of the museum and its board."

"Hmmm. It's all very speculative. We don't have anything solid to substantiate these possibilities. But maybe Jonas can dig up something." Delta typed a message to Jonas, telling him to come and talk to her as soon as he could because she wanted to share her news personally. "I'm not going to put our ideas in a message. If we're wrong, it's almost like slander. I'd rather say it to him, face-to-face, you know."

Hazel nodded. "You can't be careful enough. Marc LeDuc is *everywhere*."

Jonas breezed in around closing time. He wore a green fleece jacket and green pants, his usual look when he had been out wildlife spotting. Spud trotted by his side. Hazel crouched down on her haunches to pat him while Delta took Jonas into the kitchen in the back. "Did you look at the website screenshot I sent you?"

"Yes, the company is well known. When I was still in the police force, we worked with them, or rather we *tried* to work with them in a case of stolen plates."

"Plates?"

"As in china. Rare, valuable, and mysteriously vanished during transport to a museum that was going to put them on display. They were transferred from the villa of a private collector, who had agreed to lend them to the museum for six months. You can imagine it was a mess, with everybody accusing the other party of not having done what was necessary to ensure the safety of the plates. In the end, we discovered the whole thing was set up, as the owner was in financial trouble and wanted to cash in on the insurance money. He had the plates stolen by some thugs he hired via a cousin with contacts among criminals." Jonas made a dismissive hand gesture. "But that's not important now. What is Investo doing here in town?"

"Right. Hazel and I wondered if it has to do with Sally. She was an art expert, especially on statues, Drake told me. She came here quite suddenly, so why did she leave LA? Had she gotten into trouble at the museum where she gave her advice on art objects? A discovery or…"

Before Delta could go on to explain their entire ingenious theory, Jonas shook his head. "Unfortunately, the situation is completely different. I can't tell you much about it, as Calvin Drake begged me to keep it quiet. If LeDuc, either Senior or Junior, get their hands on this, it would mean disaster for Drake and his family."

Delta eyed him, not understanding. "How come?"

Jonas looked around him and lowered his voice. "The

Investo company is looking into the disappearance of a valuable jade statue from the museum where Sally worked. They discovered only two days ago that it was missing, since it was kept in depot, meaning it was not on display, and nobody had actually seen it for a bit. The box it was in was found empty, and they established by keycard check-ins of the door leading into the depot that Sally had been in the depot on the afternoon before she took her leave."

"So, they think *she* took it?" Delta widened her eyes. "But…Sally was fired, right? Her job there ended abruptly and… Did they already suspect her of stealing?"

"No, not at all. A colleague accused her of having made a mistake dating some objects, and Sally claimed the colleague had herself entered wrong dates into the computer. Neither of them wanted to back down, and in the end, it was decided Sally had to go. Probably because she had worked with them for only three years, while the other woman had been at the museum for her entire professional career."

"So, Sally was dumped, so to say? Can she have taken the statue out of anger? To get back at them?"

"Maybe. We can't know for sure Sally took it. If we accept that the colleague whom she had the argument with did enter wrong dates into the computer, that same woman might have stolen the statue to implicate Sally in theft. Sally shared a workspace with her, so the woman might have taken Sally's keycard from her purse or the drawer of the desk she worked at. She only had an advisory function there, not a full job, so she didn't have her own room or desk. Especially when a desk is shared, it's easy enough to take items and return them later."

"Yes, but why? Wasn't the dismissal enough? What had Sally done to this woman?"

"I don't know. This is all I know from Calvin Drake, who heard it from Sally. Whether we can trust what she said is of course doubtful. She won't have told her brother something that could cast her in a bad light if she wanted to come and work for him, right?"

"Right." Delta bit her lip. "So, Drake is now confronted with an accusation of theft against his sister, who's deceased and can't defend herself anymore?"

"Exactly. Investo wants West to search the villa for the statue. Maybe the insurance company hopes Drake will be eager to clear his sister's name and will allow the search?"

"Although maybe it's not even likely it's there. Sally traveled from LA to Tundish. If she took the statue, she could have left it somewhere. In a safe deposit box at a bank, for instance. She need not have brought it here and kept it among her things at the villa."

"Look, Delta…" Jonas leaned over. "Not a word about this to anyone. Not to those paper-crafting ladies either. I know they're your friends, but they are a little talkative, and this can't get out."

"I understand. In the hands of Marc LeDuc, it would be explosive. How about Hazel?"

Jonas held her gaze. "If I ask you not to tell her, how would you feel?"

Delta wasn't sure. It felt awkward, hiding something from her best friend, but at the same time she wanted to do what Jonas asked her. He knew what was best, and he was also a friend.

"Don't tell her yet. Maybe there will be developments soon enough, and things will become public. Then you can tell her that I asked you not to reveal it yet. Just because of the people involved. I mean, Drake is so upset that his sister died, and then this suggestion that she stole something from her former employer."

"All right. I won't tell a soul. But you keep me informed. This is getting more and more interesting with all the different angles. Does this mean anything for West's charges against the husband?"

"Nope, West will still think Jarvis was involved."

"You know West that well you can predict this?"

Jonas shrugged. "Yes, because I think along the same lines. Look, Sally Drake was a woman who had never in her life gotten a ticket for speeding. A law-abiding citizen. Why would she suddenly steal a statue from the museum where she works? That makes no sense at all."

"Unless someone put her up to it," Delta supplied.

"Exactly. And who better to assume did this than the husband who was pressuring her for more money all along?" Jonas glanced over his shoulder at the door behind which Hazel was probably wondering what took them so long. "I've got to run along now; I have a group I'm taking out in the dark to listen to the sounds of the forest." He rolled his eyes. "It's a new idea from Rosalyn for busy city people who come here to relax."

Delta grinned. "Have fun. I'm going to the community center with the Paper Posse to rehearse our part in the upcoming town festival. We're doing an outlaw song, composed by Rattlesnake Rita's husband. I really don't know how I got talked into it, but it's for a good cause. There will be an old money coffer there for people to put their anonymous donations into. They hope to raise enough to expand the mining museum's collection and draw even more tourists into town. While we're at the community center, I might sneak a peek at that boardroom Lydia and Clara changed to such mixed responses."

"The boardroom will probably be locked up. But let me know if you hear anything significant. Like odd places where Sally was seen before she died? If there is a missing statue around here somewhere, I want to be the first in line to find it."

"Is there reward money involved?" Delta winked at him.

"Just a sense of pride." Jonas's tone was as light as hers, but Delta supposed he did mean it. Sleuthing came natural to him, and he'd love to outwit West.

Jonas went into the shop and snapped his fingers at Spud, who immediately came running to him and looked up as if he expected to be put to work. The duo left the shop.

"He had a lot to tell you," Hazel said with a probing look.

"Oh, only some personal stuff." Delta straightened a pile of notebooks. "Let's lock up and head for the community center. Mrs. Cassidy is bringing her pumpkin soup and Jane her corn bread for some dinner before we start rehearsal."

"Sounds great."

Delta glanced at Hazel, who went into the back to get her things. She wasn't asking anything more about what Jonas had said?

"Of course not," a small voice pestered her, "Hazel trusts you. She thinks you told her the truth. But you haven't. What'll she think when she finds out? That you chose Jonas's side against her?"

Nonsense, she told herself. *There are no sides, and Hazel will understand that something as painful and explosive as the possibility that Sally Drake was an art thief has to stay under wraps as long as possible. Maybe, if the museum wrongly assumed she took something from the depot, we need never even discuss it.*

Still, she felt uncomfortable as they left and locked up the store. Like something had come between her and Hazel.

For diversion, she looked to the other side of the street, where the man who was working on Mine Forever's roof equipment stood at his van. The light of Mine Forever's flashy sign illuminated his features clearly.

Delta narrowed her eyes. She knew that face. Not from having seen him around the street working for the diner, but...

The party at Drake's villa. One of the caterers. Dressed in white, but that same face. Why on earth would a handyman attend a party dressed up as caterer?

She blinked as she stared at him. He lit a cigarette and got into his van. With a roar of the engine, he drove off.

"How odd." Delta stared after the disappearing van.

"What?" Hazel asked, slipping her keys into her pocket.

"That guy. I could have sworn he was at Lena Laroy's birthday party, dressed up as one of the caterers."

"That can't be. The catering company has their own people, they don't suddenly hire a handyman to help out."

"I'm pretty sure it was the same guy. I overheard this conversation between a woman in a turquoise dress— either Lena or Sally—and a man who put pressure on her to give him something. 'Tonight or else,' he said."

"Yes, so what?" Hazel looked her over. "You mean that the handyman working in Mine Forever may have crashed the party dressed up as a caterer to be able to speak to Lena or Sally? What for?"

Delta's mind was racing. She couldn't tell Hazel, but having learned Sally might have been in possession of a

valuable jade statue, the man imploring the woman to hand
something over suddenly took on new meaning. She pulled
out her phone to message Jonas, and then recalled he was
out with his group and had probably turned off his phone to
ensure total quiet during the trip. He had talked to her a few
minutes ago, so he wouldn't expect she had anything relevant to report. Did she even have to tell him or go straight to
the police? It was strange and could mean something.

And had it been Sally behind the bushes? Or Lena? She
needed to know, without a doubt, if it had been the murdered woman.

"Pumpkin soup can wait." Delta pointed at Hazel.
"We're going to the Drake villa to see Lena Laroy."

"What for?" Hazel spluttered. "And what about
rehearsal?"

"We'll come back as soon as we can. And they can start
without us." Delta made a beeline for the Mini Cooper. She
had a feeling they could really discover something worthwhile here. Another angle on the case.

Chapter Ten

AT THE VILLA, THEY FOUND THE ENTRY GATE OPEN AND could drive right through. The lights on either side of the driveway were not on. They parked the car at the garage. When the headlights died, it was rather dark. Delta assumed the lights came on as daylight faded and wondered why they hadn't today. She pulled out her phone to use as a flashlight. They made their way to the front door. Delta pushed the bell but didn't hear it ring inside. She glanced at Hazel. "That's weird. The whole place seems abandoned. Maybe we'd better go around back and see if we can find someone there?"

"Okay." Hazel looked a bit reluctant, wrapping her arms around her shoulders and glancing around like a deer ready to run at the first sight of a threat.

They rounded the house and walked past the dark windows of the study and then the large kitchen. A single lamp was on. Delta caught sight of Drake and Zara Kingsley, standing at the fridge. Zara was pointing inside it. Drake said something to her and looked around him. He went to the far wall and pressed buttons. Nothing seemed to happen. His face reddened. He reached into his pocket for his phone. Zara was pale. She backed up and stood leaning against the sink.

Delta knocked on the window. Zara jumped, and Drake dropped his phone. Hazel said, "Looks like a bad time to be calling. Maybe we had better go away again."

"Too late for that."

Zara came to the back door and opened it a crack. "What are you doing here? How did you get in? The buzzer for the intercom didn't—"

"The gate was open."

"Open?" Zara's jaw slackened. Then she glanced over her shoulder. "The fridge isn't working either. I think we have no power. It could be a simple malfunction, but Drake thinks…" She lifted her hands to her face. "If someone cut the electricity, the security system isn't working either. The killer could be here on the grounds. To slaughter all of us." She shrieked in terror.

Drake appeared behind Zara at the door. "What's up? Did you see something? Is he out there?"

"Who is he?" Delta asked.

Drake shot her a fiery glare. "What are you doing here? How did you get in?"

"The gate is open. Security is off." Zara yelped. "He's back to kill us all."

Drake looked startled. He said to Delta and Hazel, "You'd better come in." He closed the door behind them, peering through the glass panel into the darkness as if he was trying to detect motion there.

Zara breathed fast. "I should never have stayed here. I'm leaving. Right now." She turned away, but Drake grabbed her arm. "Zara, no. There's nothing wrong."

"Then why were you calling the police?"

"I wasn't calling the police; I was calling the electric company to ask if there is a problem in the area or if it's just us. I want them to send someone over right away and fix this."

Drake looked Zara over. "But if you think I should call the police…"

"What's happening here?" Lena Laroy descended on them, dressed in a flowing white dress with several long, beaded necklaces. Delta wondered in passing if they had been bought at Bessie's Boutique.

"Well?" Lena shot her husband and Zara an angry look.

Zara squeaked, "I noticed the light in the fridge didn't go on when I opened the door. Mr. Drake came to see and then tried the switches for the lights, and nothing is working. There doesn't seem to be any electricity in the entire house."

"Then how come that lamp is still on?" Hazel asked, pointing at the single lamp against the wall.

"It's solar powered, takes up sunlight during the day and then shines during the night," Drake said in a distracted tone. He put an arm around his wife. "I think we had better stay together until the electric company gets here to fix things."

Lena looked at him. "Do you think…"

"The killer is here," Zara whimpered. "He cut the power so we would be helpless and he could stab us all."

Delta had to admit that the idea of the power being cut was unsettling. After all, what for?

Lena stood motionless in her husband's hold. "Did you see anyone when you came up to the house?" she asked Delta.

"No, but it was rather dark. The lights along the driveway weren't working either. We merely had the headlights, and they don't shine far."

"Meaning someone could have been lurking on the grounds," Drake said in a grim tone. "Maybe I had better call the police." He kept his arm around his wife while he placed the call with his free hand.

Zara stared at the couple with narrowed eyes. Delta wondered if she was in love with Drake and jealous of Lena.

"Where are the dogs?" Lena asked Zara.

"Upstairs in their own playroom. I was getting myself a snack."

"Go to them. I don't want them to be alone while it's dark."

"But if the murderer is around, I could get killed."

"We're paying you to watch the dogs. Go watch the dogs!" Lena's voice became higher as if hysteria was near.

Zara edged to the kitchen exit. "Can't I wait here until the police…"

"Maybe that is safer," Drake said.

"Of course." Lena's eyes flashed. "Why don't you put your other arm around her?"

Delta kept her eyes on Drake to see how he took this.

"My sister was murdered," he said through gritted teeth. "I don't want to take chances, with anyone."

"Oh, darling." Lena wrapped her arms around his neck and hugged him.

Zara rolled her eyes as if she couldn't believe this was sincere. Delta had to admit she had her doubts as well. The Drakes made a rather strange couple.

Outside, police sirens resounded.

"That's fast," Hazel said.

Flashlights streaked across the lawn, and the back door was thrown open. West entered with a deputy in tow. Another seemed to be outside, shining his flashlight around.

"We came right away," West said. He glanced past the faces and spotted Delta. His brows went up. "What are you doing here?"

"We didn't get a chance to ask, Sheriff," Lena said

sweetly. "Just as Delta and Hazel arrived, we discovered the power had been cut."

"The power was off," her husband corrected. "We don't know if it was cut."

West said, "We'll have a look around," and barged out of the kitchen with his deputy hot on his heels.

Lena looked at Delta. "What did you come to see us about?"

"I wanted to talk to you in private. But it seems like a bad time."

"No, not at all. It will be a nice distraction." Lena raised a hand to her face and rubbed her forehead. "Tension is so bad for me. Come into the living room, please. We can wait there for what the police discover." She shot a look at her husband. "You take Zara up to look after the dogs."

He seemed to want to argue, but Lena was already using the light of her phone to guide Delta and Hazel to the living room. It was dark inside, and the eerie blue light of the phone gave Delta the feeling they were burglars sneaking in. Lena shone the light at the couch. "Sit down, please. This is all a bit unusual. But it will be resolved."

"Do you already know who sent you that perfume bottle?" Delta asked.

Lena sat in a chair, up straight, with her hands in her lap. She shone the light of her phone away from her face so Delta couldn't see her expression. "No. I doubt the police will either. There were no fingerprints on it."

"I see. And was there footage of the table? I mean, a security camera that caught whoever put it there?"

"Lots of people went near the table. I don't think that will help much."

"How stressful for you. First the threat, then the murder. Do you think they are connected?"

"Why all these questions?"

"If the power was cut," Hazel chimed in, "you might still be targeted. We have to find out by who."

Lena laughed softly. "Some fan who's not right in the head maybe. Who can tell? When you're in the spotlight, it can attract the wrong kind of people."

Time for a little bluff. Delta took a deep breath. "Like that caterer? I saw he followed you around and wanted to talk to you."

Lena stiffened. "He wanted an autograph, but I don't give those anymore. My modeling days are over. I try to live a normal life."

"You hardly have a normal life," Hazel said in a friendly but emphatic tone. "You're being threatened, and your sister-in-law was murdered on your grounds."

"I heard there was another case like it, years ago." Lena's voice was thin. "Maybe it's the same killer? Or a copycat?"

Delta shook her head. "Before we assume such a tenuous link, we must look at what is right in front of our eyes. That man, the caterer, came here under false pretenses. He's not a caterer. I saw him in town today, working as a handyman. He must be after something."

Lena released her breath.

Delta pressed, "The sheriff is here to check your house for a possible power outage. I might as well tell him I might have a lead." It seemed unlikely the caterer slash handyman had actually cut the power, as he had driven away from town right before they had headed here, but a bit of pressure on Lena to reveal something at this crucial moment couldn't hurt.

"I want to help out," Delta added sweetly.

"No." Lena sounded anxious. "You must not tell Sheriff West about that man. He didn't cut the power. I'm sure."

"But he did accost you at the party. He wanted more than an autograph. Why didn't you tell the sheriff about him? He might have put the perfume bottle on the table."

"Of course not. He wanted an autograph, and I told him no. Nothing more to it." Lena rose. "I must go and see how the police are getting along." She left the room.

Delta tried to see Hazel, but it was too dark. "Do you believe her?"

"Not really." Hazel took a deep breath. "But we can't do much about it. West never liked you or me, so if you tell him what you saw at the party, he won't do anything with it."

"I'm not so sure about that."

"Come on. He has Sally's husband under lock and key and believes he did it."

"But who cut the power then? That guy Jarvis is in a cell."

"It need not be connected. It may be a failure of some kind."

The door opened, and Lena came back in. She sounded relieved when she said, "The sheriff found out that it's something with the electricity control panel. I'm not technical, so I don't understand what it is exactly, but it cut all power in and around the house. He is turning it back on." As she said it, a lamp in the living room turned on, casting things in a nice, soft glow. Delta's eye fell on the bronze woman picking flowers. "We'd better be going."

Lena looked her in the eye. "Leave that caterer man be. He's not involved in anything."

"I'm sorry," Delta said, "but I don't believe that."

Lena escorted them to the front door. "Goodbye."

Outside, Delta said, "There is definitely more to that caterer slash handyman than meets the eye. I also think

Zara is very suspicious. I wonder how much she knows about electricity? Can she have manipulated the control panel? She acted so over-the-top panicky. It felt like an act. Maybe she hoped to fall into Drake's arms?"

"They do have a bit of tension between them," Hazel agreed. "I'm not sure what she's up to." She stretched. "We'd better get to the community center for our rehearsal, or they will be done without us."

At the community center, they saw a jet-black Buick parked close to the entrance. Delta pointed out the fins on the back. "That's Randall Drake's car. Jane told me all about it the other day. An icon from the fifties, they call it at the local garage. I wonder what he's doing here."

They went inside and turned left right away into the big assembly room with a stage that was used for all kinds of activities, including the upcoming town festival. Piano music flowed toward them, and on stage, they caught a man seated behind a piano, surrounded by the Paper Posse ladies. They all smiled at him while he played a big band classic and sang to it, in a rather good baritone. As Delta drew closer, she recognized his smooth, handsome features.

"That answers my question," she whispered to Hazel. "Randall Drake." She climbed onto the stage via the steps on the right-hand side and closed in on the group. Randall ended the song on a long note and ran his hands down the keys in a dramatic closing section. The ladies applauded him with fervor. Mrs. Cassidy said, "You're so good you should be part of the show, Mr. Drake. If you're staying that long."

"Randall, please." He winked at her. "I don't know yet

how long I'm staying." He caught sight of Delta and Hazel. "Hello. The more the merrier, I say."

"We've just come from the Drake villa," Delta said. "There was a power outage there. Most peculiar." She looked at him closely. Calvin Drake had hired Jonas, saying he didn't know who he could trust anymore. Had he also been thinking of Randall? But Randall had obviously left the villa a while ago if he had been here rehearsing with the ladies.

Randall didn't blink. "A power outage? I'm not surprised. With all the gadgets my uncle installed, the circuits must get overloaded at times." He let his fingers play across the keys. "Shall we rehearse?"

"Mr. Drake offered to help us. He was here to meet with the mayor and overheard that our regular pianist is in bed with a touch of flu." Mrs. Cassidy smiled. "Such a nice offer."

Randall waved it off. "I miss playing. I used to do it quite a lot in college. But after that… Life got serious, you could say."

"What do you do anyway?" Delta asked. "You're not in your uncle's company, are you?"

"Oh, no. Fortunately not. He's a real tyrant. Everything must be done one way only. His way."

The ladies laughed.

Delta noticed he had avoided mentioning what he did do for a living. Jonas had said he had heard in passing that Randall was a software engineer, on vacation in Tundish, but at the bakery, Jane had told her he didn't have to work for a living because his family had money. Either way, the question was: Why was he staying with his uncle when said uncle and his own father were on bad terms?

"Time to get serious." Mrs. Cassidy looked around. "Has everyone got their sheet music? Now, last time we were a bit stuck on the opening section. We have to rehearse that a few times. Jane, you start."

Jane fidgeted with her music. "I don't know if I have the right voice for this section. Shouldn't we switch it up? Maybe Bessie can do it. Or Hazel?"

Hazel paled. "Me? Start?"

Delta knew her friend had rather not been in the Paper Posse's performance at all, because she hated to be the center of attention, and quickly offered, "I can try."

Randall gestured for her to come stand beside him at the piano. "Let's try the opening keys." He repeated them a few times. "Now suit your voice to it."

Delta tried, and it didn't sound too bad. Randall smiled at her. He had melting brown eyes, and standing here with him playing and her singing, she did feel a bit like a star.

After her solo, all the ladies joined for the refrain, and Randall played with gusto as they sang about the joys of living the outlaw life. The murder case faded to the back of Delta's mind, and she just let the music carry her.

"It'll be done soon." Delta turned down the heat under her pan of pasta. Rehearsal had been fun, but apart from a cup of coffee and a slice of cornbread during the break, they had not had any dinner, and she intended to catch up now that they were home. Just some spaghetti with meatballs and sauce.

A low sound, much like a thud, seemed to come from the back door. Still a little jumpy from the odd events at the

Drake villa earlier that evening, she stiffened at once and tightly clutched the ladle she held for stirring. Hazel was in the living room, getting things ready so they could have their bedtime snack on the sofa. She sneaked to the door and peered out. To her surprise, it was the tall, statuesque figure of Lena Laroy, standing with her shoulders pulled up as if she was undecided about something. Delta opened the door. "Hello."

Lena startled. "Oh. I had no idea you were already coming to the door. I was still debating whether I would knock. It's all so awkward." She burst into tears.

Delta reached out her free hand to her. "Do come in. It's getting cold out there."

The woman passed her coming inside and shrugged out of her expensive woolen coat. She folded it over her arm and wiped away a tear. "Sorry for that. I didn't mean to be so... It's all the tension. The power cut at my home."

"You don't believe it was a technical malfunction of the control panel?"

"No." Lena swallowed hard. "I had to pretend, because my husband was watching my every move. He claims to be keeping an eye on me because he's worried about my safety but...I think something else is up."

Delta gestured for her to go into the living room. Hazel looked up in surprise when they came in. "Oh. Good evening." She looked past their unexpected guest at Delta, the question marks all over her face.

Lena dropped herself on the couch with a sigh. "It's Zara." She spread her hands in a dramatic gesture. "She gets on my nerves. I'm not sure whether it's her clumsiness, the little accidents..."

"What accidents?" Delta asked.

Lena plucked at her coat. "Last time she left the house in my husband's car, she almost drove into me. She claimed she never saw me, but...I'm not so sure."

"You think Zara wants to harm you?" Delta asked. "Do you think she's behind the threats against you?"

"It's not impossible, is it?" Lena looked at them. "I'm thinking it's someone from the outside, but what if she is under my own roof? She could have put the present on the table. The perfume bottle with the skull."

Delta nodded. "Possibly, but so could have all the other guests. You didn't see her do it. What reason could Zara have for targeting you?"

Lena wet her lips. "I have a feeling there is something between Calvin and her. I'm afraid he brought her in because they're having an affair."

"Do you have any concrete proof for this?" Delta glanced at Hazel.

"No. And at first it seemed absurd. She's so much younger than he is, a schoolgirl almost. But she obviously likes to be near him. And sometimes he looks at her, as if... they have an understanding."

"I see. Can she have cut the power in your house? I mean, would she know something about the control panel?"

"Maybe. I don't know." Lena hid her face in her hands. "I don't feel safe in my own home anymore."

"Did you discuss the car incident with your husband? When Zara almost hit you?"

"Yes, and he told me she's merely clumsy. He keeps saying that whatever she does. She can't handle the dogs either. One of these days something will happen to one of them. Oh, my poor babies."

"Why don't you fire her?"

"I can't. Calvin hired her, and he doesn't listen to me."

Delta admitted this was rather suspicious, but now that Lena was here, she wanted more. "And this man, the caterer, he has nothing to do with it all?"

"He has been after me before." Lena looked at Delta. "But the police won't do anything without evidence. I'm hoping to lure him into a situation where I can get footage of what he's doing. If I tell the police now, they will ask him a few questions; he will deny everything and go free. He did it before."

"What did he do earlier?"

"I don't want to talk about him. I'm only here to tell you about Zara and my husband and to ask if I can stay with you tonight. I don't want to be at home."

Delta widened her eyes at this unexpected request. "Stay with us, here?"

Hazel said, "We don't have a spare room available. This cottage was meant for me when I got it, and then Delta came to town and moved in for the time being. Until she has found a place of her own. Both bedrooms upstairs are taken and—"

Lena said, "I can sleep on the couch. I told my husband I was going out for a drive, and I will call him later and say I had a flat tire and I'm staying at a hotel. He'll think it's odd, but never mind. Let him and Zara have the house to themselves to do whatever they want to do."

"I thought there were more people there. Staff?" There was a housekeeper, someone had said. "And how about Drake's nephew, Randall?"

"He comes and goes when he wants." Lena shrugged. "I have no idea why Calvin even let him in when he showed up. He hasn't said a word to Randall's father in years."

"I heard in town," Delta said, "that you might have had a hand in the reconciliation. Because your husband is no longer in touch with the children from his first marriage."

"I never met them. It wasn't me their father left their mother for." Lena grimaced.

Delta noticed she avoided confirming or denying she had pressed Drake to take Randall in. The handsome, suave young man had seemed very close to her at the party, taking the role of her absent husband.

Lena's expression changed, as if she was about to cry again. "That's exactly why I worry about Calvin and Zara. She wouldn't be the first young girl to fall madly in love with him. He met his second wife when she was babysitting his children with his first wife. That girl tore his entire family apart. When their affair became known, his wife and the children didn't want to talk to him anymore. He married the babysitter, and after two years, she claimed he beat her and filed for divorce. She took a chunk of money off him too. Little gold digger."

Delta knew that people had said the same thing about Lena when she had started dating Drake, as she had always had a taste for wealthy older men. But she just said, "So you think that your husband's interest in Zara might fit a pattern? That he destroyed a marriage before after gaining interest in a girl working in his household?"

Lena rubbed her face. "I don't know. Maybe I'm getting paranoid. Alienating the people I love because I think someone is after me."

"Someone did place that threat on the gift table. A bottle of your own perfume with a dark message."

Lena shivered and rubbed her arms. "I don't want to think about it anymore. But how can I not think about it? Sally is dead and…" She suddenly jumped to her feet. "You're right, I can't stay here. You have no spare room and… Please don't take what I told you too seriously. I'm very upset. I'll go to a hotel. Thanks for listening to me."

Delta followed her into the kitchen. "You can sleep on the couch if you want to. You're too emotional to start driving around in the dark. Our rather belated dinner is almost ready." She gestured to the stove. "Why not eat with us and then have a good night's sleep and see what you want to do? Everything might look different in bright daylight."

Lena looked at her with red-rimmed eyes. "Are you sure I can stay here? That it's not a problem for you?"

"No, not at all." Delta felt sorry for the woman who apparently had nowhere to turn now that she was in trouble. "Please stay with us. We don't have to talk about the case either. We can chat about Wanted, paper goodies, anything you like." She smiled encouragingly. "Please feel welcome here."

"You're too kind." Lena answered her smile. "I don't know what I would have done if…" She stared out of the window into the darkness. "I feel so very alone."

Chapter Eleven

THE NEXT MORNING, DELTA AWOKE FEELING LIKE SOME-
thing was not quite as it ought to be. She recalled the
appearance of Lena Laroy at their back door, her story, the
dinner with an odd mix of lighthearted chatter about paper
crafting and Lena's modeling days and the moments where
Lena seemed to turn into herself and become frightened
and fragile.

Knowing Drake had met Zara at the Lodge and had
even been seen with an arm around her shoulders, Delta
wondered if Lena's bad feelings about the two were more
than paranoia. But she hadn't said so to her.

Yet.

Before showering, she decided to go downstairs to
see how their guest was doing. She tiptoed off the stairs
and peeked into the living-room area. Lena sat on the
couch, her hair tousled, her makeupless face wrinkled in
a deep frown. She had something in her lap. When Delta
looked more closely, she realized with a shock it was her
sketchbook. Lena might have picked it up to see some of
her designs, but as Delta watched the former model's deep
interest and the way her eyes shot from left to right as if
she were reading, she had a sinking feeling she was studying her case file in the back. The information about Sally's
murder.

Her thoughts raced to recall what she had written there
about Calvin Drake, Zara, Lena herself. This was extremely
painful.

And potentially dangerous, keeping in mind that Lena herself could be Sally's killer.

What had they done taking her into their home?

Delta turned around and made her way back up the stairs as softly as she had come. Her heart was beating fast, and she didn't know what to do next. Shower and dress and go down to play hostess as if nothing had happened?

But what if Lena hadn't turned up at their cottage in a panic at all, but with the conscious idea to use her stay here to find out how much they knew? What they were looking into, etc.

Delta took a deep breath. They should have sent her to a hotel anyway. But it had seemed like such a harsh thing to do to an upset woman. And Delta hadn't considered for a moment that Lena might use her time in their cottage to go through her things.

If she went down and confronted her about it, Lena would probably claim she had just picked up the book to look at her designs and hadn't known it contained anything other than drawings. Which, by the way, made total sense. Lena couldn't know she used her sketchbook for case files, could she?

Delta massaged her temples. She had to be careful, or she would become paranoid herself.

Dressed and with more determination in her step than she actually felt inside, Delta went down and found her guest lying on the sofa, apparently still asleep. *Good actress.* She gently shook her shoulder. "Good morning. Do you want some breakfast?"

Lena gave a very convincing sleepy sound. "Yes, please. Black coffee and some fruit. I don't do bread ever, and I hate the smell of anything frying. Eggs, pancakes."

Point taken, Delta thought. Lena had a very charming way of making people do exactly what she wanted. Had Calvin Drake loved her for it and then started to hate her? Bit by bit, and then he had met Zara and made a plan to get her into the house and then…slowly drive his wife insane? With the near accidents, the lights failing…

Nah. It sounded too much like something from a Victorian novel. The wife who goes crazy under the evil machinations of the young and innocent staff member.

Still, Lena had said that Zara had almost driven a car into her.

Lena had said. Yes. They only had her word for it. And for many other things she had claimed. They needed to check up on her statements. Thoroughly.

In the kitchen, she messaged Jonas: "Lena Laroy is here. Turned up last night, allegedly afraid to go home. Can't tell you more, but things feel off. Come over here like you are turning up out of the blue and talk to her. Maybe you can get more than I can?"

She put the phone away and started to make fresh coffee.

Hazel came down and asked Lena how she had slept. "Not too good at first, then I fell asleep and had bad dreams, now my head is splitting."

"You take it easy. I will get you coffee." Hazel came into the kitchen area. She looked at Delta, who whispered, "She only wants coffee and fruit. Nothing frying, so we can't make anything."

Hazel nodded and picked up the fruit bowl full of bananas, apples, pears, and grapes. She brought it to Lena and then got her a plate, knife, and napkin.

Delta listened for sounds outside, indicating Jonas's

arrival. As a former cop, he would know how to handle Lena. She hoped.

Hazel came to pour coffee for Lena and whispered to Delta, "I didn't sleep too well either. Too much on my mind."

Delta nodded. Outside she heard the hum of an engine. Relief washed through her. Jonas would know what to do with the wily former model.

The engine sound stopped, and after a few minutes, Jonas came around back with Spud darting ahead of him. The dog bounced against Delta as she opened the door for them. "Hello, good morning."

Jonas said to her in a low voice, "Anything up?"

"She read my case file when she thought I was still in bed. I wonder if she came here to find out how much we know."

"For real?" Jonas looked her over. "Are you afraid of her?"

"I don't know. She's not being fully honest about things." Why cover for the caterer at the party? If he was a stalker she wanted to ditch, she should have come forward with that information. Something wasn't adding up.

Jonas nodded. He said in a loud voice, "But I really have to discuss this with you now." He gestured to Spud to go in, and the dog shot past Delta and went for Hazel, who fell to her knees and hugged him. Jonas barged in, saying, "It will be a big thing at the Lodge, so I really need your help. I think we could… Oh, Mrs. Drake. Or should I say Miss Laroy? I can never quite remember."

"Lena is fine." Lena smiled up at Jonas, a half-peeled apple in one hand, the knife in the other. "What are you doing here this early?"

"Discussing some events at the Lodge. And you?" He nodded at her apparel. "It looks like you slept here."

"You don't have to be a former policeman to deduce that." Lena's tone was light, but her eyes flashed a moment. "I'm surprised you don't know yet. I thought in this small town the news spread fast. The police were at my home last night. Someone sabotaged our power."

Delta hitched a brow that Lena suddenly called it sabotage, while earlier she had been keen on saying it was merely a malfunction of the control panel. But then she had felt obliged to lie because of her husband, right? That was what she had explained to them last night upon arrival. What was the truth, what lies?

Jonas came to sit by her side. "Sabotaged?" he repeated as if he couldn't believe it. "Who would do such a thing?"

"Zara perhaps. Or my husband. You have no idea what kind of man he is, Jonas. Cold and possessive. But"—she lowered her eyes—"I shouldn't say this to you. You work for him."

"He hired me for a job. It's not like he owns me." Jonas leaned over. "Are you afraid of Calvin Drake?"

Delta watched in fascination how Lena's eyes changed expression and she inched closer to Jonas, speaking in a low voice. "Yes. I hate to admit it, but it's true. He's not himself anymore. He changed after Sally came to live with us."

"Sally? You just mentioned Zara."

"Yes, Zara may be having an affair with him, but Sally made him promise her things, like taking her into the company and… It was absurd. Sally knew nothing about design. She was an art expert, and not even a good one, or she wouldn't have gotten fired at that museum. But Calvin treated her like she was pure gold. He must have felt pressure to do what she wanted. He could be so curt with me. I was surprised he even wanted to celebrate my birthday. Of course, he wasn't there himself. Business was more important than me." She raised a hand. Her fingers were trembling. She put the hand slowly on Jonas's arm. "You have no idea what kind of man he really is."

"Then don't go back to him." Jonas covered her hand with his own. "If you go back, you may be in danger."

Lena held his gaze. "But I must go back. If I stay away any longer, he'll know something is up. He'll only become more difficult to live with."

"Leave him for good. Divorce him if you are that unhappy."

"I can't. I don't have a career anymore. How would I live?" Lena swallowed hard. "I had an offer to do more perfume, a whole new line, a spring collection, but Calvin said I could do a line of furnishings with Drake Design. That was until Sally came."

"But Sally is dead now." Jonas still spoke in that kind, considerate tone. "You don't have to be afraid she will take your place."

Lena stared up at him. "What are you saying? That I'm happy she died?" She pulled her hand away as if she had burned herself and jumped to her feet. "How can you think that? I'm scared out of my mind after the murder. I can't sleep, can't eat—last night with the power outage I almost ran out in a panic. Maybe straight into the killer's arms?" Her eyes went wide. "You have to help me, Jonas."

"I'm trying to. I told you not to go back to Drake if you think he can't be trusted."

Lena stamped her foot. "You don't know how it is. Like I have a choice."

"Everyone has a choice." Jonas grabbed her shoulders. "I'm offering to protect you now. But I can't help you when you're not cooperating."

Lena sank on the couch again. "I don't know," she said and started to sob.

Jonas looked down at her. Then he came for Delta and ushered her into the kitchen. "I can't tell if she's really afraid of him or putting on a little show for us."

Delta nodded. "That is hard to determine. What will you do?"

"I'm going to Drake to see how he's doing alone with Zara. I want to ask him about the relationship between them. Are you coming with me?"

"And leave Hazel alone with Lena? Is that safe?"

Jonas pursed his lips. "I'll stay here to have breakfast with you, and then you have to leave for the store. Lena will have to leave as well. We'll drive into town, and then you can jump in with me and we'll go to Drake's villa. Deal?"

Delta nodded. "Deal. There's more than one thing I want to ask him."

After they had finished breakfast and had said goodbye to Lena, who drove her own car into town to do some shopping, Delta got in with Jonas, and they set out for the Drake villa.

As they drove along the lake, Delta said, "It's such a beautiful view of the water and the snowcapped mountains. Too bad the villa seems to be the site of heartache over and over. Did you read about this fifties case? Athena Barrows? I went to see Coldard about it."

"Busy with a new book again, is he?" Jonas grinned. "He has been saying that for years now, but nothing comes out of his hands anymore. He lives in his own world of stories, of the past."

"He seemed pretty sharp to me. He told me that Athena Barrows was rumored to have had an affair with a relation of the Taylors. Anthony Taylor, who died in Italy?"

"Rumors are not facts, let alone hard truth." Jonas glanced at her. "Don't complicate the present case by bringing in that old thing. Unresolved, and it will stay that way. The only one who thinks they might be related is Marc LeDuc, who dug up that story because he thinks it's rather romantic and can get him clicks."

✐ "So, you don't think it's remarkable that a woman got stabbed near the villa in the fifties and now it happened again?"

"Remarkable maybe, but that doesn't mean the two cases are related. There's the villa. What shall we say?"

"The gate is closed, so we need to announce ourselves," Delta observed. "Too bad really. That power outage last night have meant we could approach the house without anyone caring that we did."

"Yes, so the question is…who wanted to prowl around unseen? And why?"

"I have no idea." Delta rubbed her face. "Too many questions, too little answers. All I do know is that Randall Drake was in town at the community center. He had a discussion with the mayor, and later he helped the Paper Posse rehearse for our outlaw song."

"But couldn't he have sabotaged the control panel before he left?"

Delta stared at him. "Of course! You told me you had heard in passing he's a software engineer. If he is, he might have tampered with it in a way that caused a power failure long after he left, so he wouldn't be on the scene to be implicated. Clever. But we'd have to know for sure he is a software engineer. After all, Jane said he's not really doing anything because he's heir to his father's fortune."

"Maybe he got a degree as a software engineer but never has to work?" Jonas suggested. "That way it fits."

Delta nodded pensively. "His father got the lot from Calvin Drake's father, cutting Calvin out completely. You would have expected bad blood between him and Randall, as his privileged brother's son, but he seems to have no problem with him being around. But can Randall be the person manipulating things? Drake said to you he didn't know who to trust, right? Can he have meant Randall then?"

"Your guess is as good as mine. I don't see how Randall would profit off threatening Lena." Jonas pressed the button of the speaker phone and told Drake it was him. The entry gate opened at once, and Jonas steered the Jeep through. At the house, he parked it in front of the garage, and they walked back to the front door.

Drake was waiting for them there. He stood in the open door like he wanted to block their way in. "Good morning. Is something up?" He rubbed his chin, his fingers rasping across stubble. "Did something happen to Lena?"

Jonas feigned ignorance. "Why would anything happen to Lena?"

"She got upset last night and left. She let me know she was staying in a hotel, but I had expected her to come home. She's not the type to run off in a fit of hysteria. Not over something small like a power failure."

"It was a malfunction then, nothing more?" Jonas asked.

"As far as the police could tell." Drake shrugged.

"You didn't think it had been done on purpose?"

"Nothing was cut or destroyed."

"Someone could have tampered with the control panel. Inside the house." Jonas held Drake's gaze.

Drake leaned back on his heels. "How do you mean?"

"Did you know," Delta asked, "that Zara tried to run into your wife? When she was taking your car out?"

Drake laughed. "Zara took the turn a little too wide, and she could have hit Lena, but she had no idea Lena was walking there, and to be fair, Lena shouldn't have been in the bend of a road on which cars are driving. I mean, on foot you're easy to overlook. She was putting herself in danger."

"So, the incident did happen." Delta looked him over.

"What of it?" Drake's eyes narrowed. "Has Lena turned it into a drama? Look, I know she's under a lot of pressure with these threats and all, but she's taking it too far. No one is trying to harm her, as in really do her any physical harm."

"And the perfume bottle?"

"Must the action of a psycho who enjoys terrorizing people. Those types never take real action. They are too cowardly for that."

"Still, I have a favor to ask," Jonas said, stepping forward. "The security footage you gave to the police, can I see it as well? I want to know if the gift was placed on the table in full view. If the perp is on the footage. The police won't tell me and…"

Drake sighed. "You can have a look if you want to. But it will take time and…"

"Great." Jonas stepped even closer. "I will look at it right now. Delta can keep you company."

Drake seemed overtaken, but he let them into the house. He told Delta to wait in the living room while he took Jonas up to where the security footage was kept.

Delta ambled through the living room with Spud by

her side. She stopped at the statue of the bronze woman picking flowers and looked it over. It was so lifelike.

"So." Drake entered behind her back. "Seems like we're condemned to spend some time together. Can I offer you anything?"

"No, thank you, I just had breakfast. Did Lena tell you at which hotel she would be staying?"

"No. Which means I can't call her there. I tried her cell, but she's turned it off." Drake paced the room. "I don't like it when she cuts me off like that."

She studied his prowling movements. Was he genuinely worried? Or frustrated Lena had eluded him? Randall had called him a tyrant last night, before rehearsal had started. "You asked Jonas if anything was the matter. It seemed like you were thinking your wife might be…in trouble?"

Drake sighed. He stood rubbing his hands and then said, "I might as well tell you. Lena has this tendency to exaggerate things. Take the incident with Zara. Yes, Zara might have hit her in that bend. But Lena should not have been walking there. We all have moments like that when we do something stupid, but we get away with it. No need to dramatize it. But Lena acted like Zara tried to run her to the ground or something. It's the same with the threats. Yes, there have been things delivered where Lena claims she never ordered them. Some groceries she attached some huge significance to. And that perfume bottle had the word death written on it. That is unpleasant, especially at a party with friends. But…she's sort of…" He looked for words. "She does appear afraid, but she also seems to be enjoying herself. The threats make her feel important. It's sad to say, but I have a feeling she needs that kind of attention."

"You mean, she might be making it up?" Delta reflected

on Lena's behavior to Jonas earlier. Was it a clever act? Was she not really afraid at all? "But you said it's really happening. There were groceries delivered and a perfume bottle with a threatening message left on the gift table at her party."

"Yes, but… Can't she be doing it herself? Sending herself threats? To keep the idea going that she needs help?" He pointed up at the ceiling. "I think Nord is thinking the same thing. He wants to look at the footage to see if Lena placed the gift on the table herself. He doesn't trust her."

What? Delta's mind spun. Had Drake consciously hired Jonas, supposedly to keep his wife safe, but in reality to prove that she was creating the illusion of being threatened? That she was playing all of them?

Drake would, of course, want outside evidence of that. Had he used Jonas to get it?

She bit her lip. "It's a big thing to suspect your wife of."

Drake laughed softly. "A few months ago, the thought wouldn't have crossed my mind. I loved her, and I ignored the little signs that she was unstable and eager for attention whatever way she could get it. Una did tell me once or twice that Lena was acting nasty to her and making hurtful accusations, but I thought it was a case of women bickering. Two strong personalities clashing. Only after Sally came here…"

He stared at the floor. "I've always looked after Sally. She's my little sister. And that louse, sucking her dry, then the museum firing her… It was all too much. I wanted to help her, set her up in the Drake company. But Lena took it badly. She was suddenly convinced Sally was going to prevent her from getting her furnishings line. I hadn't even promised her a line, she had raised it once, and I had said we could see. Never meaning to do anything with it, really."

He rubbed his forehead. "It was hard enough convincing

Una that Sally could be an asset to the company. I didn't need Lena giving me a hard time as well."

"You said then you started to notice things."

"Yes. Her ways to get attention from me. Acting scared, then getting angry. Mood swings. It got worse and worse."

"Instead of contacting Jonas, you should have asked for a psychiatrist to look her over."

"She would never have agreed to see one. She told me she wasn't crazy. That was it. I need not hire anyone for her. In the meantime, I did think it was odd, with the deliveries and her response to them. So, I hired Nord to ensure everything went smoothly at the party." He scoffed. "Talk about making a huge mistake."

"Jonas didn't know that…" Delta fell silent.

Drake sank in a chair and buried his face in his hands. "My little sister," he said. "She'll never be back."

Delta didn't know what to say or do. Maybe Drake blamed Jonas for what had happened, because deep down inside he blamed himself? That he had not been able to prevent Sally's murder?

Spud went to the man and leaned his head on his knee. Drake looked up and patted the dog. A smile flickered across his features.

"You seem to love dogs," Delta said. "Your wife's poodles are a bit spoiled, but they seem friendly and playful. How did you find Zara to take care of them?"

"Through an agency." Drake scratched Spud behind the ears.

"You interviewed her before you hired her?"

"I emailed her, and she came here."

"To the villa? Or did you meet her before?"

Drake looked at her. "What are all these questions?"

Delta cleared her throat. It was now or never. She might not get another chance to speak to him one on one. "You were seen at the Lodge Hotel with Zara, before she came to work for you. You put an arm around her. You seemed quite close."

She had expected him to jump to his feet and shout at her to leave his house, but he just sat there, his shoulders slumped. Then he said with a hoarse voice, "I should have known it would get out. How can I ever explain this to Lena? Especially now that she has already left in a frenzy."

Spud whined and licked his hand. Drake patted the rough head.

Delta waited patiently for him to continue. Finally, she seemed to be close to a big revelation. She could only hope it would make Jonas happy.

"Can I ask you to keep this to yourself?" Drake asked.

Delta pursed her lips. "If it's relevant to the investigation…"

"I can assure you it's not." Drake sighed. "Do you know anything about my past marriages? I mean, before I was with Lena?"

Delta felt uncomfortable. "I know you've been married twice before. And you have kids from your first marriage."

"Yes. Kids I never saw, as they were angry with me for having left their mother. Then this summer here in Tundish, a girl wants to meet me about a job for dog walker and tells me out of the blue that she is my daughter. That she wants to get to know me but without me advertising her as my daughter. You see, she hadn't heard nice things about me from her mother and wanted to see for herself what kind of man I was, without attaching herself to my name. She was skeptical, so, I knew I had to give her the chance to see me and get to know me without that pressure on the relationship. I hired her to watch Lena's dogs. Zara is not that handy with dogs but…"

"You covered her mistakes and defended her to your wife, because she is your daughter." Delta exhaled. Of course. The age difference now made total sense. "People are whispering it's an affair." She didn't want to say Lena herself thought this.

Drake turned red and made an impatient hand gesture. "People claim so much. Let them talk. I'm having a chance to get to know my daughter, at last, and I'm not letting anyone spoil that for me."

"But why not tell Lena? Let her in on the ruse? You could still have kept it a secret from everyone else."

"No, Lena wouldn't have kept her mouth shut. She would have given it away in no time. Also, to drive us apart. I know she wouldn't be able to take me getting close to anyone, not even my own child." His expression was grim. "She's possessive like that."

He sighed, and Spud licked his hand again. "I should never have married her. But I was under the spell of her beauty and her charming ways and… I wish I could turn back time and do it all differently."

Drake looked at Delta with a desperate expression. "You see, Lena will never tolerate me having a bond with Zara. Even if she knew the girl was my daughter and no threat to her… Because everyone is a threat to her, in her obsessed mind."

"Your sister Sally as well?"

Drake watched her with a frown. "You wonder if Lena would have hurt Sally? I asked myself that same question. I don't know. I really don't know." He patted Spud with a forlorn look in his eyes. "I try to tell myself she would never have gone that far. Simply because I can't stand the thought of her having…"

He swallowed hard. "And Una says they were together at the time of the murder. Una and Lena. So, neither of them could have…"

Delta blinked. "Did Una say that to you? In private? Or did she actually make a statement to that point to Sheriff West?"

"Yes, both of them did."

"But Lena and Una are not exactly friends, are they? Isn't it odd they are each other's alibis?" On the other hand, would they lie in an official statement to the police?

"You mean, they could be lying, and they weren't together at all?" Drake studied her. "And which one of them do you cast as the killer? And why would the other one lie for someone they don't like?"

Yes, that's the trouble. Delta shrugged. "I don't know, but you can always promise something the other one wants. Una wanted to stay your right-hand woman. With Sally out of the way, she could. Maybe Lena said that if Una declared they were together, she could stay in charge, and Lena would not push for any sort of role in the company. Maybe she even said she'd give up her line of furnishings. Something like that." Delta took a deep breath. "Sally may have been a threat to both of them."

"Sally was harmless." Drake jumped out of his chair. "I only wanted to help her get back on her feet. Have a life again after the misery in LA."

"Did she tell you she had been wrongly accused by a colleague?"

"Of course. She told me everything. I felt so sorry for

her. I only wanted to help her." Drake's voice broke. He stood with his head down.

Spud sat on his rear, watching him.

Delta wanted to ask if Drake had also known about the jade statue, missing from the museum's depot, but the door opened, and Jonas walked in. His expression was tense, and he stopped a few paces away from Drake. "I got it. The moment where the gift, the box with the perfume bottle is placed on the table."

"It's actually on there?" Delta shot to her feet. "Does West know?"

"If he looked, he found it. If not…" Jonas made a hand gesture. "But it's not good news, Mr. Drake."

Drake looked at Jonas with wide eyes. "Is it…Lena herself?" he asked in a whisper.

Jonas shook his head. "No. For a moment I thought so because of the color of her dress. But it was someone else."

Someone who looked like her, superficially. Delta knew the name before Jonas said it. Realized how devastating this would be for Drake.

"It was Sally."

Chapter Twelve

"No, that can't be. You're lying. Sally would never do anything to hurt Lena. To hurt me through her. She knew I loved Lena. She…" Drake clenched his hands into fists. "You're mistaken."

"Those images don't lie. I can show them to you if you want to see for yourself."

"No." Drake stepped back. "I don't want to see it. I can't bear to see her alive and well and… She's dead, Nord. Don't you have any feeling?" He turned away abruptly.

Delta said to Jonas, "Will you let West know about this?"

Jonas shrugged. "I have no choice. The person who placed the sinister gift on the table died that same afternoon. There might be a connection."

Drake swung round to him. "What are you saying now? That Lena killed her? Because she suspected her of being behind the threats and… You're destroying my entire life. My family."

Jonas shook his head, but Drake pushed on. "I should never have hired you. You bungled the case. You didn't do what you were supposed to. My sister died, and now you go digging and throwing up smoke just to cover your own incompetence."

Jonas wanted to say something, but Drake gave him no chance. "Leave my house. Now."

Jonas stepped back and called for Spud, who came to him at once. He looked back at the host, as if he wasn't sure he was doing the right thing, then left the room. Delta followed in a rush. In the hallway, she whispered, "Is the footage secure? I mean, what if he goes up and destroys it to protect his sister's good name? He seems to have loved her so much."

"I made a few screenshots with my phone. Besides, West has a copy of the footage. That's okay. I only wish I had told him in a different manner. I realized that it would be hard on him when I recognized her, but…"

Jonas shook his head as he walked with her out of the house into the bright sunshine. "I can't understand why Sally would want to threaten Lena."

"Maybe she hoped she would leave the villa and Sally could have Drake to herself? He had left his first two wives, so maybe Sally believed that he didn't love Lena much, or the marriage was under strain anyway. Or she used the perfume bottle in particular to show Lena that if she made products, those would be used to harm her. To keep her from making the furnishings for Drake Design. It seems Sally wanted into the company."

Jonas nodded.

Delta continued, "I have more. I confronted Drake with the fact that he was seen at the Lodge with Zara before she came to work for him and Lena as their dog walker. That he seemed close to her, even putting an arm around her. He admitted to me that she is his daughter, from his first marriage. You mustn't tell anyone, as Lena doesn't even know."

"Why not?" Jonas asked, looking surprised and confused.

Delta explained what Drake had told her. "He apparently wanted to give his relationship with his estranged daughter another chance, on her terms. Without anyone knowing what they really were to each other."

"Yes, I can understand that, but he gave her access to his house and his life. Judging by what you and others told me, Zara hasn't been a good influence. She's coming between him and his wife, and she's not taking care of the dogs like she should. She's behaving as if she's sixteen. A brat, testing the limits."

"Her father's limits," Delta supplied. "She must be carrying a grudge over the way he left her mother for the babysitter. Maybe she wants to make life hard for him by aggravating his new wife, while he has to defend her, and hurts his marriage without being able to explain why. It's working, because Lena fled the house last night."

"Yes, which leaves us with the open question of who caused the power outage. Was it Zara trying to unnerve her stepmother? Or Lena herself, to maintain the illusion she's under threat?"

"Illusion, if we assume the other threats were her own doing, but we now know Sally put the gift with the perfume bottle on the gift table. And let's not forget nephew Randall, who lives with them. He could have sabotaged the control panel before he left the villa to drive into town. His conspicuous car ensures everyone can vouch for him being there when the power outage happened. But he might have engineered it in advance. Have you talked to him?"

"In passing. He was at the Lodge. I asked him how he was doing after the murder, and he said he was fine. He acted a bit jumpy, but I suppose people don't like to discuss murder."

"I see. He was close to Lena at the party." Delta frowned hard. They had reached the Jeep and got in. Jonas leaned his hands on the wheel.

"I would never have believed it if I hadn't seen it with

my own eyes. Sally threatening Lena…" He looked at her. "It now seems the perfume bottle and the murder weren't two different things after all. They might have been intimately connected."

"You mean, Lena suspected Sally was behind the gift and confronted her about it, away from the party? Having brought a knife to maybe scare her into forgetting about ever doing something like that again?"

"For instance. They fought, and Lena killed her. By accident, maybe." Jonas started the engine. "Lena is highstrung enough to lash out in anger."

"And cold enough to cover it up by pretending she may be next on the killer's list?" Delta thought it over. "If we want to accuse Lena, we need to break her alibi first. That would mean targeting Una Edel, who claims Lena and she were together during the time frame for the murder."

"Now there is someone who is cold and calculating," Jonas said. "If she agreed with Lena to cover for her, I doubt we could shake her."

"But what would be in it for her?" Delta mused. "Must be something pretty big and important."

She leaned back in the car seat. "I'm going to ask Clara Ritter how the design for Wanted is coming along. With a little luck, I can ask her what she knows about Una Edel."

Chapter Thirteen

JONAS DROPPED DELTA NEAR THE OFFICES OF LYCLA Design and waved at her as she stood on the sidewalk. The tense events at the Drake villa had made her forget about her complex feelings for him. They had easily fallen back into the atmosphere of companionship she enjoyed so much. Maybe being friends was actually better than hoping for more?

She looked up at the front of the building, which held a shoe store below. Racks with discounted boots were outside, and Delta cast a covetous eye on a pair of knee-high black boots. And the mustard ankle boots beside them were not bad either.

But before she got lost extending her wardrobe, she had work to do. She entered through the door beside the shoe shop, marked with the LyCla logo on the glass pane, and went up the steep stairs. At the top, she looked into a corridor with three doors on her left-hand side. She decided to knock at the first. It was opened quickly by a smiling woman in a blue pantsuit. Her blond hair was pulled back with a band, and curls dangled onto her shoulders. Delta had a fleeting association with a country singer. "Good morning. I'm looking for Lydia or Clara?"

"I'm Lydia." The woman shook her hand. "Do come in. Would you like some coffee or tea?"

"Tea would be nice." Delta took a chair opposite a modern desk with a white top and metal legs. Models of rooms with tiny furniture sat everywhere, and in the corner, a golf bag rested against the wall. The dust settled onto it suggested it wasn't used much.

Lydia had gone to the corner where a water heater sat on a high counter against the wall and poured water into a mug. She brought it to Delta with a box full of tea bags. "Choose anything you like. I hate the herbal varieties, but Clara insists on us having them—claims they are relaxing."

Delta chose plain Ceylon and inhaled the scent as she moved the bag around in her mug.

Lydia said, "I can guess what you're here for. The design isn't quite finished yet. Clara is very busy."

Delta was surprised, and apparently it showed as Lydia began to laugh. "Clara told me about her visit to your store and the assignment you gave her. She pointed out both Hazel and you to me when we walked down the street the other day. I guess she feels a sort of natural connection to you both. We're also friends who started a business together."

"Oh, really, how nice." Delta accepted an oatmeal cookie from the tin Lydia presented before her. The thin layer of chocolate on the bottom immediately stuck to her fingers.

Lydia leaned back in her chair. "It's not always easy for women to run a business. Men don't see you as equals. Maybe in your specialty, where you deal with female customers more, it's different. But we compete directly with men all the time and…"

"Yes, it must have been a blow to you when Drake of Drake Design bought a villa here and started to get customers. He's such a big name." Delta blew on her tea. "I heard you were eager for a partnership. If you can't beat them, better join them, right?"

"Yes, we looked at the possibilities." Lydia moved a pen around on the desk. "But it didn't work out. Drake is too traditional for us. We like to be a bit more daring."

"Oh, I see." Delta took a bite from the cookie. "Yes, of course if you don't agree with the work… I'm so sorry you're facing such backlash just for being successful female entrepreneurs. I mean, Marc LeDuc wrote about Clara like…she was flirting with Drake to get into his company. It's a shame things are viewed in such a light. He must have been lurking behind a bush to get that photo." Delta shook her head. "Sad, really, when you think of it."

"Well, he also has to make a living somehow. It's old news." Lydia looked her over as if she wondered why Delta had brought it up. Then suddenly she leaned forward on her desk and said in a vicious tone, "And he didn't have to take that shot himself. Someone gave it to him."

"Oh?" Delta widened her eyes. "Someone who… wanted to harm your business maybe?"

"Actually, no." Lydia studied her French-manicured fingernails. "Someone who was a bit worried for her own position, I suppose." She looked up at Delta with wide blue eyes. "Have you met Una Edel?"

"Yes, at Lena Laroy's birthday party. Una Edel is Drake's second-in-command, I understand?"

"That's what she likes to call herself. I doubt he needs her quite that much. She is not a real designer like we are. Take those models…" Lydia gestured around her. "She can't build them. She can barely draw with a computer program. She's efficient, I suppose, and she has about taken over Drake's agenda for him and so on, but the design end of things is really not her forte. Which is why she was worried Clara or I might replace her."

"I heard she was worried about Sally Drake replacing her too."

Lydia laughed, her head back. "Sally Drake was an art

expert from LA. What did she know about design? Yes, Drake was fond of his little sister and wanted to protect her, but even he had to acknowledge she didn't know anything about his core business." She studied Delta. "You were at the birthday party, you say. What did you think?"

"How do you mean?"

"Oh, I don't know. I've been hearing all kinds of rumors. The police don't show up at a party for nothing."

"We really didn't see much. We were in our tent, doing a 3-D card–making workshop."

"Too bad. I might have found a way to work with you for little money."

Delta blinked her eyes. "Sorry?"

"I could make a deal with you to do changes to your store on a budget—in exchange for some information about the party."

"What kind of information?"

Lydia pursed her lips. "The kind of information that Drake wouldn't like to see out and about?"

Delta clutched the mug. It wasn't that hot anymore, but it felt like it burned her fingers. "I don't follow."

"You have a nice business here, and you want to pull in more customers. We could give you a facelift that will stun the town. But it costs money. I'm prepared to strike a very good deal with you in exchange for something that will help me when I go to Drake with a new proposal."

"New proposal?" Delta repeated.

"Yes. About a possible partnership."

Delta put the mug on the desk. "I really have to be going. Hazel is waiting for me. Thanks for your time."

She got up and turned to the door. Her heart pounded. Was this woman really suggesting she'd blackmail the

Drakes? A low-price renovation for Wanted in exchange for information she could use against Calvin Drake?

With the knob in her hand, she heard Lydia's chair squeak. Footsteps clicked behind her. For a moment, Delta imagined a hand on her shoulder and a threatening whisper to keep her mouth shut. But Lydia simply said, "Nice to have met you. Goodbye."

Delta raced down the steps and jerked open the front door. Outside, she took a deep breath. She was eager to get to Wanted and tell Hazel about this very odd conversation.

She almost bumped into someone and realized it was Clara. The woman readjusted the strap of her purse and said, "Um, about your design, I haven't quite—"

"Never mind. Take your time. We're in no rush." Delta breezed past her and raced across the street.

When she looked over her shoulder, she saw Clara standing in the doorway of the building, with Lydia's blond head shimmering behind her. Were they talking about her? Or would Lydia not say a word about her attempt to shake her down?

What an odd couple of women. Apparently eager to do a lot for their business.

Maybe even…kill?

Chapter Fourteen

"You must have misunderstood." Hazel nodded firmly. "She hardly knows you and wouldn't make such an offer out of the blue. Or maybe she was joking just to see if you would take the bait. I can't imagine her being serious. I mean…" She considered a moment. "No, really…"

"It was the weirdest experience I've had in a long time, and I'm going nowhere near those two again." Delta shivered. "They give me the creeps. Did you hear anything worthwhile?"

"Not really. I kept an eye on the handyman at Mine Forever. You know, the fake caterer? He seems to be about done." Hazel sighed. "I would love to know what he wants from Lena. But he's not going to tell us, I bet."

"Speaking of Lena, do you think she's still roaming about, or would she have gone back to the villa? Part of me is sorry for her, especially now that I know Drake lied about Zara, but…she does seem a bit dishonest. What was she looking for among my things?"

Delta pulled out the sketchbook and studied her case file. "Oh, boy."

"What?"

"I put up a question asking if Zara already knew Drake before she came to work at the villa as a dog walker because the two of them met at the Lodge. If that confirmed Lena's suspicions, she might be after Zara now to get the truth out of her." Delta sighed. "She thinks the two are having an affair, while actually, Zara is Drake's daughter."

"That's their own fault, I guess. If they had simply told her, it wouldn't have turned out this way." Hazel cut open a parcel with new pens and started to stack them. "I don't understand all the secrecy."

"Drake wanted to give his daughter a chance to get to know him without any pressure. That wasn't a bad idea. But he shouldn't have taken her side all of the time and gotten Lena suspicious."

"Zara can take care of herself, I suppose," Hazel said. "If Lena does quiz her about it, she has to stand her ground. What do you think? Should I put this jar with pens up there or down here?"

Delta cast a quick look. "Higher is better. Through the glass you can see the different patterns on them. I love the ones with the gold glitter, but I already have so many pens I never use, I have to resist buying them." She checked her watch. "Once we close the shop, I wonder if you'd like to go to the Lodge Hotel for dinner. Then we don't have to cook, and I wanted to talk to Ray, if he's there. Jonas dismissed Coldard's story about the Athena Barrows murder case like it doesn't matter at all regarding the present problem, but I want to know a bit more about the Taylor relative who featured in it. The one who died in Italy of pneumonia. Or something else."

Hazel grimaced. "If he was suspected of murder, the Taylors won't want to be reminded of him."

"He was never charged, let alone convicted. So why not discuss it casually? Tragic case, etc. How about it?"

"Fine with me. But I don't want to be there when you ask Ray about it. I want to avoid him in general. I'm tired of the rumors that I'm interested in him. I'm not."

Delta thought the denial was a bit emphatic but nodded her agreement right away.

They closed up for the day and left to take the car to the Lodge Hotel.

Guests dressed up for dinner were having drinks in the lobby, and the receptionist handed out keycards to new arrivals whose suitcases cluttered the way through. "They need an old-fashioned bellboy to take up the lot," Hazel whispered to Delta while they passed.

The dining room was to their left, and Hazel and Delta wanted to go in, when Delta saw Ray on the other side of the lobby, talking to his sister Isabel. Delta said, "You go in and find a table, have a look at the menu, and order drinks if you want to. I'd love a mineral water with some fresh lemon juice. I'll talk to Ray and come back to you as soon as I can."

Hazel nodded and entered the room. Delta crossed to Ray and Isabel. Isabel saw her first and flashed a smile. "Hello, Delta. What are you doing here? It isn't crafting night, is it?"

"No, I actually wanted to talk to Ray for a minute, if that's okay."

"Sure," Ray said. He nodded at Isabel. "I'll get on it and let you know." He made an inviting gesture to Delta toward the doors in the back of the lobby leading out into the garden behind the hotel. "We'll have a bit more privacy there."

A bit was the right assessment, as several hotel guests were in the garden, stretching their legs before dinner, having a drink, or quickly smoking a cigarette. The elegant lamps spread a warm yellow glow, and in the sky, a pale sliver of moon sat among a haze of cloud.

Ray moved closer to Delta. "It's chilly out here."

Delta gestured across her coat. "I'm dressed up warm. I wanted to ask you a quick question about something I heard. A bit of town history that is already way in the past. But it has to do with the Lodge, so—"

"You might be better off asking Rosalyn. She knows lots of the Lodge's history. I'm more into bringing in new guests and helping Isabel with the site, and so on." Ray leaned over and added with a wink, "Rosalyn is beginning to see it might just be helpful to have a famous brother around."

"I'm glad to hear you're getting along better." Delta put her hands in her coat's pockets. "I do hope you can help me, though. I doubt Rosalyn will want to, in this particular case."

"I can't imagine she wouldn't want to show off her knowledge of our hotel's history."

"Athena Barrows."

"Ouch." Ray halted and looked Delta over. "That is one name we like to avoid mentioning here. Although we can't really, now that Marc LeDuc decided to drag it all up again."

"So, you do know something about it?"

"As a matter of fact—but don't tell anyone you got it from me—Rosalyn briefed us all about it this morning. Following Marc's exposé on his site. She explained that there was no reason to think that our great uncle had anything to do with the young woman's murder so—"

"She briefed the entire hotel staff?"

"Isabel, me, Finn, and the receptionists. The people most likely to get questions about it. Rosalyn isn't dumb. She knew once she had seen Marc's piece that guests might see it too and have questions about it."

"And what exactly did she tell you?"

Ray shrugged. "What I just said."

"That's not the answer you'd expect to give to interested guests. A bit more would be nice. This is almost like 'no comment.'"

"Rosalyn told Isabel and me a bit more, after the others had left." Ray looked Delta over. "Do you want me to give you the details?" His brown eyes twinkled. "What do I get in exchange?"

"This is serious. Athena Barrows was stabbed, like Sally Drake. Near the same villa."

"What of it? Do you think it could be the same killer? But our great uncle died."

"I'm just looking into a possible connection. Of any kind."

Ray exhaled. They continued to walk until they stood on the platform overlooking the lake. There was no one there. Everyone had gone in, apparently, for dinner. Delta couldn't blame them, for the wind was sharp here, and the chill of an October evening invaded her bones.

Ray said, "I've never heard much about our great uncle. Probably because he died young and abroad. Now with this murder business, I wonder if it also had to do with the rumors that he was in love with Athena Barrows. She was a married woman, of course."

"Unhappily married, I heard."

Ray pursed his lips. "Hard to judge. We may think she had to be unhappy because her husband was a lot older and the marriage was probably more the choice of others than her own. But in the past, marriages were often set up that way, and not everyone was unhappy. In fact, I sometimes wonder if falling in love isn't just as silly. I mean, basing a commitment for life on a feeling that may pass…"

Delta studied Ray's serious expression. "You think marriage is a commitment for life?"

"I'd like it to be. Call me old-fashioned. Or simply romantic." He forced a laugh, but his eyes stayed pensive.

"So maybe Athena and her husband weren't that unhappy. Maybe she didn't feel sorry she had married him. Still, she was murdered. By whom?"

"That is a very good question. Suggestions have ranged from a thief wanting to steal from the boathouse, whom she caught red-handed before getting stabbed, to someone who knew her and wanted to get rid of her, using the opportunity where she was alone and couldn't call for help."

Delta nodded. "What do you think? It seems you know more about it than you let on."

"After Rosalyn briefed us this morning, I was curious, and I looked online for information."

"Do you have a library card?" Delta asked, adding with a grin, "If you get one, you can check the newspapers' online archives."

Ray grinned. "Good idea. But no, I looked online outside of those archives. Barrows was an influential man at the time, so I figured there had to be information about it. It was also part of a book some guy wrote about cold cases."

"Really?"

"Yes. I'm not going to tell Rosalyn about that, because the author seems to be a firm believer in the theory that our great uncle did it, and Rosalyn might get it into her head to sue him for slander." He winked again at Delta. "Just kidding. That book is twenty years old, so Rosalyn need not worry about it making waves."

"You never know. With Marc LeDuc digging, things might get dragged up again. Has Marc talked to you?"

"No, he knows he won't get a thing from me. Or any other Taylor. He might have tried his luck with one of the clerks or boating instructors. But I doubt they know much about the distant past."

Delta nodded. "I see. Well, seems to be a dead end then. This book, though, about the cold cases, do you remember the title and author?"

Ray gestured to the hotel. "We have it in our collection."

"What?" Delta stared at him.

"Yes, well, that's purely coincidental. Three years ago, Rosalyn bought a huge number of secondhand books to put on the shelves in the lobby, the billiard room, selected guest rooms. She likes big, leather-bound volumes with a bit of clout, so she didn't buy them through a bookshop, where she might be saddled with paperbacks, but through a guy who's a local historian and book collector."

"Coldard?" Delta asked.

"Yes, do you know him?"

"Only by name. So, Rosalyn has been to Coldard's house? Did she talk about Athena Barrows with him?"

"I don't think so. Those books came to the Lodge three years ago, and I can't imagine Rosalyn packed them up herself. Must have had some staff members do it."

"But the book about cold cases, mentioning Athena Barrows and your great uncle, was among those books?"

"Yes. Once I saw a picture of it online, it struck me as vaguely familiar. Then I recalled I had seen it in our very own billiard room. So, I need not go far to look into it. I can get it for you, and you can borrow it to look at."

"That would be great. Thanks."

Ray frowned at her. "I really wish you wouldn't be digging into these murders. Either that old affair or Sally Drake's death. It's really none of your business and... Well, Calvin Drake strikes me as a man who doesn't like interference.

Better leave this one to the police." He held Delta's gaze. "Or did Jonas put you up to it?"

Delta felt her cheeks grow warm. "I was there when it happened and… It's so odd. And I don't like loose ends. I'd be happy if you can lend me the book. Now we'd better go back inside. I'm freezing." She quickly walked ahead of him back to the hotel, hoping he wouldn't push the point about not getting involved in the murder case. She already was, and she couldn't let go.

———————

"What's that?" Hazel asked when Delta came to her table with the book Ray had fetched for her.

"Just something I want to look into. Nothing to worry about tonight. What's on the menu?"

"We're lucky. They're having a dessert buffet tonight." Hazel nodded in the direction of a long table decked out in white cloth. "In half an hour, when the first guests are ready to tuck in, that will hold the best sweet treats in the region."

"Oh, let's get started quickly then. What do you suggest for the first course?"

They enjoyed pumpkin soup and a main course of cheese baked in a rosemary and chopped-nuts crust with potatoes from the oven and broccoli. But their eyes were on the table where the staff put out cheesecakes and chocolate cake, ice cream in several flavors, whipped cream and fresh fruit, pudding and macarons.

"My mouth is watering," Hazel whispered. "I can't wait to try it all."

Ray appeared beside their table. He smiled at Hazel and said to Delta, "Can I whisk you away for a few minutes?"

"What for?" Delta was a bit worried the raspberry cheesecake would be all gone before she could try some and didn't want to leave the room.

"Come on. It's a surprise."

Delta rose reluctantly and gestured at Hazel. "You go ahead and get some dessert, if you want to." Then at least her friend wouldn't miss out.

She followed Ray out of the dining room, curious despite her annoyance at what he could have for her. In the lobby at the reception desk, an elderly lady stood waiting. Her neat blond bob swung around her ears when she turned to them. Her eyes lit, and her face broke into a wide smile. "Delta!"

"Gran!" Delta ran and locked her grandmother into her arms. She inhaled the scent of her favorite French perfume and closed her eyes a moment. It was like she was coming home to Gran's house for the holidays, feeling so warm and loved.

Growing up with two much-older brothers, one a professional athlete who had been on the road a lot, Delta had often stayed with her grandmother when she was a child and had developed a close bond with her. Over the years, Gran had always supported her dreams of drawing and crafting and, on her thirtieth birthday, even donated her the money needed to buy into Wanted. Everything Delta now had here in Tundish, she had because of her grandmother.

She lifted her head and asked, "What are you doing here?"

"I'm checking in. I was at your cottage, but you weren't there. I thought I might as well take a room here and try again in the morning." Gran gave her a rueful smile. "I decided quite on impulse to fly out to you. I should have called maybe, but it seemed like it would be more fun if I simply turned up."

"It certainly is. I can't believe you're really here." Delta hugged her again. "Welcome to Tundish. I want to drag you into town right away and show you Wanted, but you must be tired from your flight. Besides, I'm having dinner here with Hazel, and we're about ready to dive into a delicious dessert buffet."

"Why don't you join them?" Ray said. "It'll be on the house. I'll also get you a glass of champagne to welcome you to town." He gestured to the clerk behind the desk. "See to it that Mrs. Douglas's luggage is brought to her room."

"Yes, sir."

Ray offered his arm to Gran. "Allow me."

He led her into the dining room, where Hazel was just returning to their table with a plate full of treats. She put it down and clapped her hands. "I had no idea your grandmother was coming."

"Me neither," Delta said.

Ray pulled out a chair for Gran, and after she had hugged Hazel, she sat down, and he put the chair in place. He tapped her shoulder lightly. "Champagne then."

Gran followed him with her eyes as he left the room with his quick, athletic stride. "What a charming young man."

Hazel grimaced. She picked up her spoon to tuck into the pudding on her plate. "Ray is not young anymore."

"He is to me." Gran winked at Delta. "You must tell me all about him. Oh, look at that." She pointed at Hazel's plate. "French meringue."

"We're going to get our desserts now," Delta decided, "before they're gone. Come on."

She led her grandmother to the buffet, and they laughed and talked while they selected the most delicious desserts offered: raspberry cheesecake, muffins with clotted cream, chocolate truffle cake with whipped cream, and a bit of rum-raisin ice cream.

"You came at exactly the right moment," Delta said while they walked back to the table. Ray stood there with a bottle of champagne. He filled glasses for all three of them, and they toasted. "To the greatest surprise," Delta said, beaming at her grandmother. Gran smiled back at her, but for a moment, there was something in her eyes that gave Delta pause. She wondered, briefly, if Gran had really simply decided to step onto a plane and come out here.

But of course, she had. If she said so.

Delta took a sip of champagne and enjoyed the fizz on her tongue. This was going to be a fantastic night.

"I do feel a bit guilty I can't put you up at our home." Delta said, standing in the hotel room.

"Nonsense. Look around." Gran gestured at the double bed, the open door leading into the large bathroom with a tub, shower, and washing basin, with shower gel and body lotion from exclusive brands on the stand. "I have everything I need. In fact, I feel like I'm on a four-star vacation."

"As you should. In the morning, I'll drop by to pick you up and show you around. You'll love the town and the shop." Delta hugged her grandmother. "I'm so glad you're here."

"I hope it's not inconvenient. You must have things to do."

"I can arrange things so I have time for it. Hazel is so

happy you're here. And I'm sure the Paper Posse will want to meet you." Delta sighed in bliss. She had the feeling that everything was all right with the world. "Sweet dreams then."

"You too, darling. See you in the morning."

Delta left the room and heard the door click into the lock. In the corridor, Ray was waiting for her. He walked her to the elevator. "Is everything all right with the room?"

"Yes, it's perfect. You really spoiled us tonight with the champagne and all."

"Nonsense, she deserves a warm welcome. I won't put it on the bill. You're friends of mine, right?"

"Don't let Rosalyn hear it."

"I don't see Rosalyn anywhere near." Ray stepped into the elevator with her. "I passed the desk just as your grandmother was registering. Of course, the name Douglas rang a bell. I asked her if she was related to you and then told her you were having dinner with us. I offered to go and get you for her. To surprise you. She thought it was a great idea." He grinned at her. "Looks like a keen old lady to me."

"Don't call her old. She called you a young man, so you must be gracious as well."

Ray grimaced. "When ladies start calling you young man, they usually have a plan with it."

Delta flushed. "My gran…"

"Shhh." Ray gestured at her to cut her off. "Don't mind my jokes." His eyes were half-serious, half-teasing. "You had a good time, right?"

"Yes, it was great." Delta suddenly felt a little forlorn leaving her grandmother; then she remembered the book she was carrying under her arm. About cold cases, because a murder had occurred. Again, near one of her workshops. Gran didn't know about that yet.

Or did she? Had she flown out in a rush because she was worried what her granddaughter was getting into now?

Maybe there would be time for a more in-depth chat in the morning when she was going to show Gran around town.

They stepped out of the elevator. Hazel was waiting for them near the entrance. She had said she didn't want to come up. Delta suspected it was to avoid Ray's presence.

Ray said to Hazel, "There's an antique show in Boulder Saturday. Would you like to go?"

Hazel seemed startled. "Saturday?" she repeated, glancing at Delta.

Delta said, "You can go. I can take care of the shop. Gran can help out as well, now that she's here. You love antiques, so..."

Ray smiled, but Hazel said, "No, I want to do some inventory on Saturday. Good night." Then she raced out of the hotel.

Ray looked disappointed, but Delta didn't linger. He might ask her why Hazel had told him no. "Good night," she called as well and rushed after her friend.

Hazel was already in the driver's seat when Delta reached the Mini Cooper.

She dived in beside her and put the book in her lap, then buckled up. "Why did you tell him no? Might have been a nice getaway. You work too hard."

"I don't want to be seen with Ray. It will only lead to talk." Hazel backed up the car and turned into the road. "You can go if you like."

"He didn't ask me." Delta patted the book.

"He did go out of his way to be nice to your gran."

Delta hitched a brow. "Do I detect a hint of jealousy?"

"No. I only mean to point out that Ray is nice to everybody. It doesn't mean…" Hazel fell silent and clutched the wheel.

Delta stared into the darkness ahead. "You like him," she concluded.

Hazel made a scoffing sound. "Wouldn't it be sad if I did? The well-known ex-football player who's so popular with the ladies."

"Ray has his serious side," Delta said, thinking about his observation on marriage.

"Maybe." Hazel braked to turn a sharp bend. "Look, I'd rather not talk about it, okay?" After a moment's hesitancy, she added, "You don't want to talk to me about Jonas either."

"There's nothing to talk about."

"Come on. In college you always told me everything." Hazel bit her lip. "Maybe it's not like college anymore, is it?"

"That's not it. I…I don't know about Jonas. It's not like anything I ever felt before."

It was silent in the car. Hazel drove with full focus, and Delta ran her fingers along the edges of the book. Her happy mood about Gran's visit still buzzed inside of her, but other feelings churned at the edges. The complicated thing with Jonas, the murder case, still learning everything about the shop, making friends, settling in. So much was new, and it took up a lot of energy. Sometimes she was simply beat at night. And deep inside, she wondered briefly if staying in Cheyenne wouldn't have been easier. Her life had been all settled there. It had been dull at times, but maybe you could also have too much excitement?

"What's that book anyway?" Hazel asked.

Delta looked down at it. "It's about unsolved murders. It also seems to contain a section about Athena Barrows.

I don't even know what I want with it. It seemed relevant when Ray mentioned it to me. Did you know Rosalyn actually got it from Coldard?"

Hazel shook her head. "Several people told me Coldard lives in a world of his own. He still does research and types up articles, but he hasn't published anything in years. It's like he's just playing make-believe."

"He struck me as sharp and knowledgeable. I will look into this." Delta folded her hands on the book. "But first I need a good night's sleep, and then I want to put some time into Gran. She flew all the way out here to be with me." A grin came up. "We're going to have the best time."

Chapter Fifteen

THE NEXT MORNING, HAZEL TOLD DELTA IT WAS OKAY IF she wanted to go to the Lodge and have breakfast with her grandmother there—to catch up. "You can then take her into town and show her around. Come on, do it. You don't know how long she intends to stay, and you have to make the most of it."

Delta agreed, thanked her, and drove to the Lodge. When she parked the car, she saw Jonas coming from the forest at the end of the parking lot in a jog. He spotted her and waved. She waited until he had reached her. Spud brushed his head against her leg, and she patted him. Jonas said, panting, "I'm going to the sheriff's station with this." He held up a small laptop.

"What's that?" Delta asked. "Did you find it in the forest?"

"No, it's mine. I use it to look at footage I made with camera traps."

"Camera what?"

"Camera traps. They are cameras attached to trees, which are triggered by motion. If an animal passes the camera, it films the animal. It's ideal for filming during the night or to get footage of shy creatures who don't show themselves when there are humans around. I have several camera traps in the woods to study wildlife."

"And? What does that have to do with the sheriff?"

Jonas opened the laptop and turned it on. He clicked through a few screens, and then showed her some moving images. They were black and white, so she assumed they had been made at night. "That's a human being," Delta exclaimed.

"Exactly."

She leaned closer. It was a man carrying a shovel and a big backpack.

"Do you recognize him?" Jonas asked in a tense tone.

"No, not really."

Jonas made an impatient gesture. "Doesn't matter. I know who it is. The guy who's restoring the building at Mine Forever. It struck me as odd he was taking so long getting a few things done, but I thought he only wanted to make more money. Now it seems he was hanging about town for a reason."

"That guy was also at Drake's party." Delta looked at Jonas. "Dressed up as a caterer. He got into an argument with Lena Laroy. She told me it was about an autograph, but I don't believe her."

Jonas looked her over. "Did she say any more about him?"

"No. Not at first. Later, when she came to our cottage, she said he had caused trouble for her before, but the police wouldn't do anything with her statement. I had the distinct impression she was really anxious about his presence, and especially about people finding out about him. Her husband for one."

Jonas frowned. He pulled his phone from his pocket and placed a call. "Drake," he mouthed at her. "Good morning. Jonas Nord here. Is your wife around?" He listened for a few moments. "I see. No, that's all right. Thank you." He lowered the phone and gave Delta a worried look. "Drake says Lena hasn't been home all night. He doesn't know where she is."

"She left the house after the power outage. She claimed it was sabotage to hurt her. She suspected her husband of having an affair with Zara. I thought she would go back later. But apparently, she also stayed away last night. I wonder where she slept."

Jonas stared into the distance. "If that guy had some kind of argument with her and he was out and about last night with a shovel—"

Delta gasped. "Do you think he hurt her? That he might have killed her and buried her body somewhere?" A chill went down her spine at the idea.

"I hope not." Jonas looked grim. "Then I would really have failed in my assignment. Do you know where Lena might have gone for the night?"

"No, not at all. We ate out last night, so she might have been at the cottage, but we weren't there. She could have friends here or… A hotel?" Delta nodded at the Lodge.

"Could you ask if she's staying there?" Jonas turned to his Jeep. "I'm taking this footage to the police. Text me whether she's here or not. I can check other hotels and guesthouses around town."

Delta nodded. "Will do." She watched while he dove into his Jeep and turned the engine on, backed out of the parking spot, and drove off. That guy. The fake handyman, fake caterer, fake whatever. Had he killed Sally at the party? Had he now killed Lena and buried her body somewhere in the woods?

But what for?

She went into the Lodge and asked at the desk if Mrs. Drake or Lena Laroy was staying there. "I need to talk to her, it's rather urgent."

The receptionist shook her head. "She's not here."

"Delta."

Delta turned her head to her grandmother, who came from the elevator and rushed for her. "You need not have come right away, but I'm glad to see you."

"Good morning. Did you sleep well?" Delta hugged her. "Let's have breakfast together. I have to send one message first." She pulled up her phone and texted Jonas. "Lena is not here. Keep me posted on developments." Then she led her gran into the dining room to have breakfast and catch up.

When Delta and her grandmother headed into town, Delta noticed the handyman's van wasn't at Mine Forever, and he wasn't working on the roof either. She told Gran to wait for her a second and crossed the street to ask about the guy. Tammy was serving coffee to a group of women and told her in passing that the job was done, and he had left town. At least she thought he had. "He hasn't been around this morning."

Delta thanked her and went back to Gran. Her thoughts were racing, and the possibility of Lena Laroy being murdered made her heartbeat stutter. The woman had come to their cottage for help. They had turned her away. Of course, there had been more to it than that, and Lena hadn't been honest with them about the danger she was in, but still… Delta had known, through Jonas, that Lena was under threat and that her husband believed it could come from closer to home than anyone thought. Now Lena was missing, and that handyman—

"I can't wait to see the store," Gran gushed, and Delta

forced herself to focus on this special moment, where she could show the results of Gran's gift to her.

They approached Wanted, and Gran took her time, admiring the front with their notebooks and pens advertised in the spot where, in the past, the posters of wanted outlaws had hung. Oohing and aahing, she went from room to room, along the sheriff's desk and weapons rack and into the old cells, looking at everything on offer. Hazel winked at Delta. Delta was happy her grandmother seemed to like it so much, but she was also a bit distracted by the idea of what was going on outside the cozy shop. The eerie, hazy images of that guy in the woods with his shovel—

Suddenly, something Zara Kingsley had said came back to mind. The remark Delta had been looking for earlier. At the time, she hadn't been able to recall the words, even though she had been certain it was somehow significant. Now in a flash, she saw the scene again: Zara had run in to tell them there was a dead body outside, near the rose bushes, and she had mentioned that one of the poodles had discovered the body. That the dog had wanted to dig there.

Dig. Shovel.

She grabbed her phone again and messaged Jonas. "Call me as soon as you can. It's important."

Her phone didn't ring.

Delta paced the room. She messaged again.

Gran looked at her. "Is something wrong?"

"No. Of course not. It's just that uh… Could you stay here with Hazel for a bit? I need to go out and see someone." She gave Hazel a pointed look. Hazel said, "I can show you how to do calligraphy."

"Oh, that would be wonderful. I'd love to do some nice hand lettering on my Christmas cards this year."

With Gran distracted, Delta left the shop in a rush and drove out to the sheriff's station. She found Jonas at the desk, talking to the deputy. She raced up to him. "Didn't you get my messages?"

Jonas gave her a surprised look. "My battery died. I need to charge it. Is something wrong?"

"I remembered what Zara said." Delta gasped for air. "She discovered Sally's body, remember? She said that one of the poodles had wanted to dig there. Where the body lay. What if something was buried there, and the dog smelled that and wanted to dig it up?"

Jonas stared at her. His eyes flickered, as if he was processing the information. "You mean...did the guy with the shovel want to dig up whatever was buried where Sally Drake died?"

"Exactly."

The deputy leaned across the desk. "The crime scene is still marked with tape. Nobody is supposed to go there and—"

"I don't think this guy will care. Come on."

Jonas ran from the station, with Delta hard on his heels. She followed his Jeep as he took the road along the lake to Drake's villa. Her mind raced with thoughts about something buried there, the murder of Sally, Lena's jumpiness, Zara's odd behavior. Had Zara wanted to come work for Drake, not because she was his daughter and wanted to get to know him, but to get access to the villa, the grounds...

Could whatever was buried there be related to the earlier murder of Athena Barrows? Did the villa hide something valuable that people were willing to kill for?

The gate was closed, and Jonas stopped the Jeep in front. He jumped out and gestured for her to follow him. He began to run along the wall fencing off the garden. "There is open wood in the back, so we must be able to get on the grounds that way," Jonas grunted. "That guy will be long gone, I bet."

"But did he find what he was looking for?" Delta pushed a hand to her side as she tried to keep up.

Finally, they saw the crime scene tape. Jonas reduced speed and then stopped altogether. The earth within the fenced-off area was undisturbed. "No one dug here recently," he said. "I'd be able to tell. You can't quite put it back the way it was."

"Why not?" Delta asked. "Everything is covered in dead leaves. You could simply throw leaves on it and—"

Jonas put his hand on her arm. "We're not going to touch anything. We need the police to come and dig. To see if anything is buried here. It could provide motive for Sally Drake's murder."

"What on earth are you doing?" A gasping deputy appeared behind them. "I asked my colleague to man the station and came after you."

"Great," Jonas said. "Now I don't have to drive back or borrow Delta's phone to call you. You have to dig in there." He pointed at the area. "There could be something valuable hidden. It may even have to do with the murder."

The deputy looked dubious. "Dig? For what?"

"If I knew that, I'd tell you. Right?"

"Maybe the jade statue." Delta looked at Jonas. "Remember that Sally Drake left the museum where she worked in LA, and they discovered later that a jade statue was missing from the depot? They thought she might have taken it. We assumed that if she had, she'd have left it somewhere along the way in a safe-deposit box at a bank or something. But what if she hid it here?"

The deputy looked even more doubtful. "That wouldn't be very safe. Someone else might find it."

"Who would start digging in the middle of nowhere? Except for a dog, of course." Delta grinned. "Maybe those two crazy poodles will do some good anyway."

Jonas had told her to go back into town, but Delta had wanted to be part of the action and hung around while the deputy and Jonas dug. It took them about an hour to hit on the right spot. It was just outside the fenced-off area. Jonas fell to his knees and cleared away the last of the earth with his hands. Then he pulled out a metal box. It was secured with a padlock. He managed to strike off the padlock with the sharp blade of his shovel, and then the box opened.

The deputy and Delta leaned over him while he lifted out a cloth-wrapped item. He unwound the cloth, and there lay a smooth, green jade statue of a tiger with two cubs. The craftmanship was excellent.

Jonas whistled. "Sally Drake *was* a thief."

"If this is what the museum is missing."

"There won't be two jade statues lying around." The deputy tapped Jonas on the shoulder. "I'll take this in now."

"No." The sharp voice came from behind them. "I'll take it." The sound of a gun cocking echoed through the silence.

Delta sucked in air.

The handyman came from the shadows beneath the trees. He held a pistol aimed at them. "Don't be stupid. Nobody wants to get hurt over that thing."

The deputy twitched to move his hand toward the

gun on his hip, but the handyman clicked his tongue. "One wrong move, and I'll shoot."

"Let's do what he asks," Jonas said quickly. He held his hands up, palms to the man.

"Back away," the handyman ordered.

They did. The man closed in, keeping his eyes on them. The statue was on the ground. He glanced down at it. He reached with his free hand to pick it up. While he moved to get it off the ground, Jonas leapt forward with lightning-fast speed and kicked the man's gun hand. The pistol shot from his grasp and flew through the air. It landed in the leaves a few feet away. The crook shouted in pain and frustration and swung his other hand at Jonas, but Jonas grabbed him by the wrist and wrestled him to the forest floor. "Quick, handcuffs," he called to the deputy, who cuffed the criminal and pulled him to his feet.

Jonas collected the pistol from among the leaves and put the safety on. "Nice little toy."

The deputy said, "You took a risk, Nord."

Jonas laughed softly. "I had handled the box. I knew the statue was heavier than he would expect. The moment he tried to lift it, his attention would be diverted, and I could strike. I'd have to." He eyed the deputy seriously. "Who said that after he had what he came for, he wouldn't have shot us anyway? I have no idea how violent he is, and neither do you."

He looked at the man. "You can tell us all about it at the station."

The man gave him a vicious look. "I'm not talking. You got nothing on me."

As the deputy pulled him along, Jonas said to Delta, "I'll come too to ensure this passenger arrives safely at the station. Can you wrap up the statue, put it back in the box, and follow behind?"

Delta nodded. Leaning down, she wound the cloth around the tiger again. It had such quiet beauty, and apparently, a high monetary value, filling people with greed. Even someone quiet and rational like Sally Drake.

At the station, Sheriff West had to begrudgingly admit that Jonas had done a good job helping to apprehend the would-be thief. He looked at the statue, which Delta had placed on his desk, and said, "Not a very impressive thing. But must be worth something. I'll call that guy from insurance."

"Investo Insurance," Delta said. "They should be able to tell you more about it. It must be old, or else it wouldn't have been in a museum."

West shook his head. "I'm first going to run the guy's prints through the system and see if we know him. Maybe the feds are looking for him, and then I can turn him over. He'll be their hassle."

"He could be Sally Drake's killer," Jonas protested. "Or are you still sticking to the husband?"

West grunted. "I had to let Jarvis go. Lack of evidence. But the discovery of this statue sheds more light on the crime. That handyman must have been Sally Drake's accomplice in the theft. But she ran here with it, to keep it to herself. He followed her to get it back. They argued about it on the edge of the garden, and he killed her."

"But he couldn't find the statue?" Jonas shook his head. "It wouldn't have been very smart of him to kill her without having found out the statue's hiding place first."

"Who said criminals are smart?" The sheriff reached for the phone. "I have work to do."

Jonas ushered Delta along. "I guess that is as much of a thank you as we're ever going to get from him. How are you?" He eyed her worriedly. "That guy with the gun was not part of my plan."

"You handled him. That's what matters. I should get back into town. My gran dropped by to see the store and how I live here in my new hometown."

"Really? And you walked out on her to come to help me?" Jonas studied her.

Delta looked down. "I was worried, because my messages didn't seem to be getting through. I wanted the thief to be caught, not get away."

"Thanks." Jonas brushed his fingers across her cheek a moment. "You're the best." Then he turned to his Jeep and went off. Delta stared after him. She hadn't even realized until now that Spud wasn't with him. Odd.

She drove back into town and found Gran at Wanted, trying to put elegant curls on all her *g*'s and *y*'s. Hazel approved her progress and cast Delta a questioning look.

Delta gave her a cheerful thumbs-up and went into the kitchen area to wash her hands. Looking back on it, with her adrenaline fading, her legs did feel a bit wobbly, and she sat down and rested her head in her hands. It wasn't just for her own sake. Jonas could have been hurt as well. Over a statue!

"Are you okay?" Hazel stood in front of her. She spoke in a whisper, as if she was worried Gran in the store would overhear. "What happened? You were gone so long."

"Yes, it's a long story. But I don't want Gran to find out. Let's uh…close up for an hour and have some pancakes at Mine Forever."

"Great idea." Hazel went back into the store to tear Gran away from her newfound hobby. Delta realized with a stab of guilt that she wasn't after innocent diversion; she also wanted to ask Tammy about that handyman. She had to snap out of sleuthing mode, really, but at the same time she realized that the discovery of the statue and the arrest of the handyman left a lot of questions unanswered. She did need to push on, also to help Jonas.

For a moment, she touched her cheek where he had brushed it and smiled to herself. Then she sprang into action and went into the shop.

Chapter Sixteen

While Hazel gave Gran the best seat in Mine Forever, with a lovely view of Wanted on the other side of the street, Delta talked to Tammy, asking her where that handyman had come from.

"He dropped by and offered his services at a low price." Tammy grimaced. "That mention of a low price convinced my boss. He knew the equipment on top of the building needed a bit of a cleanup, but he had put it off, saying he didn't want to invest in it. So, the offer was just right. I didn't like the guy, though. Shifty eyes, if you know what I mean. And slow, slow. Like a snail. Although then he was suddenly done and packing up his things. Odd guy."

"And you don't know where he came from? He's not local?"

"No. His van had no name on it either." Tammy shrugged. "Super-shady if you ask me. But it wasn't my decision to make. Now what can I get you?"

While they enjoyed the prize-winning coffee and pancakes with bacon and cheese, Delta's fingers itched to sketch the new information into her case file. She had a feeling they were somehow getting closer to real answers, but she wasn't quite sure yet how it all fit together. Sally had left LA with a stolen statue. She had taken it from a depot, had maybe believed the theft wouldn't be discovered for a while. She had settled here, intending to work in Drake's company. But if she had known she could ask her brother for a job, why steal a statue? Not for money, it seemed. To get rid of her husband Abe? A sort of buy-off? Had they met away from the party to settle the deal? After all, Jonas had told her earlier that the divorce would leave Sally almost penniless. Maybe she had tried to get something out of it by offering her husband the statue? Or Jarvis had actually asked for it?

Or had someone else put her up to the theft? The handyman? But Lena had said he had been after her before. How had Lena's stalker gotten in touch with Sally? How would he have known she had access to a valuable statue?

It seemed more likely he had learned about the statue while he was here in Tundish, stalking Lena. For instance, at the party. But then they were left with the question Jonas had raised at the police station: Why kill the very person who knew the hiding place of the valuable item he was after? It made no sense. Other pieces didn't seem to fit as well. Sally coming into the company while Drake had wanted to work with Lydia and Clara. Who, by contrast with Sally, knew plenty about design. The models in Lydia's office had been so well done, detailed and smart. Why would a clever businessman let a woman with no experience into his company? Only because she was the little sister he loved and wanted to protect?

And where was Lena Laroy now? Why hadn't she gone back to the villa?

Was Zara merely a daughter wanting to reunite with her father?

"Delta?"

She looked up and realized Gran had asked her something. "Sorry, what did you say?"

"That you have everything so nicely organized. I'm so happy you're set up here now. That young man was very nice last night." Gran winked at her.

"Ray is really not my type." Delta glanced at Hazel.

"No? Oh, there was someone else, I think. What was his name? The ranger with the retired police dog."

"Gran! I never said that—" Delta cut up her pancake.

"I'm sorry, darling." Gran reached out and put her hand on Delta's. "Elderly people like to see others happy. I hope you are."

"Oh, yes, I am."

"It's just that..." Hazel spread butter across her pancake. "We did a workshop a few days ago at one of those big villas along the lake, and one of the houseguests was murdered. We're not involved this time, not really, but... Well, it did shock the town, of course. Everyone is a bit preoccupied."

"Another murder?" Gran sat up and stared at Delta. "This town doesn't seem to be very safe."

"The houseguest came from LA, so she might have been killed over something that happened there. Her husband could be involved. She was about to divorce him, that is. And he didn't want to let her go." *Not to mention the life insurance he's collecting now that she's dead.*

"Oh. One of those relationship dramas you read about. So sad." Gran shook her head and took another bite of her pancake.

Hazel said, "It was a very unfortunate coincidence we were doing a workshop at that party. But I had no idea that we'd encounter murder when I agreed to do it. After all, you don't tell Lena Laroy no."

"Lena Laroy?" Gran perked up. "The former model? She used to be in all the magazines I read at the hairdresser's. Didn't she marry some very rich man? Who had been married before?"

"Yes, Calvin Drake." Hazel reached for her coffee.

"Oh, yes." Gran gestured with her fork. "He betrayed his first wife with the babysitter. It was all over the tabloids. Not a new story but still very sad when you think about it. When you take someone into your home to care for your children, you don't expect anything like that. Oh, look. What cute dogs." She pointed into the street. Delta followed her movement and saw a pink-clad figure on the other side of the street, peeking into the window at Wanted. Two big, black poodles strained on their leashes.

"It's Zara," Hazel exclaimed. "What can she want with us?"

"I have no idea, but I'll go ask her." Delta rose and smiled at Gran. "You have more coffee if you like."

"It's very good."

Hazel gestured for Tammy to come over with the coffeepot, and Delta left the restaurant and crossed the street. Zara had stopped looking into windows and was typing something on her phone when Delta reached her. "Hello."

"Oh!" Zara almost dropped the phone. "You startled me." She got tugged to the right by a poodle and put her phone away. Taking a better hold of the leashes, she said, "I was looking for you."

"I thought so. I was over there having lunch." Delta gestured at Mine Forever. "What's up?"

"Drake called me. He said he had heard from a neighbor that the police had been to the house again. I didn't dare tell him that I wasn't there. I took the dogs out and had a manicure." She showed Delta her shocking-pink fingernails. "I hoped you would know more about it."

"Why me?" Delta said.

"Because you seem to know everything." Zara eyed her. "I can't face Drake later today and tell him that I know nothing about the police being at the house. I'm supposed to know."

"You're the dog walker, right, not his house sitter." Delta took a deep breath. "He does allow you a lot of freedom. Other staff members might already have been fired over smaller things."

"That's none of your business." Zara eyed her coldly. "Now what happened with the police? The neighbor told Drake you were with them at the house. Why?"

"I wonder which neighbor that was who could see everything so well," Delta said. Zara's attitude irritated her. "It sounds like he spied on us with binoculars. Then he probably also saw what happened."

"Not really. Only that you left with some box in your arms. Did you find something?"

Delta shrugged. "If Drake wants to know, he has to ask the police." She wasn't about to reveal the discovery of the jade statue Sally had allegedly stolen from the LA depot. Maybe Zara knew nothing about this, and Drake would prefer to keep it that way.

Zara straightened up. "Really?" Then she let her shoulders hang and said in an anxious tone, "You were right. I should already have been fired. It's just my luck I wasn't. I need this job. Please help me. Don't let Drake get angry with me. Tell me what you found out this morning."

"Sorry, can't do." Delta turned away and crossed the street again. She stepped into Mine Forever's hallway and pulled up her phone. She called Drake. He answered after a few rings.

"You wanted to know what happened at your house?"

"Did something happen at my house then?" He sounded confused.

"Yes, Zara stopped me in the street and asked about it. A neighbor informed you about the police being present?"

"A neighbor? No. No one called me about anything. Least of all Lena's whereabouts. I'm so worried about her. Do you know anything?"

"No. But you got no call? Zara made that up?"

"I haven't talked to her all morning. I don't know why she said that to you." Drake sighed. "Frankly, she's been misbehaving since the power outage and Lena's hysteria."

"I see. Sorry to hear that. I have to run. Bye." Delta disconnected. Zara had lied about a neighbor having seen something was up at the villa. Had she come back to it and seen the police leave? Had she wondered what was up and devised a story to find out?

But why? And how much had she known about the jade statue being buried there near the rose bushes?

Delta put her phone away and returned to the others deep in thought. This was getting odder and odder.

———————————

After lunch, Hazel said she could run the store alone for the afternoon, and Delta really had to take Gran to the gold-mining museum. "It's one of Tundish's highlights, and you have to see it right away. Buy a few souvenirs." Hazel grinned at Delta. "No objections. You need some time off. You've been far too busy."

At the gold-mining museum, with its authentic front and old mining cart advertising the opening hours and prices, Gran pinched Delta's arm. "It's been too long since we did anything this fun together."

Delta felt a bit of guilt that she hadn't visited Gran

more often or asked her to come here sooner. But she had been busy settling in and had thought Thanksgiving or Christmas would be perfect for family time.

"Zach called me last week." Gran glanced at Delta. "He wanted to know how you were doing."

Delta froze. Her strained relationship with one of her brothers was a sore point. Because she was a lot younger than Zach and her other brother, Greg, she had never been very close with either of them. But the general family dynamics had been supportive, especially of Greg's athletic career and ambitions to compete in the Olympics. Delta had never known anything but her parents catering to Greg's needs. Zach had started to feel neglected, and with his decision to marry on the day Greg had to compete in a very important contest, forced their parents to choose between attending the contest or Zach's wedding. This had caused a lot of stress and had even driven a wedge between their parents, with Dad choosing to support Greg at the contest and Mom attending the wedding. When Zach had told Delta after the wedding that he was still angry because Dad should have come, Delta had snapped and broken off contact with him. He didn't even know she had changed her life.

Gran said, "I told him you were fine. I haven't told him about the move and all. I think you should do that yourself."

Delta sighed. "I do want to get back in touch with Zach, but…I can't forget how he tried to manipulate Mom and Dad over his wedding day. I know he struggled with them always being there for Greg and not putting as much time into him, but to play them against each other like that—"

"He's sorry about that."

"Did he say so?"

"No, but he must be. Delta, you're not a prosecutor

after Zach. Or his defense attorney. Leave what he did to him. Be his sister."

"But I'm also Greg's sister and Mom and Dad's daughter. I can't separate all that." Delta pressed Gran's arm. "I will think about it. Maybe I'll send Zach a card for Christmas with my new address. But let's not discuss it now. Let's have a good time, okay?"

"Fine with me."

Inside, they found Mrs. Cassidy at the reception desk. It was decorated with a painting of a gold-mining camp, people milling about with equipment, and a lucky man in the middle holding up his find. Mrs. Cassidy, in nineteenth-century dress, grinned at Delta. "Good afternoon. Welcome to the museum."

Delta said, "We'd like to have a look around. Hazel gave me the afternoon off. This is my gran. Gran, this is Mrs. Cassidy."

"Oh, the outlaw enthusiast." Gran smiled and extended her hand. "Have you already found one in the family tree?"

"Not yet, but I keep looking."

The women shook hands.

Mrs. Cassidy asked if they'd like something to drink, but Delta told her they had just had lunch and were going to look around a bit first. They went into the room where a presentation breathed life into Tundish during the gold rush, with old photos and claims from the day. Then they moved on to the actual objects: scales, sieves, and mattocks stacked along the walls. A dummy was dressed up like a miner, and old guns told the story of violent robberies and double-crossing. Friends who had shared claims had turned on one another when the gold fever grabbed them.

"Excuse me." Mrs. Cassidy moved in and put a hand on

Delta's shoulder. "I'll tell her a bit about the actual mine. Now you go to the front. Jonas is there. He said it was urgent."

Delta nodded and left Gran in the capable hands of the museum's most tireless volunteer. At the reception desk, she found Jonas with Spud. "Hey, boy." She leaned down to rub his head. "Where have you been? You missed all the excitement when we dug up the statue."

"I dropped him off with a friend this morning who has an anxious dog. She doesn't dare go into certain places, and when Spud is present, she gets more confidence. A small thing to help out." Jonas smiled down on his German shepherd. Then his expression sobered. "Guess what the sheriff found out about our handyman friend?"

"I have no idea. Is he Sally Drake's killer?" Maybe they could have established that from finding blood on his clothes?

"Could be, but we don't know that yet. No, it's a real shocker. He's related to Lena Laroy. He's her brother."

"Her brother?" Delta echoed. "Does that mean he was at the party with her permission? But why as a caterer? Why not as a guest?"

"I don't know. It does give the impression that the two of them were up to something. Maybe Lena found out about the statue being in Sally's possession, and her brother came in disguise to take advantage of the opportunity. He had access to the house and the grounds during the party, and with so many people milling about, he was barely noticed."

"On the other hand, the presence of that many guests would make it tricky for him to start digging for a missing statue. Or didn't they know at that time that it was buried?" Delta stared at the floor, deep in thought. "The argument I overheard did allude to giving something, handing something over."

"See." Jonas nodded. "Now the trouble is that he won't talk, and she's nowhere to be found. Maybe she fled out of state, even."

"Because she knew her brother was about to get caught?" Delta mused. "We assumed she was an innocent victim of the circumstances, who might even have been killed by that handyman, and now it appears they could have been in league with each other."

"We don't know for sure, of course, but she doesn't seem to be as innocent as we first assumed. We need to find Lena and put pressure on her to tell her side of the story. That brother of hers is tough and won't crack under pressure. But she has a name and reputation to protect. Do you have any idea where she might be?"

"No. Sorry."

Jonas nodded. "Oh well, you can't know everything." He turned away from her, then said, "I'm glad nothing happened this morning. When I took you to the villa, I had no idea we'd run into any kind of danger. It's a risk I should have anticipated. I can understand if you're mad at me."

"Of course I'm not mad."

"You shouldn't have been there. Me, the deputy, okay, it's our job, but you're just a shopkeeper from town. If something had happened to you—"

"But nothing did. And you are here now to ask me where Lena is. So, we're still on the case, right?"

Jonas turned to her. He shook his head slowly. "I don't know, Delta. This could be getting out of hand. Where is Lena? What does her brother know? What were they up to?

How does Sally's murder fit in? We should be very careful from now on. Maybe…leave this to the police?"

"What about your promise to Drake?"

"He wanted to protect his wife. But now it turns out she was the one plotting something. There's much more at stake than we knew when we started." He took a deep breath. "Do you have any idea what that statue we dug up is worth?"

"Fifty thousand?"

"More like two hundred thousand."

Delta's eyes widened. "Really? It looked like a normal statue, you know, made of jade, maybe, but—"

"It's a matter of age, provenance, heritage. This thing seems to have been in the hands of a powerful ruler and was also made by a master craftsman, who left only a few art objects after his death. Sally knew exactly what to take from that depot. It was the most valuable piece they had." Jonas thought a moment, then said, "Take care, Delta. Don't go after leads by yourself, and tell Hazel and those crafting friends of yours the same thing. I don't want any of you to get hurt."

He walked away with Spud by his side. The dog looked up at him as if he sensed his tense mood and wanted to cheer him up.

Delta's heart sank. It had all turned complicated, but they couldn't leave it be at this crucial stage. Where was Lena? What was Zara up to with her interest in the precious statue? Her story about a neighbor having seen events at the villa this morning had clearly been a lie.

How much had Drake known or suspected? Would Sally not have confided in him when she came to him?

But she had tried to get a place in his firm, which suggested she was low on cash. So, had she actually stolen the statue for someone else? Her husband, Abe Jarvis?

Lena's brother?

But how could Sally have ever gotten in touch with Lena's brother?

Delta rubbed her temples. She would write down all her new information. Perhaps if she connected a few dots, a clearer picture would emerge.

"I'm so sorry," Delta said to Gran, "that I didn't have as much attention for you today as I should have."

They were standing on the platform at the back of the Lodge Hotel, overlooking the lake with the lights of the houses and boathouses along it and the snowcapped mountains against the velvet sky. The moon was strong tonight, and the evening air seemed alive with the sounds of nature.

As often when she regarded the beauty around her new hometown, Delta was filled with gratitude that she had been able to make the move from Cheyenne to here and do what she loved most: draw and develop stationery. Gran had made that possible for her, and Gran was with her now. Still, she had left her several times today to go after the murder case.

"Don't worry about it, Delta." Gran placed a hand on her arm. "I know you have a lot to take care of here. And that young man, Jonas, is very nice, I heard from Mrs. Cassidy."

Delta groaned inwardly at the idea of the well-meaning Paper Posse women trying to pair her off with Jonas. "We're just friends."

Gran nodded. "Of course. You need friends now that you're building your life here. It's such a nice, quiet little town, with so much history. Those murders bother me, though."

"They have nothing to do with me. I merely try to help out with what I know." Delta pulled up her shoulders. "It's a sort of intellectual challenge. I enjoy it."

"You used to be good at puzzles." Gran smiled at her. "You always wanted to try ones for an older age group. And you could even finish them, because you were so determined."

Delta wrapped her arm around her grandmother. "I can't believe you're actually here. I hope you don't mind I didn't put you up at the cottage. But we have no spare room and…" Maybe she should have given Gran her own bed and slept on the couch?

"This hotel is fine. Ray Taylor is taking good care of me." Gran winked. "I feel rather flattered, at my age."

Delta grinned. "Ray can turn on the charm whenever he wants to." She thought a moment and added, "I think he really likes Hazel. But she doesn't want to give him a chance, because he's been such a ladies' man in the past."

"People can change." Gran looked pensive. "But more often than not, they stay basically the same. It takes a strong woman to deal with a man who has been in the public eye and will get attention wherever he goes. If Hazel can avoid it…"

Delta studied her expression. "Do you think it would be better for her if they don't get together? You're probably right. I have a soft spot for Ray. I know he's more serious than people think. And he did have a hard time coming back here and sensing how hostile part of his own family was. He did patch things up with Rosalyn, a bit, but… I guess it's not easy to run a hotel with so many different opinions. Rosalyn wants to change the look of the main rooms, with help of Calvin Drake, and…let's say not everyone sees the need."

"This Calvin Drake seems to be quite a force around town. I heard he also made changes to the community center?"

"No, that was done by those two ladies, Lydia and Clara. You can see it when we go rehearse for our part in the town festival again. Some consider it true design, others an eyesore."

Gran took a deep breath. "Delta—"

Delta's phone beeped.

"One moment, Gran." Delta pulled up her phone and checked the screen. An unknown number. She hesitated a moment, not sure she wanted to answer. But Gran gestured at her. "Go on, answer it."

"Hello?"

"Delta Douglas?"

"Yes? Who's this?"

"Lena Laroy."

Delta almost dropped the phone. "Lena? Everyone is looking for you. We thought you…might have been hurt."

"I need to talk to Jonas Nord. Can you bring him to a meeting place if I tell you where?"

"Why don't you ask Jonas yourself?"

"I don't have his phone number. I got your number off the card you gave me for the card-making workshop. Please help me."

The woman's tone was anxious, and Delta bit her lip. "Where do you want to meet?"

"There's this steakhouse along the road to Boulder. It's called The Bull Horn. I'll be at a booth in the back. Don't take forever. I don't feel safe here. Bye."

Delta lowered the phone and stared at it. "This is really odd. Lena Laroy wants to meet Jonas at some steakhouse.

I have no idea what she wants him for or… I should have given her his phone number instead of playing messenger for her." She exhaled. "Well, nothing to be done about that now. I'd better call Jonas."

"You can go with him to this steakhouse. I'm going up to my room anyway. It's been a long day." Gran smiled at her.

"I'll walk you to the elevator." Delta called Jonas as they went along. He answered at the third ring. "Yes, Delta? Is something up?" He sounded a bit on edge, and Delta recalled his instructions not to go after leads alone. Lena's brother was a hardcore criminal who had waved a gun at them. Was Lena any better?

"Lena Laroy called me. She wants to meet us at a steakhouse. She gave me instructions to get there. Can you come pick me up? I'm at the Lodge."

"I can go by myself. Tell me where it is."

"No. I'm coming. I have no idea what she wants. She played the helpless card before, and I fell for it, even taking her into my cottage. But she went through my sketchbook, maybe not out of curiosity, but on purpose. Because she's been up to something with that brother of hers all along."

"I don't think—" Jonas sighed.

"Come and pick me up. Bye." Delta disconnected.

Gran looked up at her. "Be careful, darling."

The concern in her eyes tore at Delta's heart. "It's a public place," she assured her. "Nothing will happen to us there. I wouldn't have agreed if it was somewhere in the forest or…you know." She leaned over and pecked Gran on the cheek. "Good night."

"Call me after this meeting so I know you're okay."

"I will. But Jonas won't let anything happen to me."

"And you won't let anything happen to Jonas." Gran

gave her a knowing smile. "Have a good evening, darling." She stepped into the elevator, the doors closed, and Delta was left alone. Jonas didn't really need her to take care of him, right? He was strong, able, and he had his police force experience. Still, it was nice not to have to do things alone.

With a smile, Delta walked out of the hotel to wait for Jonas. His Jeep breezed into the parking lot soon enough. He jumped out and rounded the vehicle to her side. She thought he wanted to open the car door for her, but Jonas said, "I'm not taking you, Delta. Tell me where it is, and I'll go handle it."

"No way. Lena called me, not you. Besides, we have no idea what she's really up to. Why did she vanish? Is she afraid of Zara or someone else? Or did she know her brother was around with his gun and she didn't want to be at home when he struck? She probably figured he'd get away with the jade statue, and his real identity, his relationship to her, wouldn't get out."

Jonas shook his head. "That doesn't matter now. Let me handle it. I know what I'm doing."

"I'm sure, but I want in on it. Please?"

Jonas held her gaze. "Why? Because it makes a good story for your crafting friends?"

Delta felt a little hurt, but saying she wanted to make sure he was all right wouldn't make it better. He'd never accept that. "I won't tell you the directions to the meeting place, so let me into the Jeep, huh?"

"Okay." Jonas opened the door with a sigh. "You're really something."

Chapter Seventeen

DELTA SETTLED INTO THE SEAT AND BUCKLED UP.

Jonas got in and started the engine. "Where to then?"

Delta told him as they went. The radio was playing a country song, and she would have enjoyed this if the atmosphere hadn't been so charged.

"You do realize this is only going to get us in trouble," Jonas said. "You should have told Lena to go to the police."

"Sure. But she wouldn't have listened, and we would have known nothing. Are you not a little bit curious how much she knew about her brother's activities? And how he got to know about the statue buried in the garden, the one Sally Drake probably stole from her employer?"

Jonas shook his head. "If Lena suspects her brother killed Sally, she won't tell us the full truth. She's had time to think up some story, and she wants to sell it to us and then have us help her sell it to West. I'm not game for something like that. I want West to solve this case and avoid getting charged by Drake because Sally was killed near the house while West was present on the scene. If we somehow contribute to West being led astray, we're helping the criminals in this case. Maybe we'll even let a killer get away."

"We can listen to her story. We need not take her side. Maybe it can give us a clue as to who the killer is. She might know something vital."

Jonas sighed. He let the wheel roll smoothly through his hands. Delta realized how safe she felt by his side. She only wished he also valued her input. Jonas was a loner who liked to do everything by himself. Someone you couldn't really get close to.

"There it is." She pointed ahead to where giant, fake bull horns sat on top of a square, one-story building. The parking lot was full of SUVs and pickups, and Jonas squeezed the Jeep into a narrow space. As they got out, they could already smell roasting meat. And stale beer.

Jonas grimaced. "Classy spot for a meeting."

"It was Lena's choice. Probably because it's such an unlikely place for her to go to. You lead the way, I'll follow."

Inside, a roar of voices washed over them. To their left, men were playing darts and pool. Balls clanked against each other, and the maker of the good shot waved his cue in the air, almost stabbing another man in the eye. Beer glasses were everywhere. Waitresses wearing cowboy hats moved quickly through the crowd.

To the right were booths along the wall with diners. Mainly men, probably truck drivers or bikers. Delta felt like all eyes were on her when she walked through the steakhouse searching for Lena. The former model had to have drawn attention coming in here.

"There." Jonas nodded to the last booth.

Delta didn't see what he meant. In the booth, a figure sat slumped over a beer, with a woolen knit hat pulled down over their hair and a tattered blanket around their shoulders. There was an empty beer glass on the table and a plate with the remains of a steak dinner.

Jonas walked over and sat down opposite the figure. When Delta slipped into the booth beside him, the figure looked up. Lena Laroy's startling blue eyes peered at her. Delta gasped. "With that disguise I would never have guessed it was you."

"Good job making this all even more dramatic than it already is." Jonas leaned back and folded his hands on the table's edge. "But I want some answers and fast. You knew your brother was in town. You knew he was at the party, trying to get his hands on something. You should have reported that to the police. Anonymous or otherwise, if you were worried about him finding out it had been you giving information to the cops. But you let it pass. You did nothing to alert anyone, and you let him walk about freely. With a gun. This morning, he could have shot the deputy. Or Delta."

He didn't mention himself.

Lena said, "He wouldn't have shot anyone. He's not really violent." She wrung her hands. "At least, I hope not. Look, he ruined my life before. I didn't want it to happen again."

Jonas looked cynical. "I'm not here for a sob story. I advise you to call the police and tell West what you know. Maybe it can save your skin. Maybe not. But I don't care either way." He moved like he wanted to get up.

"Jonas." Lena reached out quickly and put her hand over his. "Please hear me out. Calvin hired you to protect me. He knew I was under strain. He didn't know where the danger was coming from, but—"

"You should have told him." Jonas sounded tight, but he didn't pull his hand away. Was he seeing how far she'd go to play him? Or did the beautiful model really have some influence over him? Delta's heartbeat skittered.

Lena said, "I knew my brother was back in my life, because he had had some groceries delivered. Things he knew I liked from the days we were in college together. We shared rooms then. I was trying to get my degree, but my brother was coasting. Going to parties, off on vacations. He always knew how to fall in with the right crowd."

"The wrong crowd, you mean," Jonas corrected.

"No, the right crowd. Rich people who could offer him free stuff. He made friends with the boys, became entangled with the girls. He was always at some resort enjoying free drinks and meals and… He was smart, but he was also greedy. He stole a diamond necklace from a girlfriend's mother, and although no one ever proved it was him, it damaged his reputation, and he wasn't asked on trips as much as he used to be. I told him it was his own fault, but it only made him angry and more determined to make everyone pay. My modeling career took off, and I started a relationship with a country star. My brother, whom I hadn't talked to in years, suddenly appeared and wanted me to give him money. I did, a few times, and then it became other demands. Stuff from the villa where I lived with my fiancé."

She stared ahead, her eyes shiny with tears. "I got caught. I didn't want to turn my brother in, so my fiancé believed I was stealing for myself. He loved me enough not to report me, but he did break up with me."

"The breakup no one understood," Delta said. Lena nodded.

Lena nodded. "I was so depressed after that. I told my brother I never wanted to hear of him again or I would turn him in. He seemed to have listened."

"Until he came back into your life, here in Tundish," Jonas supplied.

"Right. This time he wanted parts of Calvin's art collection. I told him Calvin would notice right away, and I'd be in deep trouble. He said that I had to lie that I had seen someone else take it. The dog walker or a housekeeper or someone who did chores for us. Anyone I could think of. He told me I was clever enough to shift the blame." Lena chewed her lower lip. "I didn't know what to do. At the party, he put pressure on me again."

"So, you told him about Sally, the art expert who had left LA in a rush, and he went after her," Jonas said quietly.

Lena perked up. "Sally? No, I... What about Sally? She didn't have anything. She had lost her job and was about to get a divorce that would leave her with practically nothing. She whined about that every day. What could my brother get off her?"

"The jade statue she stole from the museum before she left LA. Come on, admit you knew about that."

"What statue?" Lena's eyes were wide. "Sally didn't tell me anything. She was close to Calvin, not me."

"She would have told Calvin about it?" Delta pressed.

"I don't know. She valued his opinion, and she wanted into the company, so I doubt she would have told him she'd stolen something." Lena grimaced. "She wanted him to like her and trust her, and that wouldn't have helped, right?"

Jonas glanced at Delta. She wasn't sure whether she believed the woman.

Lena said, "I don't see why he would have wanted anything to do with Sally. Her murder must be unrelated. I mean, it was her husband who came after her."

"Yes, her husband. Did you know Jarvis? Did you see him at the party? Did you know he was going to meet her?"

"No, I had no idea he was even in town."

"And Una Edel?" Delta asked. "Were you two really together at the time of the murder?"

"Yes. Una was inside the villa with me, discussing some things she had noticed at the party that weren't up to par, you know, a caterer slacking off, that sort of thing. She's a master of organization."

"And when you talked to her, she didn't have the key chain in her hand?"

"No. I didn't see it at all that afternoon. One of us either has it or it's in a porcelain pot on the sideboard, so whoever needs it can get it."

"Who could have fetched it from there?"

"Calvin, Una, Zara, Randall. Everyone who lived at the villa, really. If I were you, I'd look at Zara. There's something off about that girl. I have no idea why Calvin is so protective of her. Other than he's having an affair with her. After all, he betrayed his first wife with the babysitter. What can I expect?"

"If you didn't trust him, why did you marry him?"

"I did trust him before."

"But then you also knew he had betrayed his first wife with the babysitter."

Lena blinked. "I'm sorry, but my private life is really none of your business. I want to make it very clear that my brother ruined my life before and I won't have him do it again."

"Then go to the police and tell them what you've told us so West has something to charge him with." Jonas grabbed her hand. "You could be in danger as long as your brother has a chance to walk away free. He's a dangerous man, and he won't spare you just because you're his sister."

Lena stared into his eyes. "Oh, Jonas..." She burst into tears. "I can't go on like this anymore. My husband doesn't love me, he's betraying me with the dog walker, and...I feel so terrible."

Delta couldn't believe she was making a scene like this,

with another woman present. What did she expect? That Jonas would lean over and wrap her in his arms? Across the table?

"Come, come, it can't be all that bad." Jonas patted her hand. "Maybe you misunderstood what's happening between him and the dog walker. You also owe him an explanation about your fears when those groceries were delivered. He has no idea your brother sent them as a reminder he was near. The perfume bottle with 'death' on it came from him as well, you think?"

"Probably."

"But footage shows Sally putting it on the table," Delta pointed out. "Does that mean Sally did know your brother and was in league with him?"

"*Sally* put it on the table?" Lena stared at her through wet lashes. "Are you sure?"

"Yes. The parcel holding the perfume bottle was put on the gift table by Sally. Images don't lie."

"That little snake." Lena hissed through gritted teeth. "She must have been working with my brother. I have no idea how they met or why she'd help him, but—"

"No idea at all?" Delta said. "You must have sensed the tension between her and you. She wore a similar dress to your own party. That's rude to say the least. Taking attention away from you as hostess."

"When she came down in it, I asked her to choose something else, but she snapped back that I had to change, if it mattered that much to me. I had bought my dress especially for the occasion, so I wasn't going to change it for her." Lena's voice carried a venomous edge. "Sally always wanted what I had. Calvin's affection—" She swallowed hard. "If my brother contacted her to somehow harm me, Sally might have agreed to help him. And then he killed her because she knew too much." She sobbed in her hands.

Jonas looked at Delta. His frown told her he wasn't sure what to believe. But Delta had the impression Lena was genuinely shocked by the idea that Sally had put the threatening bottle on the gift table. Maybe she had never given her quiet sister-in-law much credit? But from what they knew now, Sally had stolen a valuable statue from the museum's depot and had threatened her sister-in-law during her birthday party. Not exactly what you would have expected, based on people's opinions of her.

Jonas pressed, "You do have to go to the police. You know things about the household that can be really helpful. I'll go with you if you like."

Delta inwardly shook her head. West didn't like Jonas and might not even want to talk to Lena, but on the other hand, he would see the importance of Lena Laroy's testimony for the case and might even appreciate that Jonas had brought her in.

Lena took a deep breath. "Look at me now. I'm sitting here in this miserable joint, with my dog walker lounging on the sofa at my home, and my brother possibly having…" She sniffed. "If that gets into the papers, I can forget about ever having a life again."

Jonas gestured at her. "Shall we go?" A waitress who halted at the table to take their order scowled when he told her they were leaving. He asked, "How much was the lady's tab?"

"Ten for the steak, five for the two beers," the waitress said.

"Here's twenty, keep the rest. The lady isn't feeling well, and we're taking her home." Jonas got up and put an arm around Lena, who hung against him like a wilting lily. The waitress hitched a brow but pocketed the twenty without comment and disappeared to serve other guests.

Outside, Jonas asked, "How did you get here?"

Lena whispered, "With my own car. It's in the back of the lot."

"We'll go to the police in that one, I'll drive." Jonas pulled out his car keys and threw them to Delta, who caught them with one hand. "You take my Jeep. Follow us."

―――――――――――――

"What time did you come home last night?" Hazel asked the next morning while she poured coffee.

"I don't know." Delta yawned. She had sat at the police station for a while, waiting while Jonas and Lena were in with the sheriff. Jonas had come out for a few minutes to tell her the sheriff was putting Lena up at a safe place for the time being, and he was also required to make a statement about their meeting at the steakhouse. "You'd better leave before he wants your statement too. Call a cab or something."

Delta had taken his advice and been glad to roll into bed. She rubbed her gritty eyes. "I hope this will be a quiet day. I just want to sell washi tape and eat Jane's cake for a bit." As she said it, her phone beeped, indicating new messages.

"Hmm, I doubt it will be quiet," Hazel commented amid continuing beeping.

With a groan, Delta fished for the phone. Several Paper Posse members alerted her to a new article on Marc LeDuc's website, saying "Security expert pointed out risk before murder." She scanned it quickly. The man who had put up security cameras at Drake's villa had told LeDuc that he had advised Drake to have a camera film the edge of the forest where Sally Drake had been murdered, but Drake had not seen the use for it. LeDuc emphasized that said forest led down to the boathouse where, back in the fifties, Athena Barrows had been murdered, which made it all the more poignant that Drake hadn't listened to the well-intentioned advice.

Hazel shook her head when Delta told her. "I bet that security expert is only eager to avoid people whispering that his system wasn't good enough to prevent the murder on Drake's premises, and him losing business. I mean, why else would he even talk to the press? So unprofessional when you work for high-class people who value privacy."

"Right." Delta yawned again and reached for the coffee Hazel put in front of her. "I feel like not even the strongest coffee can fully wake me up today. I wish I could get back into bed for an hour."

"Why don't you? I can drive out to the shop by myself and open up. I used to do it on my own when you weren't here yet."

"I know but—"

"Come on. Do it." Hazel pulled the coffee away from her. "A bit more sleep, and then you will feel brand-new."

Delta did admit that the idea of her soft bed was tempting and dragged herself out of the kitchen and up the stairs. As her head hit the pillow, she vaguely thought that something about Marc's observations could be relevant, but she had no idea what or why. Her eyes slipped closed, and she drifted off.

When Delta woke up, there was bright light seeping through the curtains, and she pushed herself into a sitting position and checked her alarm clock. Eleven? Then she recalled Hazel had sent her back to bed and gave a relieved sigh. She felt a lot better and showered and dressed at leisure. Coming downstairs, she thought she heard a sound in the kitchen. Had Hazel come back to see how she was?

A bit on edge, Delta sneaked to the kitchen door and peeked in. Gran was standing at the sink, putting lovely flowers into a big vase. Delta opened the door. "Good morning. What are those?"

Gran swung around. "Good morning. I hope you feel better. These are for you. I admired the fresh flowers on the breakfast table at the Lodge Hotel, and Ray kindly told me where they get them. He took me over there, and I bought these for you, and then he dropped me off here."

Delta grinned. "Ray is going out of his way to be nice."

Gran eyed her with a serious expression. "He might have felt obliged to help an old lady who was a bit… emotional."

"Emotional?" Delta narrowed her eyes. Suddenly, all her senses were on full alert. "Why? Is something wrong? Do you miss your own home? I know how much you hate to go away." She went over and hugged her grandmother. "I'm sorry. It's selfish of me to want to have you here."

"I'm forced to leave my house, Delta." Gran stared up at her. "I got a notice that they are going to change the neighborhood. They are buying people's houses for a new road. It's all been decided. No way to protest against it. I have to move."

"No." Delta couldn't believe her ears. "You've lived there for all your life. Dad was born there. You love that house."

"I looked into every possible way to stop it, but…the lawyers tell me I don't stand a chance. Other house owners have already accepted all the money they can get, and the road is important for the area. I have to go as well." Tears shimmered in her eyes. "I came here to tell you personally. I wanted to do it last night, but…that phone call interrupted and—"

"I'm so sorry. I feel like I haven't been there for you."

"You're more there for me than anybody else. I came to you because I know you'll understand what the house means to me. You grew up there."

Tears pricked behind her eyes at the memories of all her holidays spent there. Delta hugged her gran tightly. "I can't believe it. What will you have to do? Where can you live?"

"I do have money in the bank. And they will pay a fair price for the house. So, I can actually choose what to do. Which state, what kind of house. A fresh start full of opportunities. Your father told me to take a cruise first and delay my decision. I don't feel like cruising right now."

"I understand." Delta stepped back and held her gran by the shoulders gently. "I'll help you work through this. You can stay here for as long as you like, and then…we'll see. I can also help you pack up your things when the time comes. It will be less sad doing it together. We'll remember all the good times we had in that beautiful house."

"I knew I could count on you." Gran smiled through her tears. "I do feel guilty about taking you away from your life here and… You are your own person now."

"But I'd love to do it. You can always tell me anything. I'm there for you." Delta kissed her. "And thanks for the lovely flowers."

"You really have to thank Ray for those. He insisted on getting them for me. He paid for them as well." Gran winked at her. "Are you sure it's Hazel he's interested in and not you?"

"Quite sure." Delta thought a moment. How complicated would everything get if, besides Jonas, she also had to think about Ray. "I'll thank him, though. They are gorgeous."

Together, they finished putting the flowers in the vase and giving the bouquet a good place in the living room. After a quick cup of coffee and some chocolate chip cookies, Delta drove Gran back to the Lodge Hotel. She wanted to thank Ray personally for the flowers and his care of her grandmother.

Ray was at the boathouse, she heard, and she ran down the path to meet up with him before he could take a boat out and escape her. He was just putting in some fishing gear, and Delta waved at him. "Hold on a sec!"

"Good morning. I was about to cast off. Want to join me?"

"No, thanks, I'm already skipping school, so to speak. Hazel is at the shop, and I'm having a leisurely morning off."

Ray gave her a quick look, and she nodded. "I met Gran. Thanks for the flowers."

"Oh, that's okay. I can't stand to see old ladies crying."

"She was crying?" Delta's gut clenched.

"Yes, uh, I guess she felt a bit lonely, away from home and all." He shrugged. "I came across her in the garden, and…I had to do something to cheer her up."

"You're a good guy, you know that?"

Ray huffed. "Can you tell Rosalyn? She's mad with me, again. I don't think we need an expensive remake of the hotel."

"Calvin Drake's design?"

"Exactly. She seems to be a bit under his influence. I don't want the same fate to befall the Lodge as did the community center. Controversy, haters versus fans. You know what I mean?"

"Yup. Say, is Rosalyn in?"

Ray looked surprised. "You're actually going to put in a good word for me?"

"Maybe." Delta winked at him. "Have a nice boating trip."

Chapter Eighteen

SHE TRACKED BACK TO THE LODGE, CROSSED THE LOBBY, and knocked at the door to Rosalyn's office.

"Come in."

She opened the door and peeked in. The Lodge's manager was behind her desk, dressed in one of her crisp pantsuits, leafing through paperwork with one hand while scrolling on her phone with the other.

"I see you're busy," Delta said quickly. "I wanted to ask you one thing. You were with Drake, right, on the afternoon of his wife's birthday party?"

"Yes."

"What time did he leave here?"

"Around five thirty?"

Delta frowned. "It's not far to the villa. That means he could have been back there before the murder happened."

"I don't think so. He told me he wanted to pick up a present for her. He must have done that before he went to the villa."

"Oh, I see. What kind of present?"

"I think it was a diamond necklace or bracelet or some such thing." Rosalyn made a careless gesture. "He had ordered it from a jewelry store but didn't have it delivered at the villa so she wouldn't know about it in advance. I think he had to pick it up at the post office." She pursed her lips. "So thoughtful of him to ensure it stayed a surprise."

"I don't think he gave it to her." Delta frowned. "I mean, a present like that would have made an impression. Why would Lena doubt that he still loves her if he got her a present like that?"

"Does she doubt he loves her?" Rosalyn's lips curled in a vague smile, as if it amused her.

"Yes, because of the dog walker," Delta couldn't resist saying.

Rosalyn seemed to shrink. "That young girl? Is he having an affair with her?"

"That's what Lena thinks," Delta said truthfully.

Rosalyn snorted, but she did look undone. *Good*, Delta thought. Her admiration for Calvin Drake could better die a quick death. The designer seemed to be surrounded by too many issues. After Rosalyn's previous relationship had ended in heartbreak, Delta wanted something better for her than a flighty married man who was probably only flirting with women to indulge in a sense of superiority.

"Anything else you want?" Rosalyn asked. "Because I'm busy."

"I'll leave you to it," Delta rushed to say and left the room. She messaged the Paper Posse. "On the afternoon of Lena Laroy's birthday party, Calvin Drake went to the post office to pick up a parcel for his wife. Probably a piece of jewelry. Does anyone know what time he left the post office with it to go to the villa?"

Delta was familiar with the rush at the post office just before it closed at six, so she could imagine that Calvin Drake had been there for a bit before he could drive to the villa. Which meant he had indeed reached it after his sister was already dead.

The replies came dinging in. Rattlesnake Rita said he had been there around three thirty. Wild Bunch Bessie confirmed she had seen him in the street before a quarter to four when she had let a customer out of the boutique who had to make it to a hairdresser's appointment at ten to four.

Delta frowned. She wanted to message that it couldn't have been then, because Drake had told Rosalyn he was going to pick up the present when he left the Lodge at five thirty. But Mrs. Cassidy had already sent a message saying, "I'll check with the post office clerks. I know them well."

The next few minutes seemed to last forever. Delta was certain that the clerks would tell Mrs. Cassidy that Drake had been in between five forty and six o'clock, which would give him an alibi for the murder.

But what if they didn't?

Her mind was racing. Sally had wanted into her brother's design company. But even if her brother loved her and wanted to help her after her job loss and with the upcoming divorce, which put her in financial trouble, he couldn't employ someone in a leading position who knew next to nothing about his business. Still, he had wanted to do just that. Even upsetting his second-in-command, Una Edel.

Why?

Could it possibly be because Sally had made him an offer he couldn't refuse? The jade statue she had stolen from the museum?

Calvin Drake loved fine art. Maybe he had longed to own something special?

Delta shook her head. She was merely speculating.

Her phone dinged. Mrs. Cassidy wrote, "The clerk remembered quite well. The parcel came from a NYC jewelry store and was insured because of the value of the necklace included in it. It was picked up at three forty."

Delta asked, "Are you sure it was three forty and not five forty? This could be significant."

Mrs. Cassidy confirmed, "Quite sure."

Delta clutched the phone. So, Drake had lied to Rosalyn. He had lied to the police. He had come to the villa earlier and…he had killed his sister? But why?

Had Sally not wanted to go through with the delivery of the statue to Drake? Had she hidden it because she contemplated giving it back to the museum? That afternoon she had looked troubled, not at all in a festive mood. Had she told Drake away from the party that she wanted to admit to her guilt and return it? Had he blamed her for that?

Delta thanked the Paper Posse for their help and stood deep in thought. Drake was a clever man. He hadn't fallen under suspicion from the police yet, mainly because he had been quite active in subverting suspicion. The threats against his wife, Sally's husband being in town, the mystery surrounding Zara—it had all worked to his advantage. Nobody had seen him as a serious candidate for the murderer. But why not?

It had happened on his terrain, which he knew well. And hadn't Marc LeDuc talked to a security expert who said he had advised Drake to put a camera near the murder scene and Drake hadn't wanted that? So, he had known he wouldn't be filmed there. It all fit.

Delta took a deep breath. It was never pleasant to suspect another human being of murder, but it was extra terrible when the killer was a close relative of the victim. Drake had claimed to love and protect his little sister. Had that been an act?

Or had he believed he was protecting her by taking the stolen goods off her hands?

Maybe Sally had stolen the statue on impulse, angry about her colleague's wrong accusations and her dismissal.

And had she then despaired and called to tell her brother? Maybe Drake had told her not to confess but leave LA, hoping the theft from the depot wouldn't come to light for months, maybe years. It could have started as a genuine attempt to help Sally, not get her into trouble, let alone kill her.

Delta rubbed her forehead. If Jonas and she took this to West, he would never do anything with it. He liked to protect the people with clout in town, and Drake hadn't drawn any attention so far. Could they somehow incriminate him? Lead West to him?

Or even better, get a confession?

Delta tapped her fist in her other hand. It could be done, maybe.

If played right.

But they'd need help from a third party. Who might not be too eager to participate?

For various reasons.

Still, she wanted to try.

———————————

"Hello." Delta stepped from the brush onto the path right in front of Zara, who was walking the poodles. One of them jumped up against Delta, knocking her back.

"You startled us," Zara spat. She looked picture-perfect in a yellow coat on brown pants and boots.

"Sorry," Delta said, "but we wanted to talk to you."

"We?" Zara looked past her at Jonas, who was standing quietly with Spud by his side.

"Oh." Her expression changed, and she smiled coyly. "Hello there."

Jonas nodded. "Hello. How are you? I had expected

you might want to leave, after the power outage and the trouble at the villa."

"Trouble?"

"Didn't you hear what happened? How we were almost shot by a madman in the garden?" Delta widened her eyes. "He was after the statue."

"What statue?" Zara looked from Delta to Jonas and back.

"Close to where Sally's body lay, a statue was found. I think the dogs wanted to dig for it. You said so when you came rushing in after having discovered the body. That they had led you to the back of the garden and wanted to dig."

"Oh. So, there was something there. I wondered if Sally was up to something. She seemed so secretive."

"In what way?"

"Hanging around Drake all of the time. Lena didn't like it. And Una even less." Zara shrugged. "But she was his sister, and he adored her."

"And how did you feel?" Jonas studied her. "After all, you are his daughter."

Zara turned pale. "How do you know that?"

"Drake told me."

"That's it? Drake told me?" She mimicked his casual tone. "He promised me he wouldn't tell a soul, and he tells you? What on earth for?"

"I work for him to secure—"

"You're no detective. Else you'd have prevented the murder."

"I couldn't have prevented the murder. Because the killer had cleverly diverted me."

"I thought policemen weren't tricked by criminals."

Jonas snorted. "More often than you'd think. Especially if that was the plan from the start."

"I don't follow."

"I was hired to keep an eye on Lena Laroy. But she was never the intended target."

"Don't let her hear you say that. She believes she is under threat. And how about that perfume bottle?"

"Yes," Delta said, "that perfume bottle. Placed on the gift table by the later murder victim. How convenient Sally could no longer tell us who had asked her to put it there."

Zara blinked. "I didn't ask her to put it there, if that's what you're thinking."

Jonas shook his head. "I'm merely saying the killer led me astray. I was watching the wrong woman, never suspecting Sally was in danger."

"And why would you have? Sally did no one any harm."

"Still, she died." Jonas stepped forward. "What do you know about the art in the house, Zara?"

"Art? Not a lot. It's valuable, and I shouldn't touch it." Zara shrugged. "I'm not the cleaning lady, so why would I want to touch it at all?"

"You're his daughter. Maybe you came to work for him to see what your inheritance might entail?"

"You have a nerve." Zara pulled the poodles to her and started to turn away. "I'm going back to the villa."

"Why did you come to work for Drake, Zara?" Jonas's voice was urgent. "He told me that it was so you could get to know him without the whole world knowing who you were. Is that true?"

"Yes." She swung back to him, her eyes flashing in defiance. "Is that so terrible? My mother told me so many stories about my wicked father, who had betrayed her with the babysitter, that I finally wanted to see for myself what he was like. It was never about money. I have enough of my own. My mother remarried, and my stepfather lets me have anything I want. I don't need Drake's money."

"Still you love to wreak a little havoc in his life." Jonas watched her through narrowed eyes. "You cut the power so Lena would panic."

"You can't prove that." Zara shrugged.

"Or maybe…" Jonas leaned back on his heels. "You made a plan with Drake when you came to the villa to terrorize Lena?"

"No. What for?" Zara blinked nervously. "I don't understand what you're driving at."

"You came out here to get to know your father." Jonas waited a moment. "How much about your father do you want to get to know?"

Zara shifted her weight. "What he's really like."

"And what did you discover so far?"

"He's pretty vain. Preoccupied with his work and his art."

"A man who gets what he wants?"

"Probably." A smile played around Zara's lips. "I inherited that trait."

Jonas wasn't smiling. "Would you say that to get what he wants, he'd kill? Literally?"

"Kill?" Zara's expression froze. "You mean, Sally? I told you she was harmless. No one would want to kill her."

"Still, she's dead. And your father may have something to do with that."

"I can't believe that."

Jonas held her gaze. "Are you willing to find out?"

"Find out what?"

"Whether he's a killer?"

"You must be crazy. How? And why would you think

he has anything to do with Sally's death? He wasn't even at the party."

"No. But we found out he came back to the villa earlier than he said. He lied about that. I wonder why. He also knew that there were no cameras filming the stretch of garden with forest where Sally died. She also buried her statue there. Now who could have told her it was unguarded? It seems your father knew about the statue."

"If he knew, he would have told the police. The statue, if it's what you say it is, could provide motive for murder."

"Yes, *his* motive for murder." Jonas leaned over to her. "Zara, I hate to do this to you, but you need to know if your father is a killer. And we need to get a confession from him, a guilty response or something, to have a case."

"So, you actually have nothing against him?" Zara sounded satisfied. "Then I'm leaving."

"Wait." Jonas caught her arm. "Don't you want to know the truth? What if he did kill Sally? His own sister. Would you want to live under the same roof with him if he did that? Would you ever feel safe again?"

Zara hesitated. "I don't understand. Why are you telling me this?"

"Because we need your help. You have to confront Drake and tell him you know about the statue and the murder. That you saw something, and you want money to keep your mouth shut about it. If he's guilty, he will make a move on you."

"You mean, try to kill me as well? Why should he? That would be crazy." Zara shivered. "I'm going home."

"Home to a father who might be a murderer. Help us prove it, Zara. Either way. If he's innocent, you'll know. We'll know."

"But you don't think that. You think he's guilty."

"He lied about coming back to the villa before the murder happened. Why was he absent anyway? On his wife's birthday party. It doesn't make sense unless you accept that he planned the murder. In advance."

"He's obsessive about art." Zara bit her lip. "My mother once told me that he wanted a painting a friend had, and he tried anything he could to get it. Offers of money, other compensation. When the friend refused, because the painting had special meaning to him, my father seemed to have accepted it. A few weeks later, during a party at the friend's house, someone threw acid at the painting, and it was ruined. My mother said she was certain my father had done it. It was never proven of course, but… She told me she was sometimes afraid of him. That even though she hated him for having betrayed her and divorced her, she was also glad to be out of the marriage with him and his obsessive side."

"There you have it." Jonas nodded. "I need not tell you anymore. Now will you help us?"

Zara inhaled slowly. "How do you want to do it? Will it be safe for me?"

"It's never completely safe. I think that in order to kill, you have to be different than normal people. Somehow deranged in your mind. Even coldblooded killers who are far from crazy are still different, in the sense that they can kill without remorse. So, you never know what a person like that might do when he realizes that he's caught out. But we can discuss how to handle it to make it as safe as possible for you. I know the place where we can do it. It's remote, and he will feel like he has the advantage."

"I don't like the sound of that at all." Zara ducked into

her collar. "Why would I even do this? Apart from wanting to know who my father really is. I never liked Sally."

"Or Lena, or anybody around here." Jonas gave her a direct, hard stare. "That's what you tell yourself. But I think you want to belong. And by helping us solve this case, you can belong. With us."

Zara eyed him. Delta wasn't sure what she was thinking. Were they even right in trusting this girl, who had proven herself to be manipulative and volatile?

But what other choice did they have? Drake wouldn't give himself away. If a stranger claimed to know something, he might work his way out of it. But if it was his own daughter confronting him, claiming to have seen him walk away, and showing off her greedy nature by asking for money to keep her mouth shut…

Delta suppressed the nerves wriggling in her stomach. She could only hope they were not making a terrible mistake.

Chapter Nineteen

THE MORNING SUNSHINE WAS PLAYING THROUGH THE trees, casting shadows on the path leading to the water. Zara stood there, shivering in her coat. She had her back turned on the water and the beautiful rainbows shooting across it while the breeze wrinkled the surface.

Jonas and Delta sat in hiding with full view of the spot where, once upon a time, the villa's boathouse had stood. The boathouse where a young woman had been stabbed— Athena Barrows. Delta wondered whether she had felt any sense of discomfort or alarm when she had come to the boathouse on that fateful day. Had she met someone there? Or had the killer been lurking, waiting for her to appear and take a boat out on her own?

They might never know. But they would know, soon enough, what was going to happen right in front of them.

She glanced at Jonas. His expression was full of focus, not easy to read. If he was worried, he didn't show it. But worrying now didn't serve a point. They were past that. They had decided to do it, and it had to work, somehow.

"Where did you leave the dogs?"

The sudden voice made Delta jerk. Drake appeared on the path. He wore a dark-blue woolen coat and strode toward his daughter.

Zara shrugged. "Does it matter? You don't like them. Neither does Lena, when push comes to shove. They're symbols of her rich wife's life."

Drake laughed softly. "Isn't it a bit early to be so cynical?" He halted in front of her.

Delta admired that Zara didn't flinch or move back, betraying that she knew something.

"This kind of meeting isn't smart." Drake stamped his feet as he stared past Zara and across the water. "Lena may not be around to notice, but people could see things. It's such a small town, full of busybodies."

"Don't worry. We only have to do this once." Zara smiled at him. "You see, I'm not coming back to the villa. I'm taking my leave. And I'd like to take a little something along...for my trouble."

"That is sudden." Drake let his gaze roam her face. "Any reason?"

"Other than the murder, the power outage, Lena on the run?" Zara made a hand gesture. "Need I go on? I've had time to get to know you. I know enough."

"Really? I don't understand this." Drake gestured around him. "Why not talk at the villa? So much more comfortable. And if you want money, I could have written you a check right away."

"Yes, but I'm not quite sure what you have in the drawer of your desk besides a checkbook." Zara smiled at him. "I feel better here in the open."

Drake shifted his weight. Delta felt Jonas tense beside her. They had no idea what the man was going to do.

Zara said, "I'd like to leave Tundish with enough money to make a few of my dreams come true. Travel the world. See faraway places. How about one hundred thousand?"

Drake laughed. "You can travel the world for as little as ten thousand if you work in the places where you're staying. Would teach you something too."

"I learned enough here. How about it?"

"Not a chance." Drake stepped away from her. "You've been acting like a spoiled brat, and I've been sorry I couldn't send you to your room like I should have done long ago. I'm not giving you that kind of money."

"Not for anything in the world? Not even my silence?"

Drake froze. "Silence? Do you intend to go to lurid news sites and sell your story? 'How I infiltrated my father's household as dog walker?'" He held up his hands as if unrolling the headline on a banner. "I don't think they will be very interested."

"How I infiltrated my father's household as a dog walker and caught him committing murder." Zara's voice was low. "It would make an excellent headline."

"Murder?" Drake frowned at her as if the word was foreign to him.

"Yes. My aunt. Sally? You killed her. I saw you do it."

"Oh, no, Zara." Drake shook his head. "I'm sure you didn't see anything of the kind."

"Because you are so careful?" She laughed. "You think no one knows, no one understands. But I know everything. About the statue she stole and the offer she made you to have her come into the company. You killed her for the statue. Which unfortunately will never be yours, because the police have it now. But to prevent the police from getting you as well, you're going to pay me one hundred grand. Come on. It's nothing to you. You have millions in the bank. I'm just asking for a little money to travel. I'm your daughter. Let me have some fun."

Drake eyed her. Delta wasn't sure he believed her or that the mention of the statue even struck any response in him. Maybe they were barking up the wrong tree, and Drake was now wondering if his daughter had completely lost her mind with this attempt to wring one hundred thousand dollars away from him.

Zara said, "You write me ten checks for ten thousand. I won't cash them all at once."

"I could simply cancel them, one by one."

"Then I will talk." Zara sounded cold. "I came here to get to know you. I've come to know you all right. You're ruthless when it comes to what you want. And you know, I am just like you."

"You're nothing like me." Drake closed in on her. "I worked hard for everything I have. You've never worked in your life. Not a single day."

"I took care of the dogs—"

"You call that work? You couldn't control them. You let them roam. You behaved like you were entitled to everything. You don't understand what work means. Or why it matters."

"Matters?" Zara laughed. "I'm a rich man's daughter. I need not work. You give everything to me."

"You sound exactly like Lena. She also wants me to give everything to her. You see, people think I'm a giving person. But I'm not. I have a credo. You can get something off me. But only in return for something else."

"Then my deal should appeal to you. I get the money in exchange for my silence, which means you don't go to jail for the rest of your life. Isn't that fair?" Zara's eyes flashed. "How much is freedom worth?"

Drake grabbed her. It happened so fast that Delta almost missed it. His hands were suddenly around her throat, and he was wringing all the air out of her.

A male voice called out from the brush, "Put your hands up in the air. You are under arrest. Put them up."

Even though Delta had known the deputy was hiding there, his sudden cry startled her, and her heartbeat stuttered. But Drake didn't seem to hear anything. He kept squeezing. Jonas jumped to his feet and ran for the man. He gave him a well-placed blow to the shoulder just where the neck began. Drake crumpled. Zara staggered back and almost fell into the water. Jonas grabbed her and steadied her. "You okay?"

The deputy closed in and knelt to cuff Drake. "You shouldn't have run into my line of fire," he groused to Jonas. "That wasn't the deal."

"He didn't hear your call to surrender. He was livid with rage. He would have killed her sooner than have put his hands in the air." Jonas took a deep breath. "But thanks for coming. You could have told me to get lost with my crazy idea."

"I should have. West will have my hide for this. Yes, I deliver him the killer, but he won't like who it is. And I still doubt we have proof enough to get him convicted."

Jonas gestured at him. "Your experts must have gotten DNA off the body. They always have something, even if it's miniscule skin particles on clothing. They can compare it to Drake's DNA now that we have him for the attack on his daughter. And the knife… There must be something on it of his as well. He might have wiped it, but you can never clean away all DNA traces. You will get him. I promise you."

The deputy nodded and leaned down over Drake. He was coming to and making spluttering sounds.

Zara rubbed her throat. She looked down on her father. "I got to know you better than I ever wanted to." She burst into tears, and Jonas put an arm around her and led her away.

Delta followed, looking back over her shoulder at the

place where, decades before, Athena Barrows had died. This whole situation had given her an idea. Was it possible that Athena had been killed by her own husband? Who had used the remote place and the nearness of Athena's alleged lover to divert suspicion? Several options had been discussed in Coldard's article in the book about cold cases Ray had lent her. An unknown intruder. Tony Taylor, with his poems possibly inspired by Athena's beauty. Never the husband.

She had to let Coldard know about her idea and see if he would delve into it and maybe find something to support it. That would give him a nice, new challenge. He needed to stay busy to keep the melancholy of old age away. Maybe Gran would like to meet him.

Delta grinned to herself. Now that Gran couldn't stay in her old house, she had a plan for her future. Right here in Tundish. But how to convince her that it was a good idea? Gran would, of course, not want to impose on her, etc. She could already imagine all the reasons.

But wouldn't it be perfect? Her new hometown, the shop, friendships, and family close as well?

Chapter Twenty

THEY TOOK THEIR BOWS, AND THE ENTIRE ROOM CLAPPED and cheered. Delta was glad to get out of the bright stage lights and disappear backstage. Mrs. Cassidy gushed that it had never sounded so fine and offered her something to drink. "Too bad, though, Randall Drake left town in a hurry and couldn't perform with us tonight. He was so charming."

"Yes, but after his uncle got arrested for the murder of his aunt, he wasn't too keen on all the attention. I guess he will be driving about in his Buick elsewhere, charming the ladies."

Delta was just savoring the cool juice when Gran popped up with Jonas on her one arm and Ray on the other. They were both dressed up in suits and looked the part for this grand night of entertainment at the town festival. Gran beamed at Delta. "I loved every minute of it. Good thing you persuaded me to stay for it."

"I intend to persuade you to stay much longer."

"I don't know yet."

Delta wagged a finger at her. "No discussions now." She looked at Ray. "Weren't there some after-show drinks in the entry hall?"

Ray nodded and led Gran away. Jonas said to Delta, "Great song."

"Thanks. I couldn't see much of the audience. The lights were glaring."

"The room was full. So many familiar faces. Even Lena Laroy. She put an envelope into the money coffer for the good cause, so I'm counting on a big donation to the gold-mining museum."

"I'm surprised she wanted to show her face here after her husband got accused of murder. I mean, Randall Drake ran, and she's sticking around?"

"I think she believes in the adage that any publicity is good publicity, even if it's bad publicity, if you get my drift. In fact, Marc LeDuc shared breaking news on his website while the performance was on that Lena will be writing a book about her life with a criminal brother and then a criminal husband."

"No."

"Yes. And I guess it will be a bestseller. People love to gobble up that kind of thing."

"I can't believe she would try to cash in on it like that. She must feel terrible, knowing she lived with Drake after he killed his sister in cold blood. I can still see him come in and go for Lena like he was so worried about her. He knew full well who had died and why. He had done it!"

"Calm down now." Jonas patted her back. "He's behind bars where he will stay. His lawyer got him to sign a full confession, of course twisting things to his own advantage. He claims Sally threatened to lie and tell the police that he had forced her to steal the statue from the museum depot and deliver it to him. Then he got in a panic that she had actually stolen something. To keep her from implicating him in the theft, he stabbed her. But it doesn't hold water. Where did he suddenly get a knife? He claims she had it with her to threaten him, but that's so unlikely. And why lie to Rosalyn about when he was going to pick up the present for his wife? That was *before* he was confronted by Sally and fell into this so-called panic. No, there never was any panic on his part, and I'm quite sure we've got it right when we reconstruct the case as Drake having planned on killing Sally at the party all along. He had even hired me to be at the party to keep an eye on Lena to divert attention. Sally had to put the present with the bottle on the table when he had gone to create a scene. Later, she couldn't tell it had been him asking her to do it for him, because she would already be dead. It was fiendishly clever. And Sally never saw it coming. She trusted him. Or she wanted a way out of her situation. Lost her job, about to lose her marriage as well."

"I feel so sorry for her." Delta shook her head.

"Me too." Jonas looked around him. "Nice backstage area. Do you want to do things like this more often? You seem to have a talent for singing."

The compliment was great, but it also made her a bit uncomfortable. "I wouldn't call it a talent. And tonight was for a good cause. A one-time occurrence."

"I wouldn't say that off the bat. You need time off, hobbies. Can't just work at the store or be at home designing new paper stuff. You need to get out and about every now and then."

"I know." Delta lowered her voice. "Any news on the property front?"

"Not yet, but I'm keeping an eye out. I'm sure we can find something perfect for your grandmother and you to live in."

"I hope Hazel won't feel like I'm abandoning her. But I always intended to get my own place, and with Gran now losing her home and having to move—"

Jonas tapped her arm. "You can discuss things with Hazel once you've found something you like. Maybe you can stay with her on weekends or whatever. It's not like you're moving away to the other side of the country. It's just Tundish."

Yes, it was just Tundish, their little town with a heart of gold that had banded together tonight to support their mining museum. It was Tundish, where something was happening all of the time, and friends could be counted on to be by your side. Tundish, her new home and maybe Gran's new home as well.

Delta couldn't wait to see what the future had in store for the both of them, for Hazel, Wanted. Their Paper Posse pals.

And Jonas and she...

He had seemed concerned for her, getting closer to her. She was still not sure she actually wanted to exchange the comfort of their easy friendship for more, but she could explore her feelings at leisure. After all, she wasn't going anywhere.

She had arrived.

Acknowledgments and Author's Note

I'm grateful to all agents, editors, and authors who share online about the writing and publishing process. A special thanks to my amazing agent, Jill Marsal; my wonderful editors, Anna Michels and MJ Johnston; and the entire dedicated Sourcebooks/Poisoned Pen team, especially Katie Stutz, Shauneice Robinson, and Anne Werthiem as well as Dawn Adams and Kelly Lawler for the adorable cover.

This series combines two of my loves: stationery and the great outdoors. I had a fabulous time building the fictional little town of Tundish, which was inspired by real-life towns in Montana's Bitterroot Valley, and developing the characters who make up the community, including the canine stars Spud, Nugget, and for this installment, the spoiled poodle duo, Pearl and Emerald, who even, unwittingly, contribute a vital clue. Dogs just bring a book to life for me, and I love writing their very different personalities as much as I love writing my human characters.

For those who are inspired by the Paper Posse's outlaw names, have a look online for the intriguing histories of individual outlaws and gangs, especially the female gang members. That they willingly posed for photos while they were wanted described their attitude to a tee. I'm delighted that the Paper Posse's Wild West names can keep some of their stories alive.

And thank you, reader, for your visit to Tundish and to Wanted. I hope you will be back for Delta's next adventure in her brand-new hometown, "the town with a heart of gold."

Don't miss out on any of the Stationery Shop Mysteries!
Read on for an excerpt from

Last Pen Standing

Chapter One

EVEN THOUGH THE SIGN OF HER DESTINATION WAS already in sight, calling out a warm welcome to Tundish, Montana, "the town with a heart of gold," Delta Douglas couldn't resist the temptation to stop her car, reach for the sketchbook in the passenger seat, and draw the orange-and-gold trees covering a mountain flank all the way to where the snow-peaked top began. From this exact point, their autumnal glory was reflected in the water of a clear blue lake that stretched without a ripple. Delta could just see this image reproduced on wrapping paper, notebooks, or postcards.

Until today, all her ideas for her own line of stationery products had lived only in her sketchbook, hidden away in her bag while she worked hard at her regular job as a graphic designer for a large advertising agency. But on Delta's thirtieth birthday, Gran had handed her an envelope. The elderly lady had had a mysterious smile that had made Delta's heart race. Leaning over and pecking her on the cheek, Gran had whispered, "Why wait until I'm dead? You're my only granddaughter, and I'd rather have you spend it now, while I'm still here to see what you do with it."

Inside the envelope had been a check for an amount that to some people might have represented a trip around the world, a boat, or the down payment on an apartment. But for Delta, it had symbolized independence—a way to leave her steady but stressful job with too many tight deadlines and finally do what she had always dreamed of: start her own business.

During summer holidays at Gran's as a little girl, Delta had sat at the kitchen table for hours drawing her own postcards, experimenting with watercolors and crayons, charcoal and felt-tips. Gran had arranged for her to man her own stall at the church fair and sell off her creations. It had been amazing to see her work bring in actual money. Some locals had even placed orders with her for Christmas cards, which she made back home and sent out to Gran to distribute. That sense of accomplishment had always stayed with her, and in her free time, she had continued to draw, cut, and paste with purpose, creating a portfolio of fun ideas that brightened her days. And suddenly, with Gran's gift, her own stationery shop was finally within reach.

It hadn't taken Delta long to take the plunge: she handed in her resignation at the agency in downtown Cheyenne, Wyoming, and crossed off the days until she could clear her desk, clean out her apartment, and drive away from the city she had called home for more than seven years. With every mile of her two-day road trip to the Bitterroot Valley, she had felt more excitement rush through her veins. She was now officially her own woman, ready to take a leap of faith and dive into a brand-new adventure in the small community tucked away at the foot of these glorious mountains.

Delta breathed in the spicy air, which still carried the warmth of summer. The sun was high in the sky, and the wind that had been tugging at her car during the ride had finally died down. She felt almost hot in her thigh-length knit vest, black jeans, and boots. Sneakers would have been better, but they were safely packed up in the trunk with the rest of her limited luggage. Since she had rented a furnished apartment in Cheyenne and donated to a charity shop most of the small stuff she didn't want to lug around, she hadn't had to pack a lot of things for the move. Just clothes, her many sketchbooks, pencils and other drawing materials, and laptop. In Tundish, she'd move in with her best friend from college, Hazel, who ran the stationery shop where Delta was going to be co-owner. Her heart beat faster just thinking about it. Her own shop, and the freedom to design products for it. She couldn't wait to get started. Having put the sketchbook with her brand-new autumnal design back on the passenger seat, she hit the gas and zoomed into town.

Tundish had been developed when settlers migrated to Montana for gold and logging. Most houses were made of wood and built in a sturdy Western style, some with dates carved into the front, placing these builds firmly within the nineteenth century. The word *gold* appeared everywhere: in street names, on signs pointing in the direction of an old mine site or to the gold-mining museum. However, Delta wasn't looking for gold. She was on a hunt for something even more precious: the old sheriff's office that housed the shop of her dreams.

Painted powder blue with black trim, the building sat on Mattock Street like a dependable force. It still had the hitching post in front where riders had tied up their horses before storming in to bring word of a bank or train robbery. The faces of the culprits had soon appeared on wanted posters between the barred windows, and even today, such posters were on display, but they no longer advertised the faces of notorious bandits, instead sporting the latest offering in stationery supplies: collectible erasers, washi tape, notebooks, and planners. A chalkboard on the sidewalk invited everyone to a Glitter Galore workshop on Friday night at the Lodge Hotel with a note at the bottom stating: *All materials included and mocktails to celebrate the results.* Sounded like a ton of fun, and Delta would be there.

Her eagerness to take in everything as she drove past had reduced her speed to about zero, and behind her, a car horn honked impatiently. Waving apologetically at the driver, who probably couldn't even see it, Delta accelerated and passed the neighboring hardware store and grocery shop, spying a parking lot beside the town's whitewashed church. She left her car there, then walked back the short stretch to the stationery shop's invitingly open doors. Over them, a wooden plank carried the name *WANTED* in tall letters burned into the wood, underlining that Western vibe. Delta grinned to herself, anticipating Hazel's expression when she saw Delta amble in. She could have called when she was almost there but had decided a surprise was that much more fun.

When she was a few feet away from the doors, her friend darted out of the entrance with a bright-yellow paper arrow gingerly held between the fingers of her outstretched right hand. Whirling to a stop in front of the wanted poster advertising notebooks, Hazel tilted her head to eye the poster, her blond bob swinging around her ears. She positioned the arrow over the right edge of the paper, moving it up and down as if to determine the perfect spot to stick it on. It read *two for one.*

Delta said, "That probably means I'll buy four. Do co-owners get a discount?"

Hazel swung around and whooped, the arrow still dangling from her finger. "Delta! I hadn't expected you yet."

She rushed to Delta and hugged her, then stepped back and held her by the shoulders, looking her over. "It's been too long. I mean, we did chat and all that, but it's not the same as a real meeting in the flesh. I can't believe you'll be living here now! The guest room at my place isn't all that big, but you can find something for yourself soon enough, once leaf-peeping season is over, and the cottages aren't all rented out to tourists who want to snap pictures of the trees."

"I'm in no rush to find something," Delta assured her. "Rooming together will be just like college." She surveyed Hazel's deep-orange blouse, chocolate-brown pants, and green ankle boots. "Wow, your outfit is fall to the max! Are there boutiques in town with clothes like that?"

"Sure." Hazel pointed across the street. "Right beside Western World, with all those Stetsons and boots on display, we have Bessie's Boutique. I've got a closet full of their pants. They're the perfect fit, and that's so hard to find. Besides, the owner is a friend of mine, so I get first dibs on all the new stock."

"Sounds great. Can I meet this friend?"

"Soon enough. She'll be attending our first workshop together." Hazel gestured at the chalkboard.

"Glitter and mocktails. Sounds posh." Delta nodded at the cocktail glasses drawn beside the workshop title.

Hazel laughed. "On Friday nights, the Lodge Hotel offers live entertainment for the guests and the locals. A big band for dancing, that sort of thing. This Friday night, it's their gold miners' annual party, a sophisticated affair that's a throwback to the hotel's heydays when tourism was just beginning to boom. It's really fun, and I thought we should have the workshop tie in to that. Of course, we'll be in our separate space, away from all the high-profile guests dancing the night away, but hey, at least we'll be able to breathe the glam atmosphere."

"Sounds fabulous. I'll snap some pictures for Gran to show her what I'm up to."

"Great. Now…" Hazel clapped her hands together and said, "Guided tour of my shop. *Our* shop, I should say. Come on in." She led the way through the entrance's double doors.

Delta followed with a pounding heart. She had seen photos of the shop, but she had never been to Tundish in person. This would be her first real-life view of her new enterprise.

Hazel gestured around her at all the warm woodwork and the authentic hearth where a pair of dusty cowboy boots stood ready, as if the sheriff would appear any moment to jump into them and set out with his posse. "This used to be where the sheriff sat to wait for news about a bank robbery or a gang of cattle thieves. You can see that I kept his desk and used it to display the newest notebooks."

Delta jumped toward the notebooks, eager to pick through the stacks and take Hazel up on the two-for-one offer. But Hazel laughed and pulled her away. "No, no browsing yet. First, you have to see the rest. There, along the wall, I have shelves for crafting packages. You can find anything, from designing your own planner to making a birthday calendar. Then in that old cell…"

Hazel walked through a barred door that led into a small space with a wooden cot pushed against the wall. Above the cot, replicas of original newspaper pages displayed the faces of the Old West's most notorious gang members, some of them smug, others defiant.

"A few of them spent time in here," Hazel explained, gesturing around her. "And I put up that bit of rope"— she gestured to a rope tied around one of the bars in the narrow window—"to refer to all the escape attempts made. They tied the other end of the rope to a horse and gave it a scare so it would gallop off and tear the bar right from the window. Crude and often not very effective."

"I love it." Delta fingered the rope.

"If you have ideas to give it even more atmosphere, just say so. I'm constantly switching it up to attract people who normally might not walk into a stationery shop but who do want to breathe everything Western. In my experience, once they are sold on the shop's atmosphere, they also buy a little something, if only to show their appreciation for the way in which I preserved it."

"You did a great job," Delta said. "And that's all the washi tape?" She pointed at countless glass jars filled with rolls of tape.

"Yup. I have unique offerings from Japan and Australia that you can't get anywhere else in the country. You should see me salivate when those parcels come in. I was tempted to keep all the ones with the pandas to myself. And in the other cell, I have all the collectible erasers."

Delta followed her into the second cell, which had a rough table against the wall where small glittery objects were lying beside old-fashioned scales and yellowing papers, folded and unfolded so many times that they were torn along the edges. A plasticized card with information warned visitors not to touch the objects because they were authentic and breakable, while also explaining that mining had often been the seed of crime as people sold fake claims or ended up in fights about gold found.

Hazel gestured across the papers. "Real stake claims donated to me by the gold-mining museum. They have a ton of those and didn't mind me having some. They get attention here instead of sitting in an archive."

"I love the fake gold clumps. At least I assume they are fake?"

"Created by a loving volunteer at the mining museum who also puts these into small wooden mining carts they sell as souvenirs." Hazel gestured to the bunk bed against the wall. "There's our offering of collectible erasers."

Delta wanted to sit on her haunches to study the products closer, especially the miniature makeup replicas, including a blusher box that could be opened to reveal two colors and a little brush inside. But Hazel tapped her on the shoulder and gestured to follow her out of the cell, back into the main space where the sunlight through the windows gave the wooden surfaces an extra-warm glow.

Hazel pointed. "Now, there in the back we have the old umbrella stands with all the wrapping paper. Above, an old clothes rack with gift bags."

Bags in several shapes and sizes were hung by their ribbon handles from the rack. They came in bright colors with glitter or in intricate geometric patterns that created visual depth. Delta closed in and spotted a few Christmassy ones among the offerings. Picking out one with a cute design of cocoa mugs and sweet treats, she held it up to Hazel. "Candy canes already?"

Hazel laughed. "Christmas themes sell well all year round. There's just something quintessentially cozy about them. I've already scheduled some early November work-shops we can do to teach people how to make menus and name tags to use on the dinner table, or teach pro-wrapping skills where we turn simple presents into gifts *extraordinaire*. I'll show you my idea list later on. I'm sure you have lots you want to add."

Delta nodded eagerly.

"But first to wrap up our tour: here's the old weapon rack where the sheriff could grab his double-barreled shotgun, now used to hold all my wrapping ribbons, stickers, and tags. The puffy stickers are selling especially well with kids."

Hazel smiled widely as she encompassed the whole shop with a wave of both her outstretched arms. "Now you're free to take a closer look at whatever you want to. And yes, co-owners do get a discount."

Delta made a beeline back to the old sheriff's desk and took the top notebook off a stack. "These dogs are adorable." Her finger traced the rows of small dachshunds, poodles, and Labs that marched across the hard cover. "In the city, I never got around to having a dog, you know. I was away most of the time, and it just seemed sad leaving him or her alone in the apartment all day long. I wonder if I could have a puppy here."

She opened the cover and leafed through the pages. "Wow, every page actually has a different dog. Aw, this border collie puppy is chasing a ball!"

"Remember that it's two for the price of one now! Speaking of, where did I put that arrow?" Hazel checked both hands and then began to look around her. "Maybe I dropped it outside?"

"Then it must be gone. There was a strong wind when I drove over here. Or someone stepped on it and it stuck to their shoe."

Ignoring Delta's predictions, Hazel ambled outside, scanning the pavement for the missing arrow.

Delta was completely engrossed in choosing the four notebooks she planned to purchase. Four initially seemed like a lot for someone who already had more notebooks than she knew what to do with, but in no time, she had selected six and was eyeing two more: one with dancing flamingos and one with letters that formed hidden words. Why not take them all?

Vaguely, she heard a footfall behind her, probably Hazel entering the store.

Suddenly, she felt a slight tug at her hair, and someone said, "Two for one. Yes, please."

Turning around, Delta found herself face-to-face with a grinning man with wild blond curls and brown eyes, a dimple in his cheek. He wore a crisp, white shirt, unbuttoned at the neck, and dark-blue jeans with a silver belt buckle of a running horse. He held up the bright-yellow arrow. "This was stuck to your back, half in your hair."

Delta flushed. "It must have gotten hung up there when Hazel said hello to me. She's looking for that arrow. I'll take it out to her." She reached out her hand, and the man put the arrow in it. His infuriating grin stayed in place. "I haven't seen you here before. New to town?"

"I'm coming to live here. To run Wanted, with Hazel."

"Really? She didn't mention that to me." The man looked puzzled. Delta couldn't figure out why this man would think Hazel should have told him that Delta was moving to Tundish. Could it be her friend was dating him? Hazel hadn't mentioned anything about it, but then again, over the past few weeks, their conversations had been focused on practical details for Delta's move and the financial arrangements for co-ownership of Wanted, so maybe Hazel had figured she could tell her once she was in town.

Hazel's most recent relationship had ended in heart-break when she found out the guy had been cheating on her. Delta had assumed her friend wouldn't have been eager to dive into something new, especially not one with a man whose athletic physique and cute dimple probably got a lot of female attention.

"Oh, there it is." Hazel buzzed up to Delta and reached out for the arrow with a smile. "I had no idea where it had disappeared to." Ignoring the man completely, she hurried outside again to put it in place.

To make up for her friend's rather brusque behavior, Delta asked quickly, "Is there anything you need from the shop?"

The man picked up a notebook with peacocks, their large purple-and-turquoise feathers adorned with little sparkly gold foil elements in them. It was the first on top of the stack, and he didn't look inside or check the price, just handed it to Delta as if he couldn't wait to get this chore over with. "Can I have this?"

"Of course, but"—Delta knew men often didn't like shopping, but still, he was entitled to a second notebook, under the deal advertised outside—"it's two for the price of one, so you can pick another for free. I can find you one that matches what you already have. Blue and gold..." She wanted to dig into the stacks, to extract those spines that looked like they might offer a color match, but he waved her off. "I only need one. Can you gift wrap it for me?"

"Certainly." Telling herself that the customer was always right, no matter how illogical their decisions might be, Delta took the notebook from his hand and walked to the cash register, feeling a little giddy at making her first sale. This was awesome, even better than she had imagined. She detected several rolls of wrapping paper stacked under the counter. "Blue and gold would be a perfect match." Delta tore off a piece the right size for the notebook. "Now, where's the tape dispenser?" She glanced across the length of the counter, then knelt down to look for it below.

Tilting forward to peer behind a stack of paper bags imprinted with the Wanted logo, she pushed herself up a little. The top of her head made contact with the counter's edge, and she winced.

"Are you OK?" the customer asked, leaning his hands on the counter.

"Yes." Delta rubbed the sore spot. "But a tape dispenser is nowhere in sight. Maybe I can dig out scissors somewhere. And a loose role of tape. Ah, here. No, this roll is empty. Let's see what's in here."

She pulled a plastic basket toward her that was brimming with elastic bands, pens, pencils, and scraps of paper with illegible notes written on them. This space needed to get more organized. She dug through the items in a rush. "Sorry about the delay."

"No problem." The customer rocked back on his heels, a surreptitious glance at his watch belying his casual reply.

Hazel came back in, and he immediately turned to her and lowered his voice in a tone of confidentiality. "I'm not eager to get back to the Lodge. Rosalyn is having a fit over the gold miners' party. The photographer she managed to get after lots of calls to friends in the right places decided to drop her like a brick for a chance to shoot some pop group in Vegas. I told her I could take a decent shot, but she just glared at me like I was suggesting she hire the seven dwarves. But she'll come around. She can't get anybody professional on such short notice."

"Why doesn't she ask Jonas?" Hazel said. "He's a professional, even if he usually has deer in front of his lens and not people."

"Now, there's an idea." The man smiled at Hazel, who kept her aloof expression in place and started to reorganize the gift bags, which were already perfectly aligned.

Delta finally found tape and wrapped the peacock notebook, putting a gold ribbon around the parcel. "There you go."

He put a ten-dollar bill on the counter. "Never mind the change. See you Friday, then." Picking up the parcel, he walked out with an easy, athletic stride.

"Never mind the change?" Delta hitched an eyebrow at Hazel. "I thought people only tipped waiters."

"Oh, that's Ray Taylor. The Taylor family used to own half of the town. People worked at their Lodge Hotel or delivered goods to it or organized trips for guests staying at it. They're a household name in the region. You just work with them, not against them."

"The Lodge Hotel is where we're doing the workshop Friday night, right?" Delta wasn't sure if she was pleased or annoyed at the idea that she might run into Mr. Taylor again.

Hazel nodded. "Ray never wanted any part of the hotel business and left town to play football. He did very well for a couple of seasons, had a string of high-class girlfriends and was even set to be drafted into the NFL. But he was injured last spring, and there are rumors his career is over. Ray is the last person to say a word about it, but the fact that he's back in town and suddenly snuggling up to his father suggests he's looking for a way back into the family fold. Needless to say, the other Taylors are not pleased."

Delta frowned. "Let me guess. He has an older brother who worked his butt off for the hotel and now sees charming Ray sailing back into town and into his father's good graces."

"*Her* father's good graces. The eldest Taylor is a daughter. Rosalyn runs the hotel like a pro. Made a lot of changes, pulled in new guests. Saved it from mediocrity, really. I mean, there are so many places to stay now. They can't depend on their former monopoly in the region anymore. Mr. Taylor Sr. doesn't seem to see that clearly, but Rosalyn does. She's invested everything in the hotel's survival. It's still a family business; her younger sister, Isabel, is working at the hotel as hostess, welcoming the guests and arranging for all the entertainment. She got Finn a job there."

Delta stared at Hazel. "Your brother Finn?" She had had no idea that Hazel's brother had moved to Montana. Hazel hadn't mentioned him in ages, suggesting they were barely in touch. Last thing Delta knew about him was that he had graduated college with flying colors and started a job with a top-notch insurance agency in Los Angeles. And now all of a sudden he was living in Tundish?

Hazel grimaced, as if the subject were painful to her. "Yes, he came here last summer for the boating and mountaineering. Then he met Isabel, and they fell in love. She got him a job as wildlife guide at the hotel."

"Wildlife guide?" Delta echoed. "I thought Finn was in finance. Insurance and that sort of thing. Or am I confusing him with someone else you told me about?"

"No, he was in insurance, but it just made him unhappy." Hazel made a wide hand gesture. "He was always sporty and loved water, the great outdoors, a sense of freedom. He hated city life with all the concrete and the never-ending hum of the traffic. He's much more at ease here, bunking with another guide who has a cabin in the middle of nowhere. The deer are at his window in the mornings, he says. It would all be perfect, if Isabel would just stop pestering him about getting engaged at Christmas this year."

Delta tried to gauge her friend's feelings on the subject. Did Hazel not like Isabel as a person, or was she uneasy about the idea that her brother would become a part of an influential family whose lifestyle might be miles away from her own? Did she think that Finn, who hadn't liked high-pressure city life, wouldn't cope well with the demands his new family might make on him?

She tried to sound casual as she probed, "And you're not a fan of the match?"

Hazel sighed. "I'm not sure if they're really a fit. They're like day and night, you know, Isabel always in high heels, Finn in a fleece jacket and shoes full of mud. He still has this college student attitude, showing up for work when he wants to and calling off when he has suddenly thought up something else to do."

Delta wondered for a moment if Finn had also had this attitude during his work in LA. His bosses wouldn't have liked it. Had Finn really given up on his insurance job because he didn't like the city, or had he been fired?

Hazel continued, "On the other hand, Finn did think up some clever ideas to entertain the hotel guests, and Isabel incorporated them into their activity calendar. She claims they're a golden duo. That is, they used to be until Ray showed up, disturbing the balance."

Yes, Ray Taylor was someone who could disturb things, Delta readily accepted. He had a self-confidence that was hard to overlook. Maybe his siblings were afraid that, even after many years away, Ray had the power to convince his father he was the best person to run the Lodge Hotel.

"Why were you so rude when he came into the store?" Delta asked.

Hazel shrugged. "There have been rumors I'm after Ray because I'm doing my workshops at the hotel. People whisper that I just want to see him. But I don't have the space needed for the workshops here at Wanted. I guess it's because Finn is with Isabel now, and people are sure I want a part of the Taylor pie as well."

Hazel shook her head impatiently. "I know trouble when I see it. Ray isn't the type to stick around. He'll just stir things up all over town and then run off again, leaving others with the mess. When he does leave, I don't want to be caught in the middle. Same goes for Finn."

Delta studied her friend more closely. Hazel sounded a little too protective, given the fact that her brother was a grown-up who had to make his own choices and even his own mistakes if need be. There had to be more to Finn and his job at the Lodge Hotel that Hazel wasn't telling her right now, but she figured her friend would confide in her later when she was settled in.

Hazel smiled again. "I'm so glad you're here now and we can do things together, starting with the workshop on Friday night. It's fully booked, with twenty participants. Some of them are regulars. They call themselves the Paper Posse."

"Posse?" Delta repeated, not sure she had heard right.

"Yes, that was Mrs. Cassidy's idea. She has a slight outlaw obsession. You know these genealogy sites where you can build your family tree, dating back centuries, to see whether you happen to be related to royalty or to a famous inventor?"

Delta nodded. "I've thought about giving it a try, but it's a lot of work, I heard. Especially if you want to go back farther than just a few generations."

"Right. Mrs. Cassidy has been searching for years now, not for a link to the British Crown, but to find an outlaw in her family tree. To quote her, 'Those who stray outside the law are often more interesting than those who adhere to it.'"

"That's an original opinion. Well, as long as she doesn't bring any outlaws to our workshops, I guess it can't do any harm."

Delta looked around her and breathed the scent of paper. The sun slanting in through the windows made all the colors come even more alive. Outside, traffic hummed, and a pigeon cooed as he strode by the open shop doors, pecking the pavement in search of food scraps.

Everything was just that little bit more leisurely here, laid-back, at ease. Finally, a break from hectic city life, late-night hours, and deadlines. And all because of Gran. The love of crafting that had been born at her kitchen table all those years ago would now provide Delta's bread and butter. Play with paper and make money off it too.

Delta smiled and vowed to herself that she was about to make her grandmother very proud.

Chapter Two

Hazel cleared her throat. "Ready to leave?"

Delta spun around, feeling kind of caught red-handed, standing in front of the long mirror in Hazel's narrow hallway. She smoothed down the sleek, ankle-length dress she had worn before to office parties. "I'm just worried about the color. Is the red too vibrant? Maybe as workshop host I should blend in with the wallpaper? Like a good butler: there when you need him and otherwise invisible."

"Not at all. They have to get to know you tonight and the outfit is their first clue to your personality. Without frills, energetic, and bright." Hazel winked at her. "Fits you to a tee. What do you think of my pantsuit?" Spreading her arms, Hazel turned in a circle so Delta could admire the black, velvet suit from all sides. She knew her friend hated dresses and hardly ever wore them. "Perfect," she assured her. "That gold blouse underneath adds a festive touch. Just right for a Glitter Galore theme. But what's that green stuff in your hand?"

"Oh…" Hazel glanced at the leaves. "Fresh mint I just cut for the mocktails. I'll put it in this bag with the other ingredients. Sparkling water, juices, fresh raspberries. The Lodge will provide the glasses, shaker, and strainer. And Rosalyn assured me a waiter would take in the ice we need around the time we're done with the crafting and ready to create our own mocktails. You carry this bag, I'll take the box with paper goodies." Hazel grabbed the big cardboard box from the side table at the front door and gestured for Delta to follow her.

Outside, they got into Hazel's Mini Cooper and turned left onto the road that led to the Lodge. Like the rest of the town, it was built on the edge of the lake, but higher up into the foothills, so it offered a gorgeous view of the water and the snow-capped mountains behind it.

Delta drank in the scene, half-twisted backward in her seat, while Hazel steered the car up the drive leading to the hotel's large parking lot. It was so full they had to drive around a couple of times to find an empty space.

"Glad I didn't come in something like that." Hazel nodded at a large, dark-gray SUV parked a few spaces away from them. "It would have been hard to fit into this narrow space. Can you squeeze out?"

Delta opened her door carefully and managed to wring herself through the opening with the bag full of fresh ingredients. The invigorating scent of the mint wafted at her.

A horse neighed in the distance. Delta turned her head around to locate the sound.

Hazel laughed. "Welcome to Tundish. That's not just any horse, but a Taylor horse. The stables are down that road there. They have a couple of horses of their own and stable some for friends. Both Isabel and Rosalyn did show jumping when they were teens, but I suppose they don't have time for extensive training anymore."

Voices resounded from the hotel entrance where people were gathering, exchanging greetings and interested questions about how they had been since last year.

"You said the party was an annual thing, so for how many years has the hotel been organizing it?" Delta asked.

"About a hundred, I guess."

Delta glanced at her friend. "You're kidding me, right?"

"Absolutely not." Hazel grinned at Delta's astonishment.

Balancing the cardboard box with crafting materials in her arms, she fell into step beside her. "Gold miners' parties are a really old tradition in the area. They started in the twenties when tourism around the lake began to develop. People wanted to get out and explore the great outdoors, but they also wanted to enjoy the comfort and luxury they had at home. The hotel offered just that. Entertainment was part of the experience. They hired singers, dancers, pantomimists. And they also had the guests perform little plays and sketches. They've held on to that tradition ever since. The guests' contributions are a major part of the show tonight."

They were at the entrance now, and a tall woman with straight, dark hair, dressed in a purple gown with silver embroidery on the bodice, came over to them. Elbow-length gloves emphasized the twenties vibe of her outfit. "Hazel! Everything is ready for the workshop in the boardroom. I hope you emailed your participants to turn right immediately after entering the hotel? We don't want them mixed up with our party guests." There was a slight hint of disapproval in the woman's voice.

Hazel said quickly, "Of course. Delta, this is Rosalyn Taylor. She manages the hotel."

"Pleased to meet you." Delta shook the woman's hand. She tried to find a resemblance to Ray in Rosalyn's features, but the guarded eyes and polite but chilly smile formed a stark contrast to the golden-boy joviality Ray exuded. Here was a woman who took life seriously. Someone who probably made a lot of demands on herself and others.

Delta said, "The hotel is in a stunning location. The view of the lake is breathtaking."

"Thank you." Rosalyn's gaze fell over Delta's shoulder. "Jonas! You're late."

A tall man with dark hair came over, looking slightly uncomfortable in his tuxedo. He had a professional-looking camera with a long lens around his neck and a dog leash in his right hand. A large German shepherd bounded beside him, sniffing the air and wagging his big, bushy tail.

Rosalyn Taylor frowned down on the dog. "I'd hoped you'd have the sense to leave the dog at home. You're here to work."

"I always bring Spud when I come to work. He'll stay wherever I put him and wait until I'm done." Jonas spoke without raising his voice.

"I can take Spud into our workshop," Hazel offered. "Hey, boy." She seemed to want to free a hand to pat the dog, but the big box in her arms wouldn't let her. "How does the theme Glitter Galore grab you?"

The German shepherd barked enthusiastically, as if he couldn't wait to get started.

Hazel laughed and said to Delta, "He's hardly a puppy, but I'm sure you'll love him anyway. Can you take the leash?"

Rosalyn Taylor turned impatiently to Jonas. "We want to do the family photo at the fireplace before the party starts. I'll tell everyone to assemble." She marched into the hotel on her high heels, Jonas following her after he had pressed the dog lead into Delta's hand. "Introductions will have to wait till later," he called to her as he left.

Spud watched his boss go without pulling to go after him. His tail was low and his eyes alert.

Hazel whispered, "That's Jonas Nord. He's a wild-life photographer working in the area. He also helps Finn with guided tours when it's a busy season, like with the leaf peeping tours now. Apparently, Ray listened to me and told Rosalyn to hire Jonas for the photos tonight."

Hazel sounded as if she was slightly surprised at her own success. With a grin, she added, "I bet Jonas had to borrow that tux. He's not the type to have a closet full of suits."

"It does look good on him."

Hazel looked at Delta curiously. "Oh?"

Recognizing the implications of that *oh* from prior occasions where Hazel had tried to pair her off with friends she considered totally right for Delta, Delta added quickly, "Just a factual observation. I'm here to settle in and work, not…get entangled in anything, you know." At least for the first few weeks she could do without matchmaking attempts.

"Sure." Hazel didn't sound convinced, but as people came up behind them, they moved on inside.

About the Author

Always knee-deep in notebooks and pens, multi-published cozy mystery author Vivian Conroy decided to write about any paper crafter's dream: a stationery shop called Wanted. Her other loves, such as sweet treats, history, and hiking, equipped the series's world with a bakery, gold-miners' museum, and outdoor activities. Never too far from a keyboard, Vivian loves to connect with readers via Twitter under @VivWrites.